THE COOL CODE

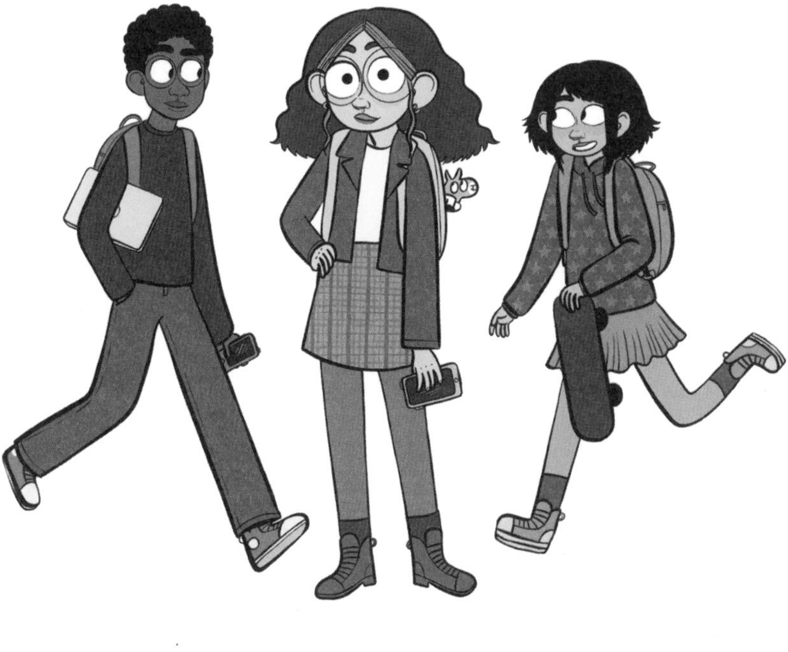

DEIRDRE LANGELAND

illustrated by

SARAH MAI

CLARION BOOKS

Imprints of HarperCollins*Publishers*

HARPER alley

FOR FREDDIE SPAGHETTI
—D.L.

TO LINDA AND DAVE,
THE COOLEST PEOPLE I KNOW
—S.M.

Clarion Books is an imprint of HarperCollins Publishers.
HarperAlley is an imprint of HarperCollins Publishers.

The Cool Code
Copyright © 2022 by HarperCollins Publishers

Library of Congress Control Number: 2022935798
ISBN 978-0-35-854932-1 (hardcover)
ISBN 978-0-35-854931-4 (paperback)

The artist used ProCreate to create the digital illustrations for this book.
Lettering by Whitney Leader-Picone and Natalie Fondriest

23 24 25 26 TC 10 9 8 7 6 5 4 3 2
❖
First Edition

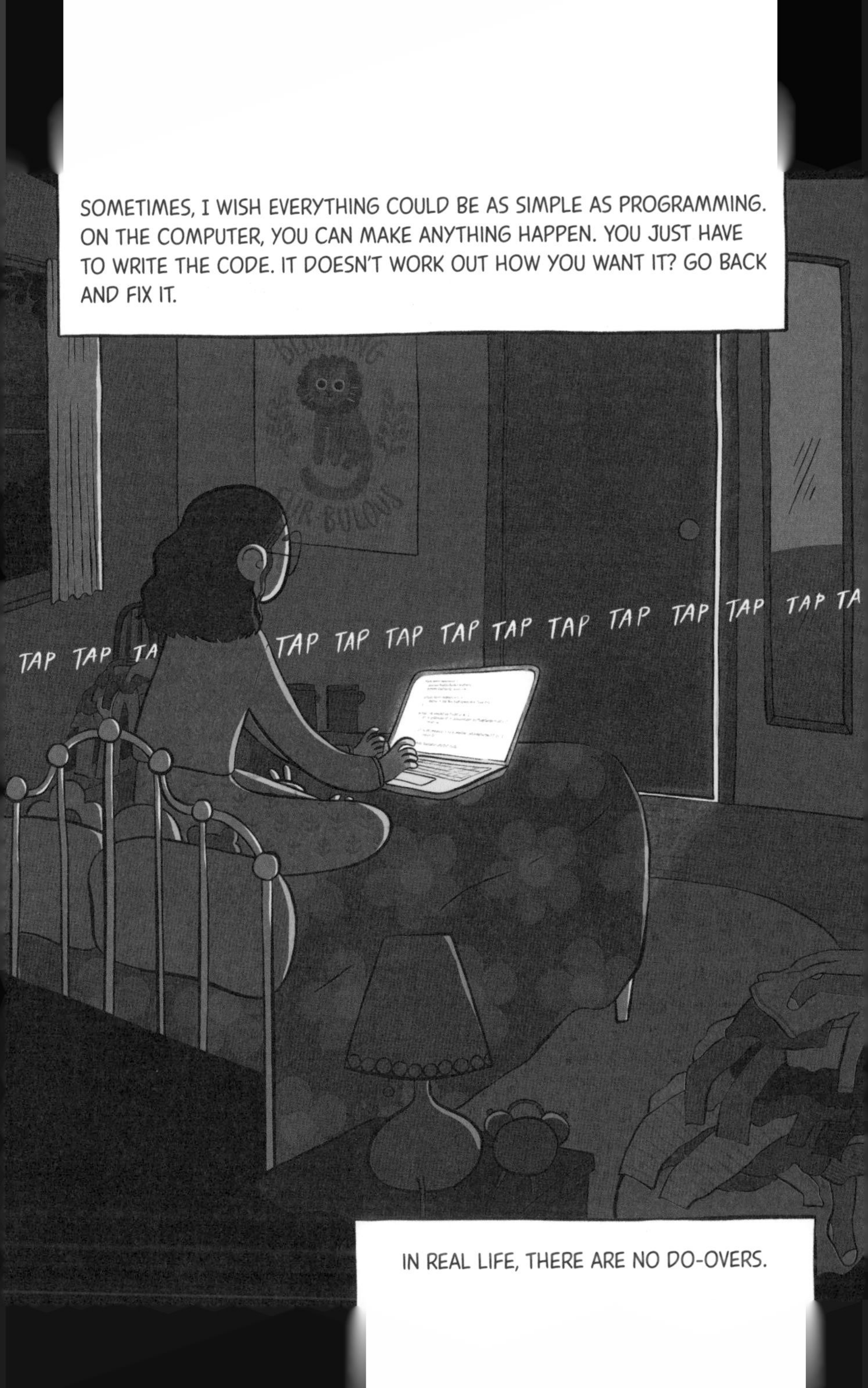
SOMETIMES, I WISH EVERYTHING COULD BE AS SIMPLE AS PROGRAMMING. ON THE COMPUTER, YOU CAN MAKE ANYTHING HAPPEN. YOU JUST HAVE TO WRITE THE CODE. IT DOESN'T WORK OUT HOW YOU WANT IT? GO BACK AND FIX IT.
TAP TAP TA
TAP TAP TAP TAP TAP TAP TAP TAP TAP TAP TA
IN REAL LIFE, THERE ARE NO DO-OVERS.

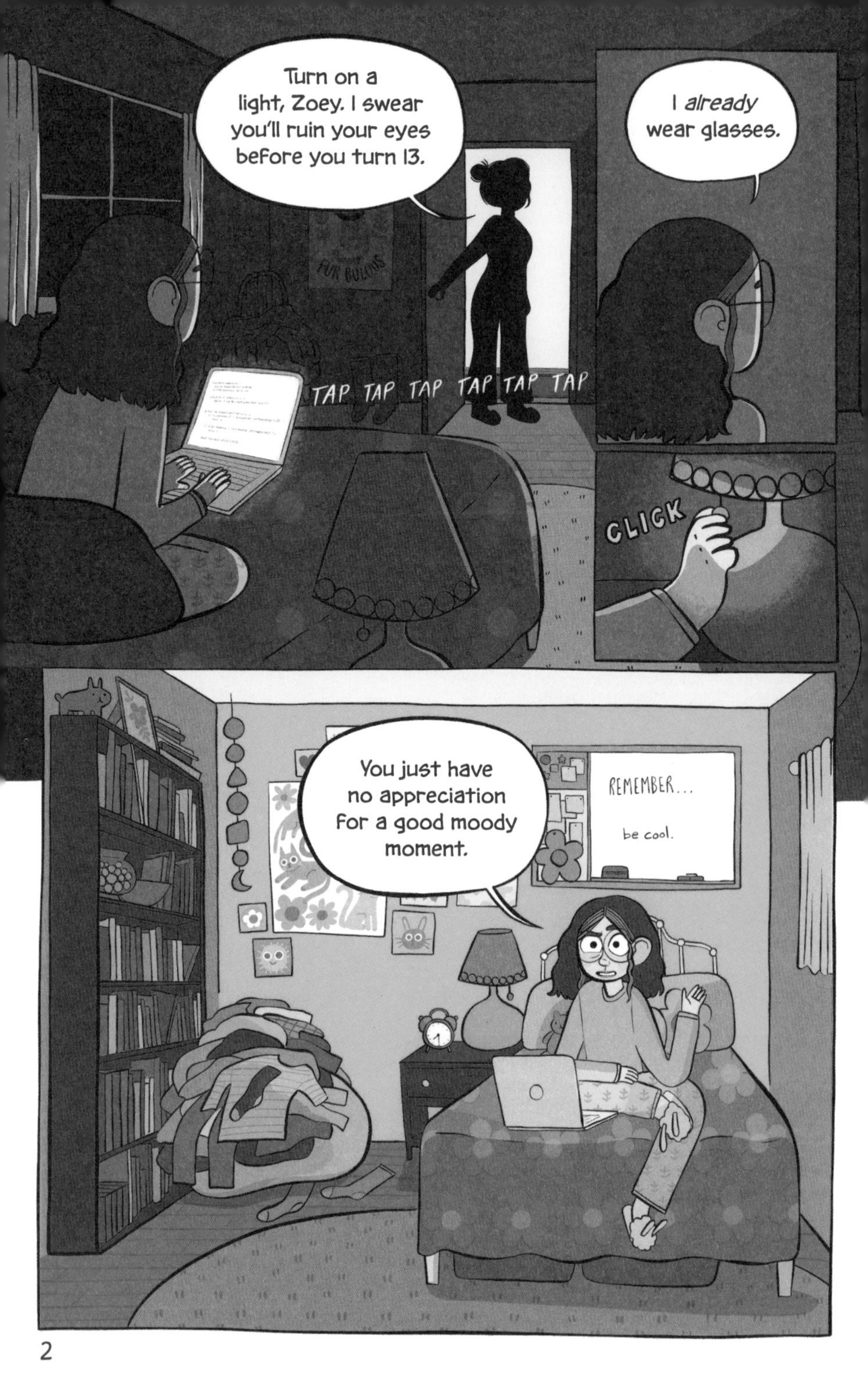
Turn on a light, Zoey. I swear you'll ruin your eyes before you turn 13.
I *already* wear glasses.
FUR BULOUS
TAP TAP TAP TAP TAP TAP
CLICK
You just have no appreciation for a good moody moment.
REMEMBER...
be cool.

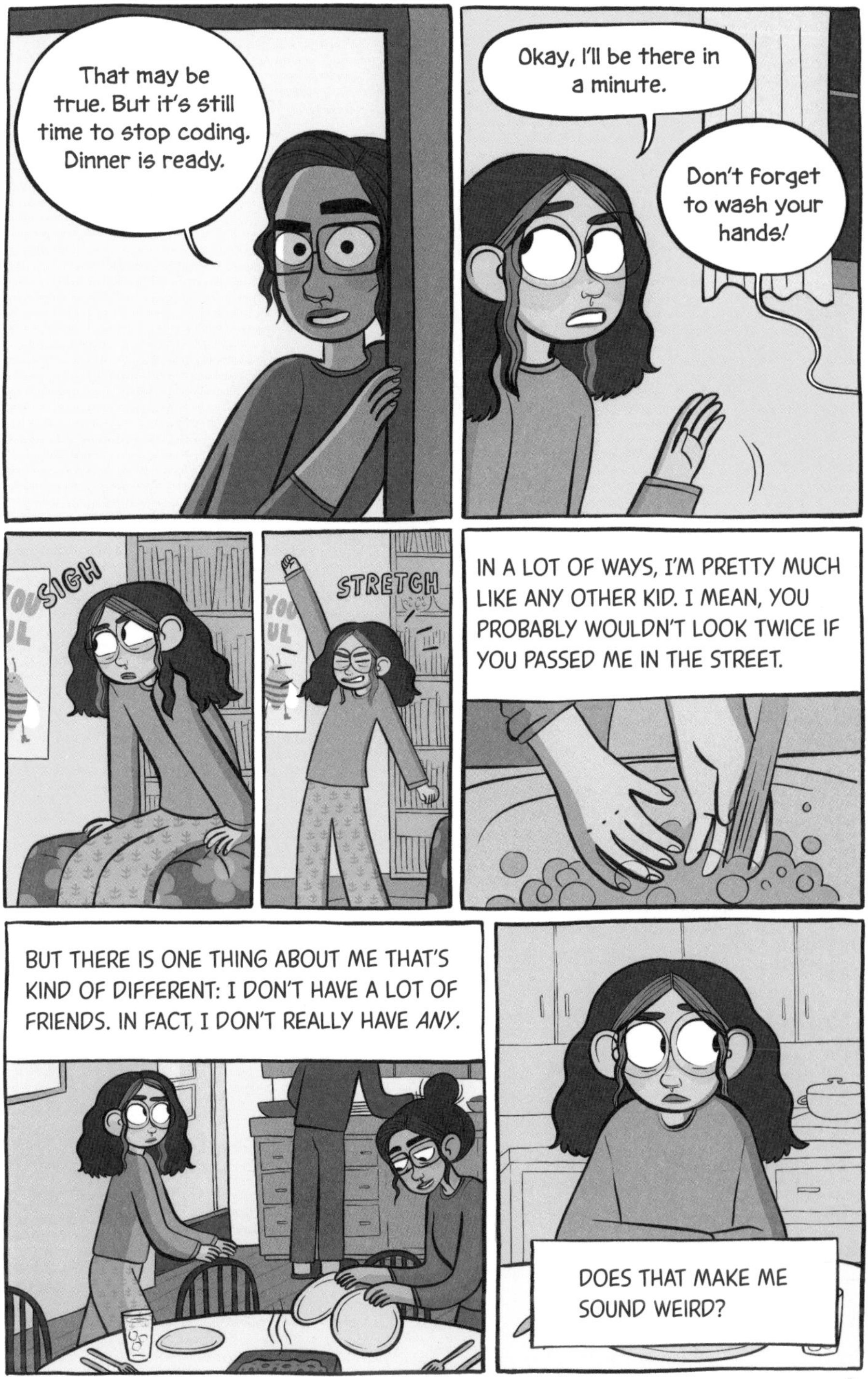
That may be true. But it's still time to stop coding. Dinner is ready.
Okay, I'll be there in a minute.
Don't forget to wash your hands!
SIGH
STRETCH
IN A LOT OF WAYS, I'M PRETTY MUCH LIKE ANY OTHER KID. I MEAN, YOU PROBABLY WOULDN'T LOOK TWICE IF YOU PASSED ME IN THE STREET.
BUT THERE IS ONE THING ABOUT ME THAT'S KIND OF DIFFERENT: I DON'T HAVE A LOT OF FRIENDS. IN FACT, I DON'T REALLY HAVE *ANY*.
DOES THAT MAKE ME SOUND WEIRD?

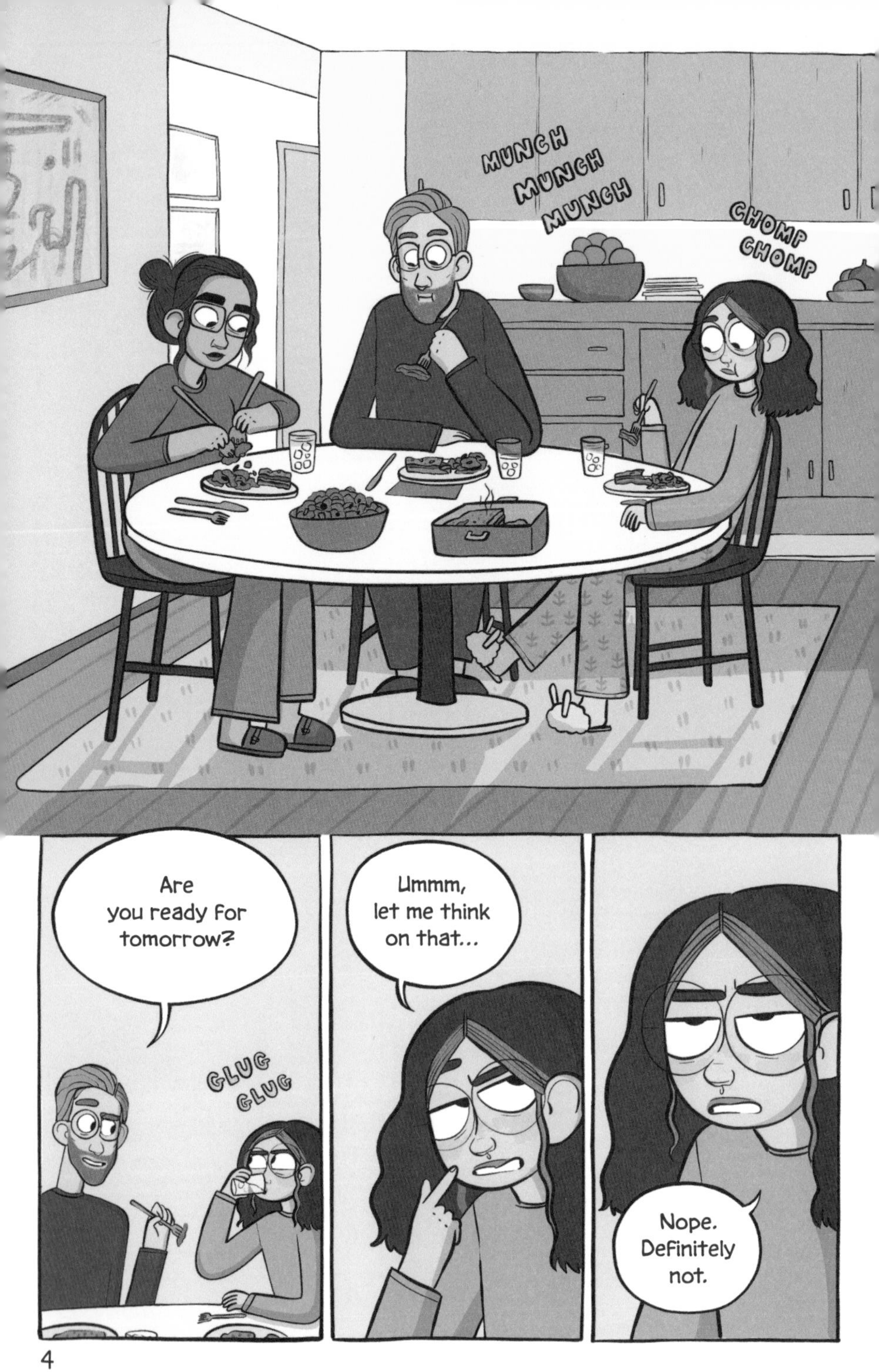
MUNCH
MUNCH
MUNCH
CHOMP
CHOMP
Are you ready for tomorrow?
GLUG
GLUG
Ummm, let me think on that...
Nope. Definitely not.

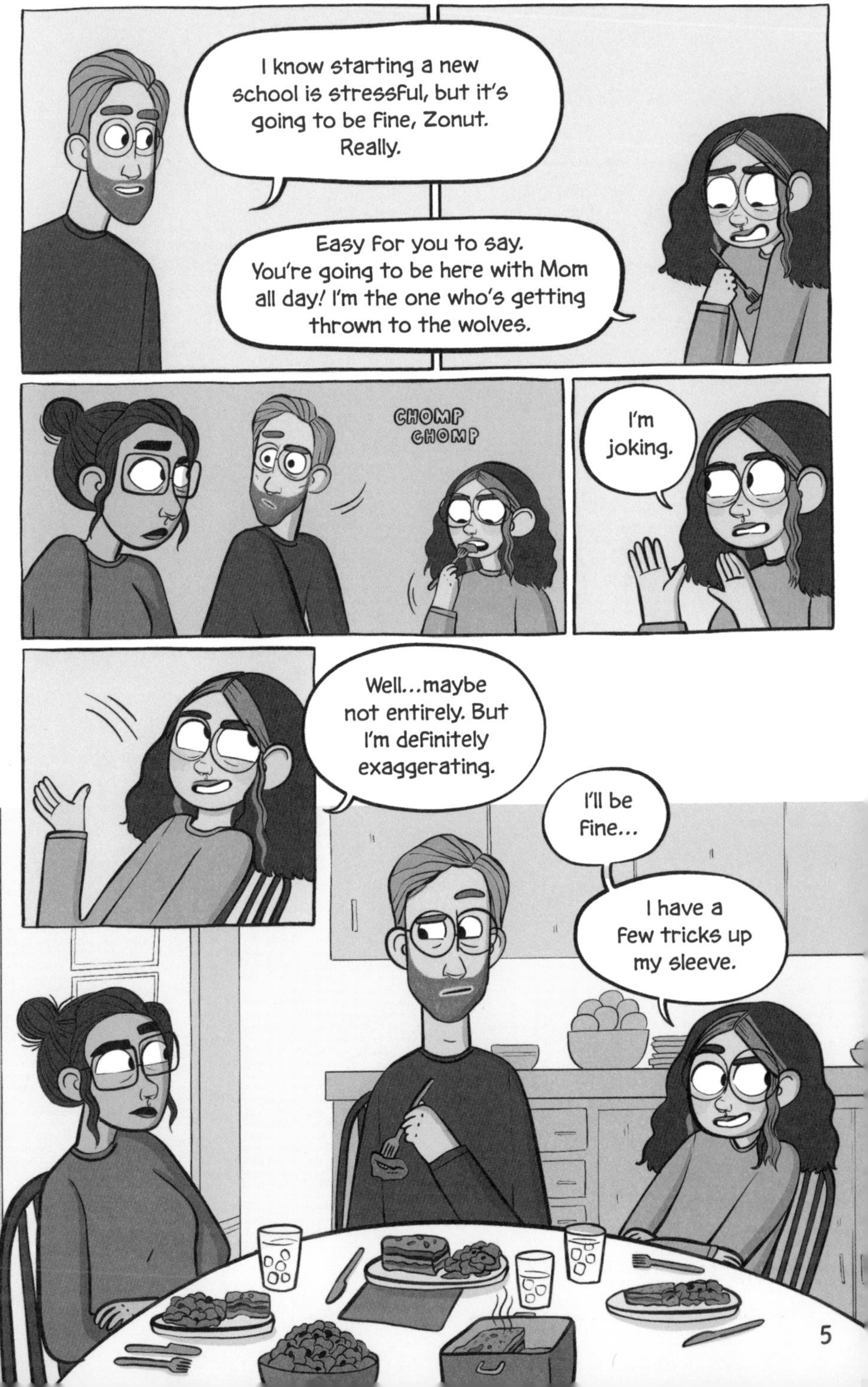
I know starting a new school is stressful, but it's going to be fine, Zonut. Really.
Easy for you to say. You're going to be here with Mom all day! I'm the one who's getting thrown to the wolves.
CHOMP CHOMP
I'm joking.
Well...maybe not entirely. But I'm definitely exaggerating.
I'll be fine...
I have a few tricks up my sleeve.

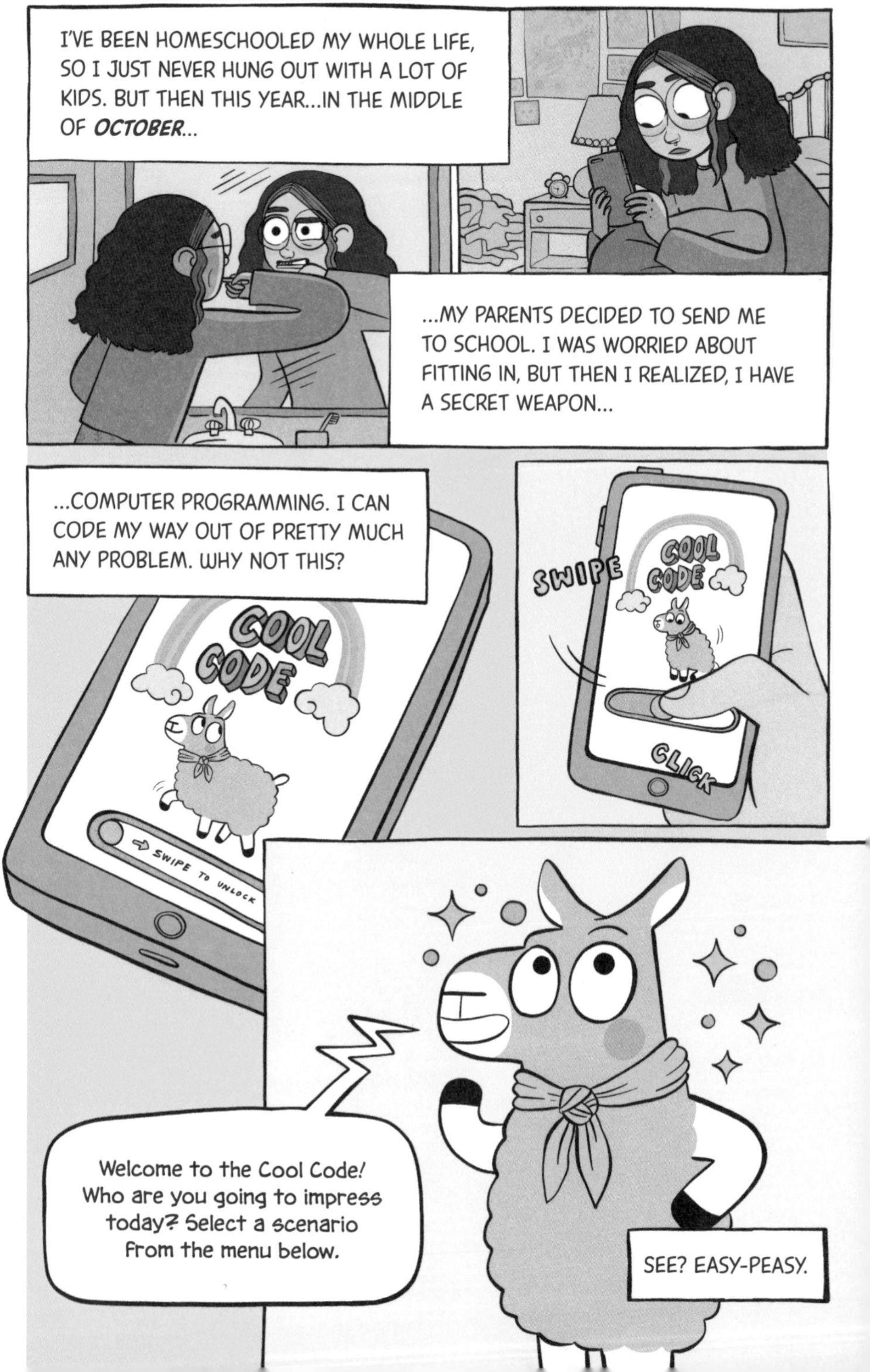
I'VE BEEN HOMESCHOOLED MY WHOLE LIFE, SO I JUST NEVER HUNG OUT WITH A LOT OF KIDS. BUT THEN THIS YEAR...IN THE MIDDLE OF *OCTOBER*...
...MY PARENTS DECIDED TO SEND ME TO SCHOOL. I WAS WORRIED ABOUT FITTING IN, BUT THEN I REALIZED, I HAVE A SECRET WEAPON...
...COMPUTER PROGRAMMING. I CAN CODE MY WAY OUT OF PRETTY MUCH ANY PROBLEM. WHY NOT THIS?
COOL CODE
SWIPE TO UNLOCK
SWIPE
COOL CODE
CLICK
Welcome to the Cool Code! Who are you going to impress today? Select a scenario from the menu below.
SEE? EASY-PEASY.

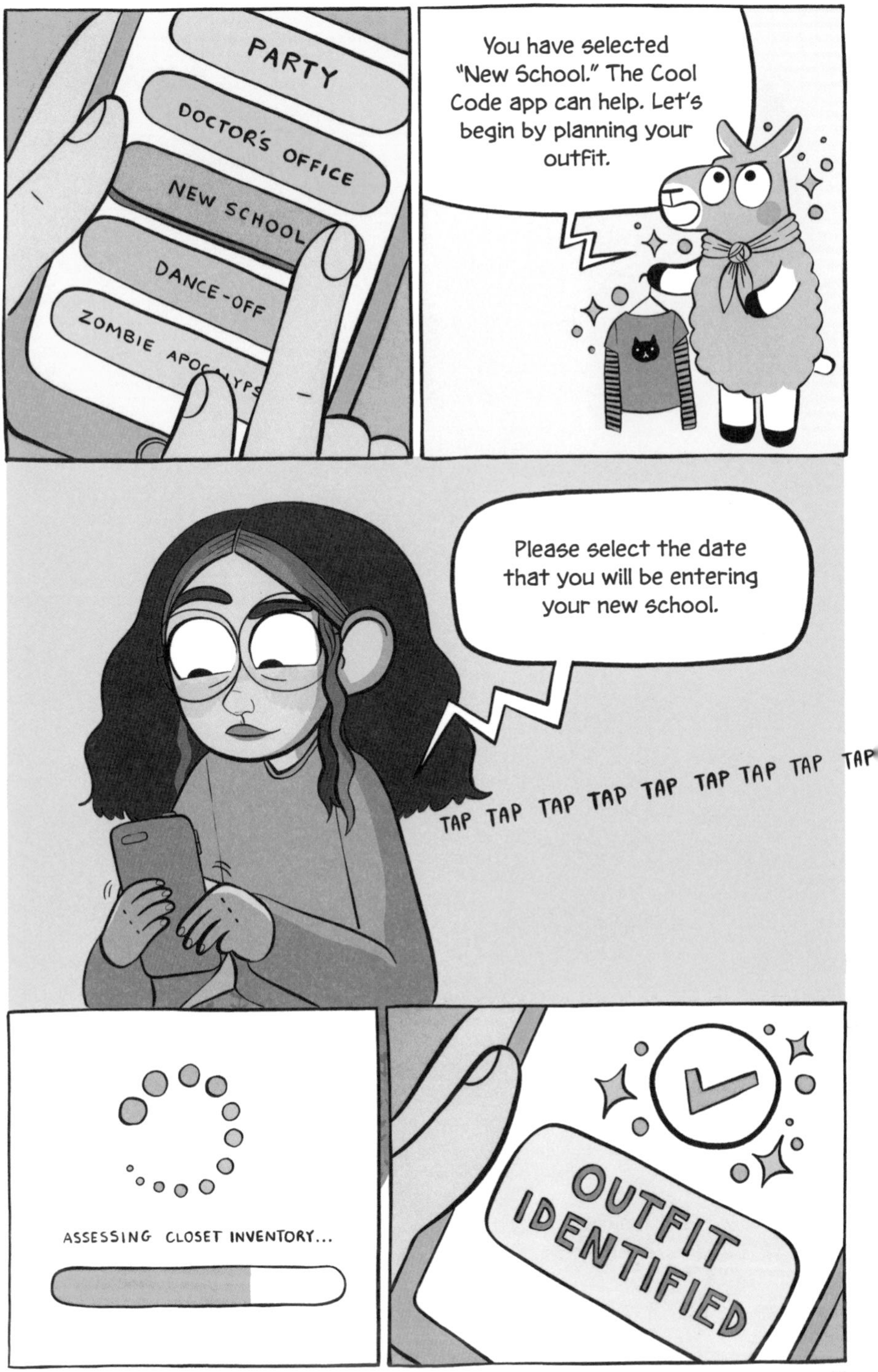
PARTY
DOCTOR'S OFFICE
NEW SCHOOL
DANCE-OFF
You have selected "New School." The Cool Code app can help. Let's begin by planning your outfit.
Please select the date that you will be entering your new school.
TAP TAP TAP TAP TAP TAP TAP TAP TAP
ASSESSING CLOSET INVENTORY...
OUTFIT IDENTIFIED

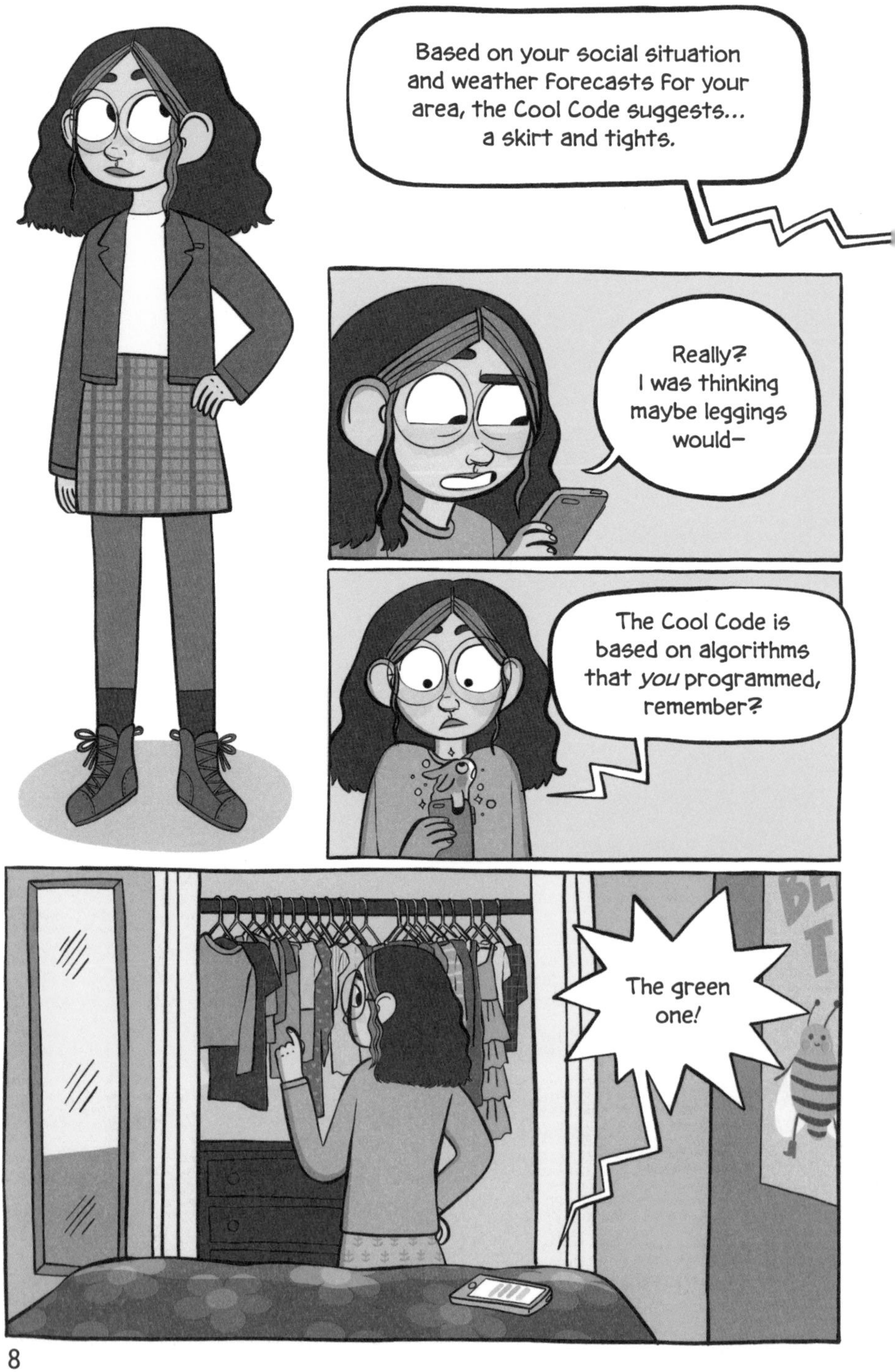
Based on your social situation and weather forecasts for your area, the Cool Code suggests... a skirt and tights.
Really? I was thinking maybe leggings would–
The Cool Code is based on algorithms that *you* programmed, remember?
The green one!

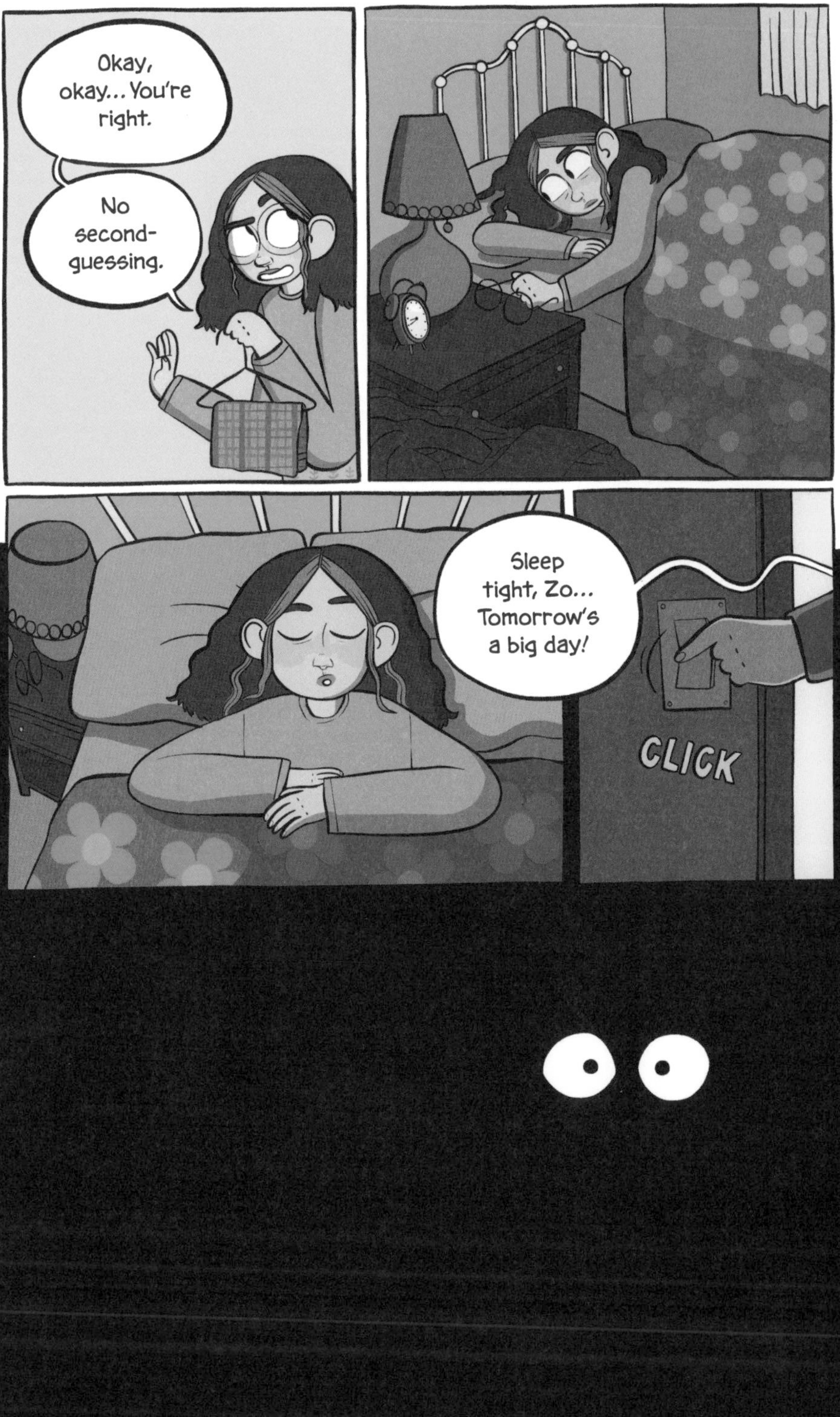
Okay, okay... You're right.
No second-guessing.
Sleep tight, Zo... Tomorrow's a big day!
CLICK

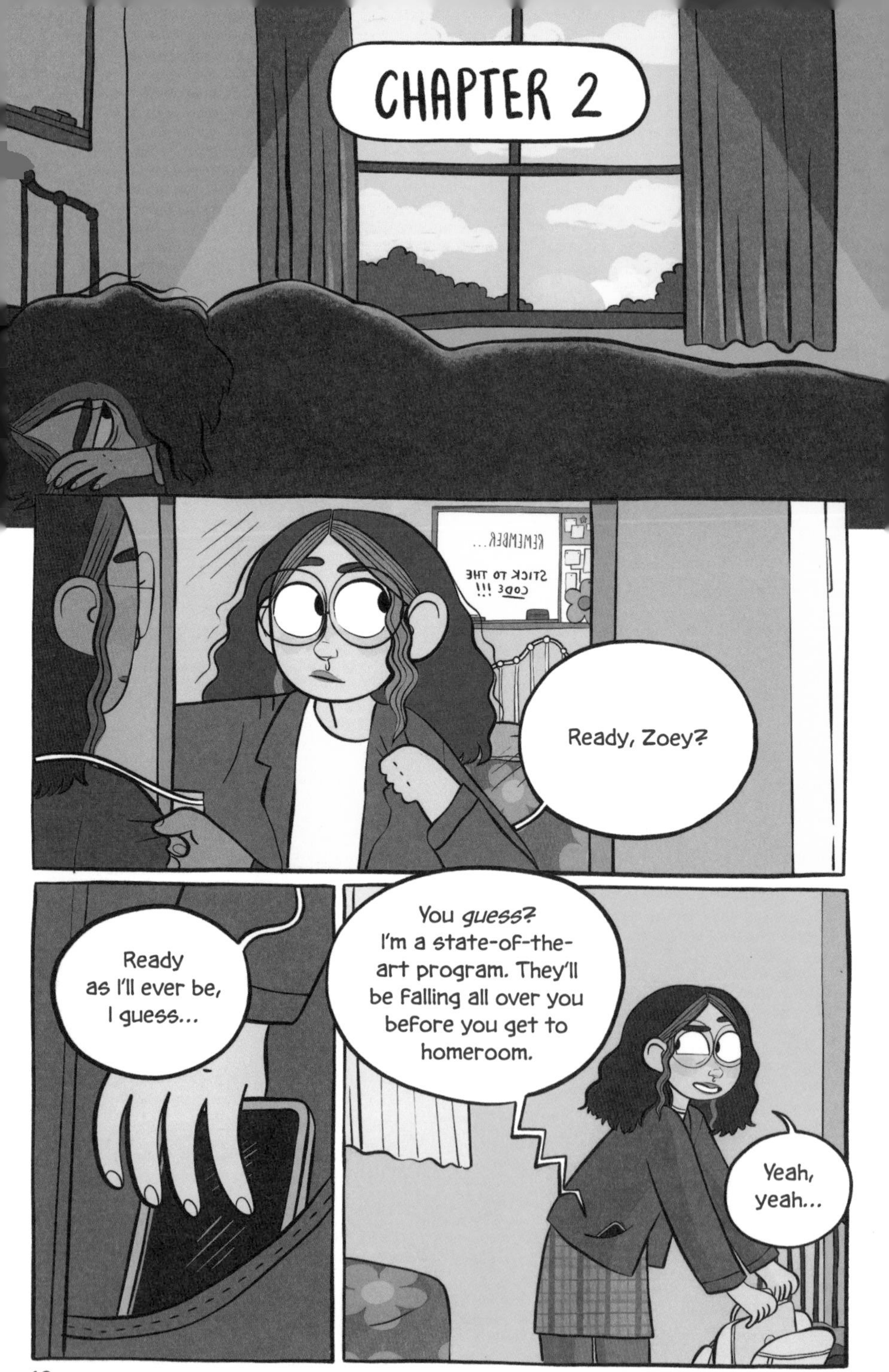
CHAPTER 2
REMEMBER... STICK TO THE CODE !!!
Ready, Zoey?
Ready as I'll ever be, I guess...
You *guess?* I'm a state-of-the-art program. They'll be falling all over you before you get to homeroom.
Yeah, yeah...

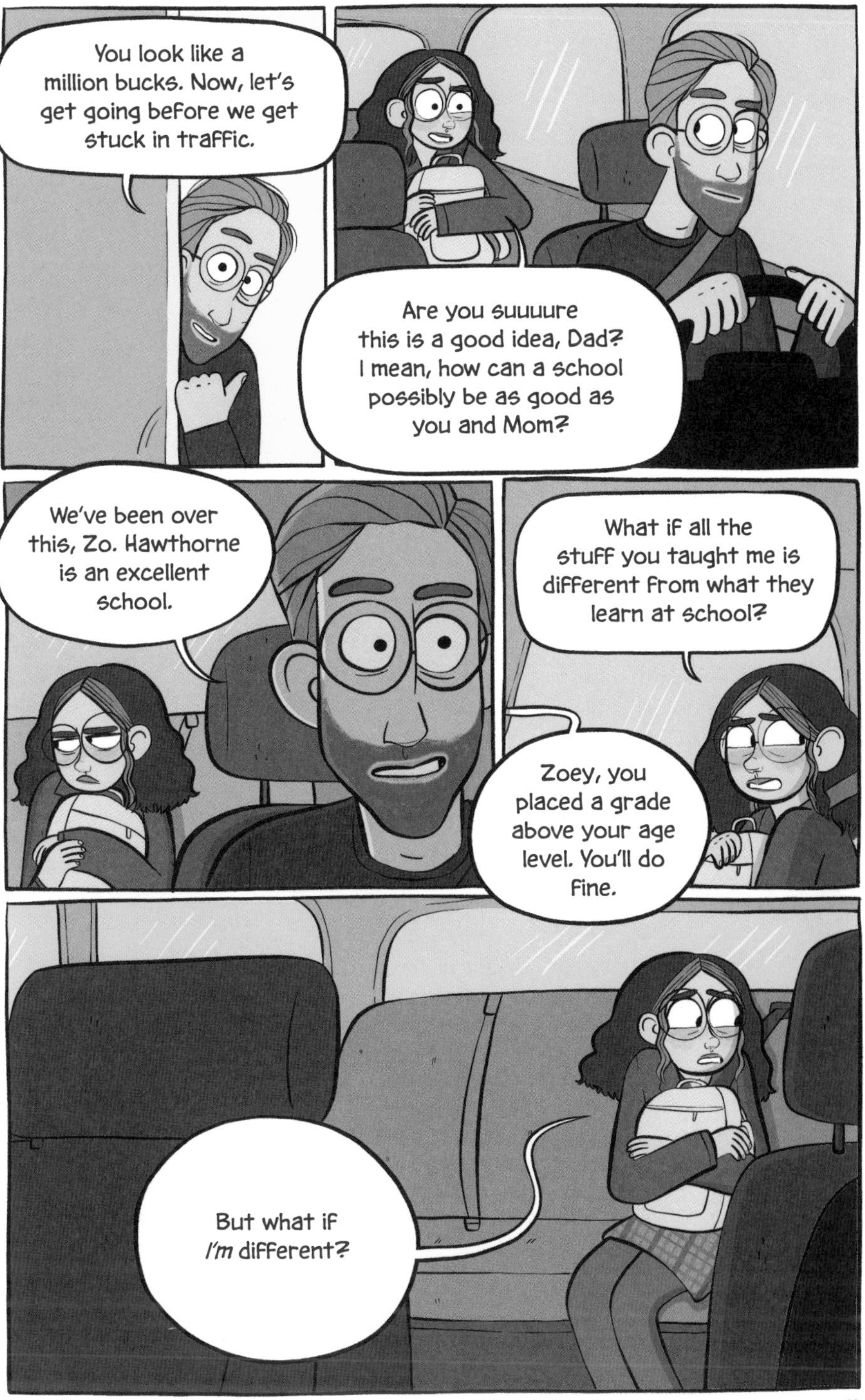
You look like a million bucks. Now, let's get going before we get stuck in traffic.
Are you suuuure this is a good idea, Dad? I mean, how can a school possibly be as good as you and Mom?
We've been over this, Zo. Hawthorne is an excellent school.
What if all the stuff you taught me is different from what they learn at school?
Zoey, you placed a grade above your age level. You'll do fine.
But what if *I'm* different?

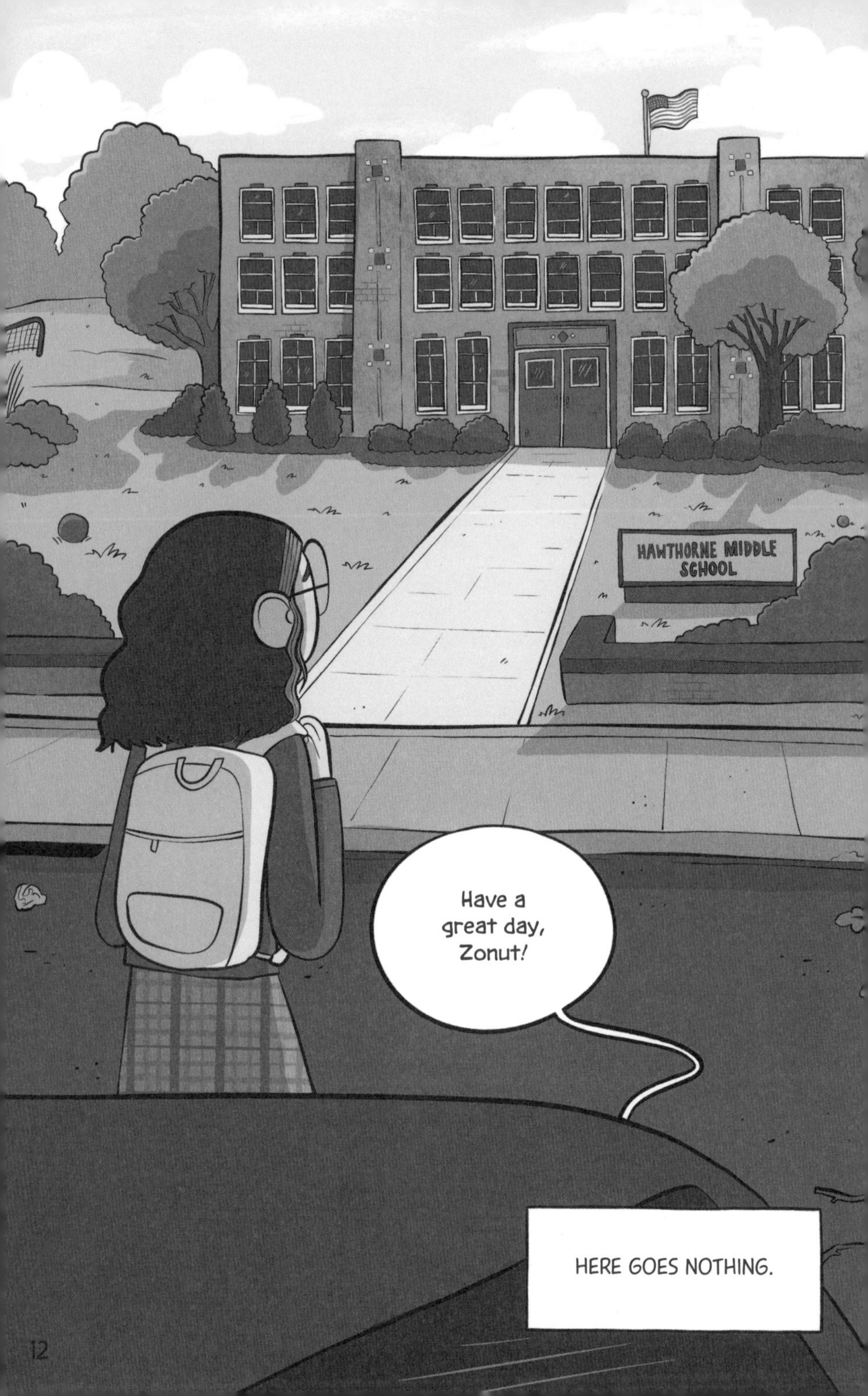
HAWTHORNE MIDDLE SCHOOL
Have a great day, Zonut!
HERE GOES NOTHING.

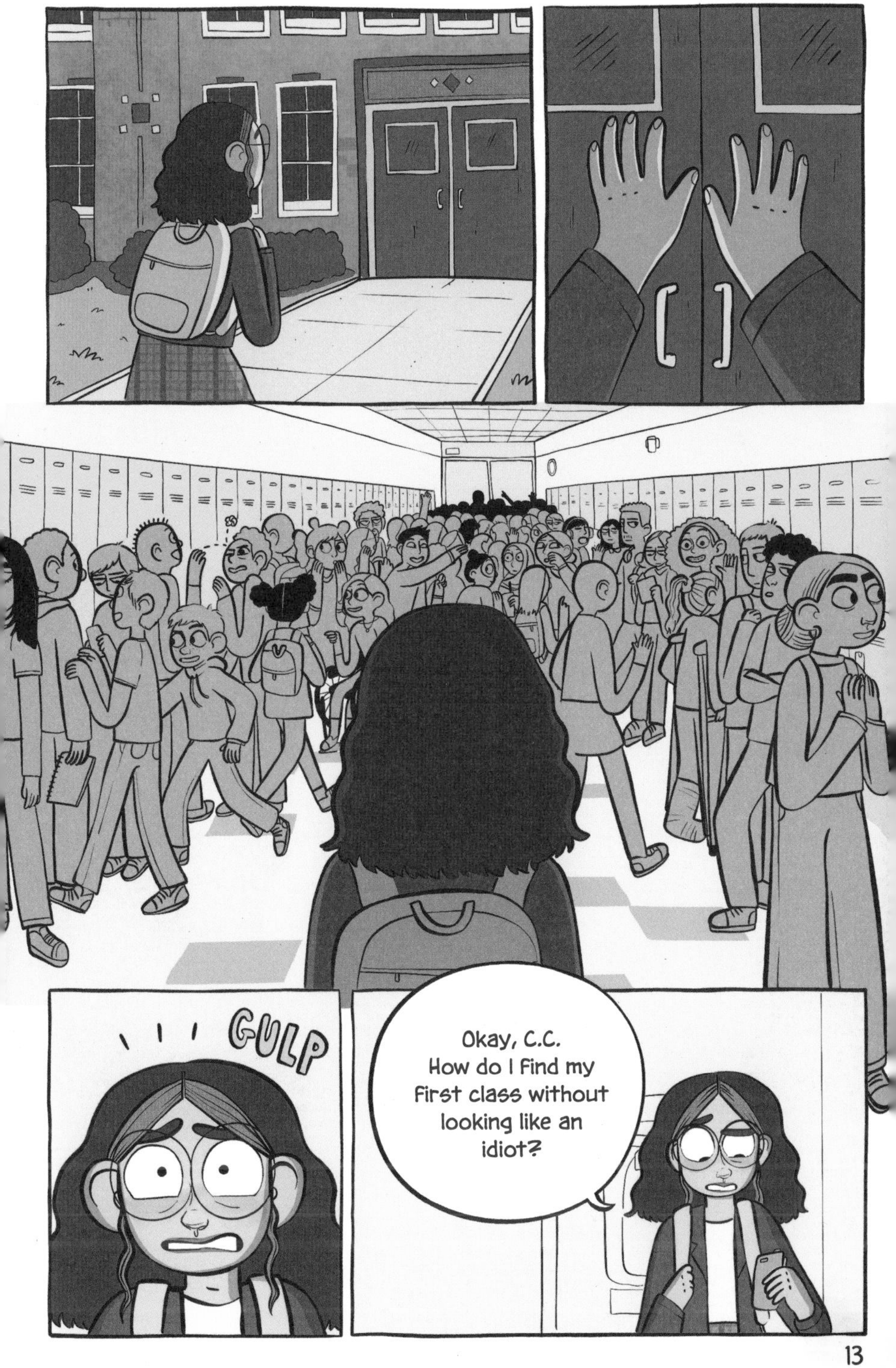
GULP
Okay, C.C.
How do I find my first class without looking like an idiot?

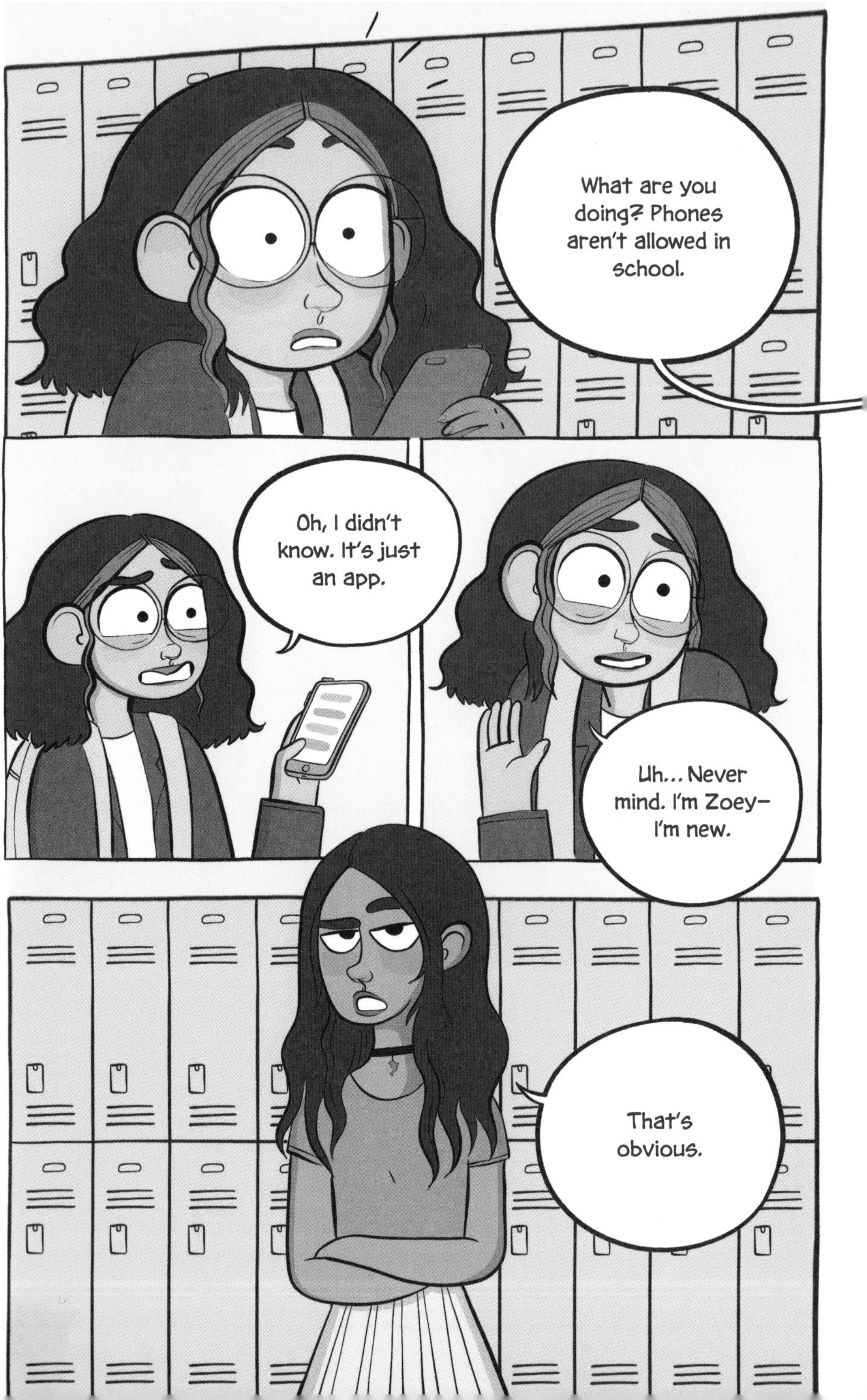
What are you doing? Phones aren't allowed in school.
Oh, I didn't know. It's just an app.
Uh... Never mind. I'm Zoey—I'm new.
That's obvious.

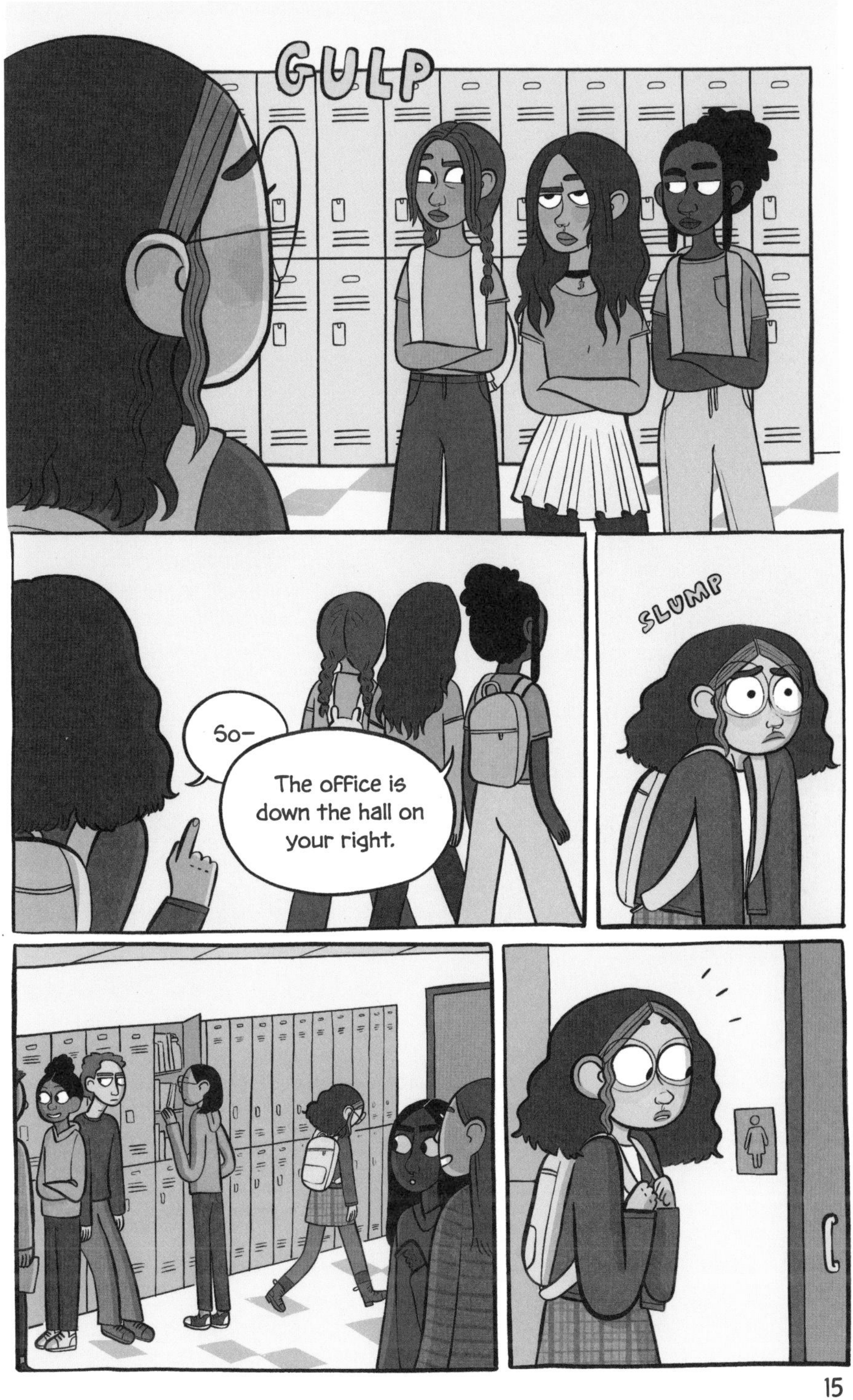
GULP
So–
The office is down the hall on your right.
SLUMP

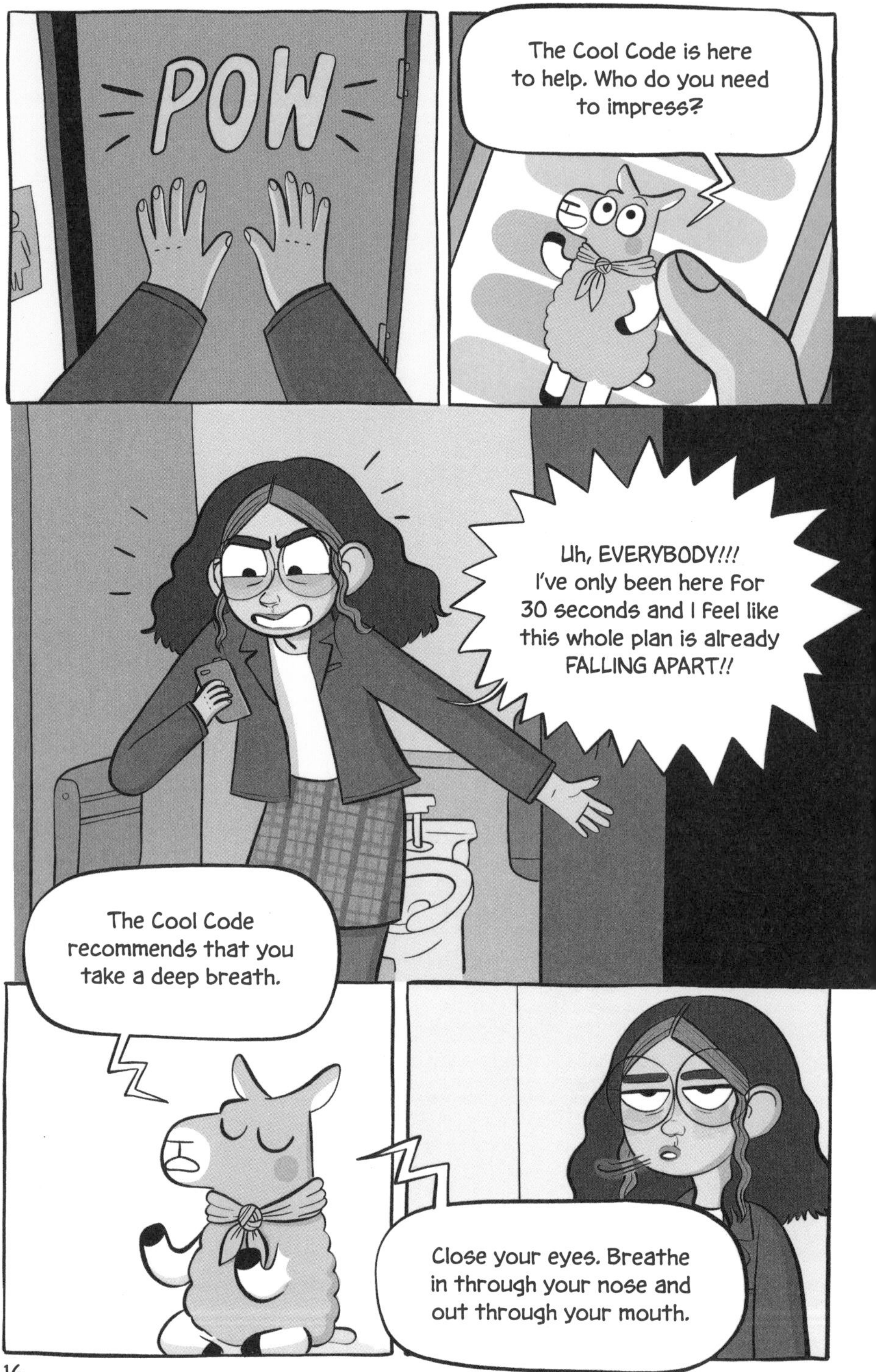
POW
The Cool Code is here to help. Who do you need to impress?
Uh, EVERYBODY!!! I've only been here for 30 seconds and I feel like this whole plan is already FALLING APART!!
The Cool Code recommends that you take a deep breath.
Close your eyes. Breathe in through your nose and out through your mouth.

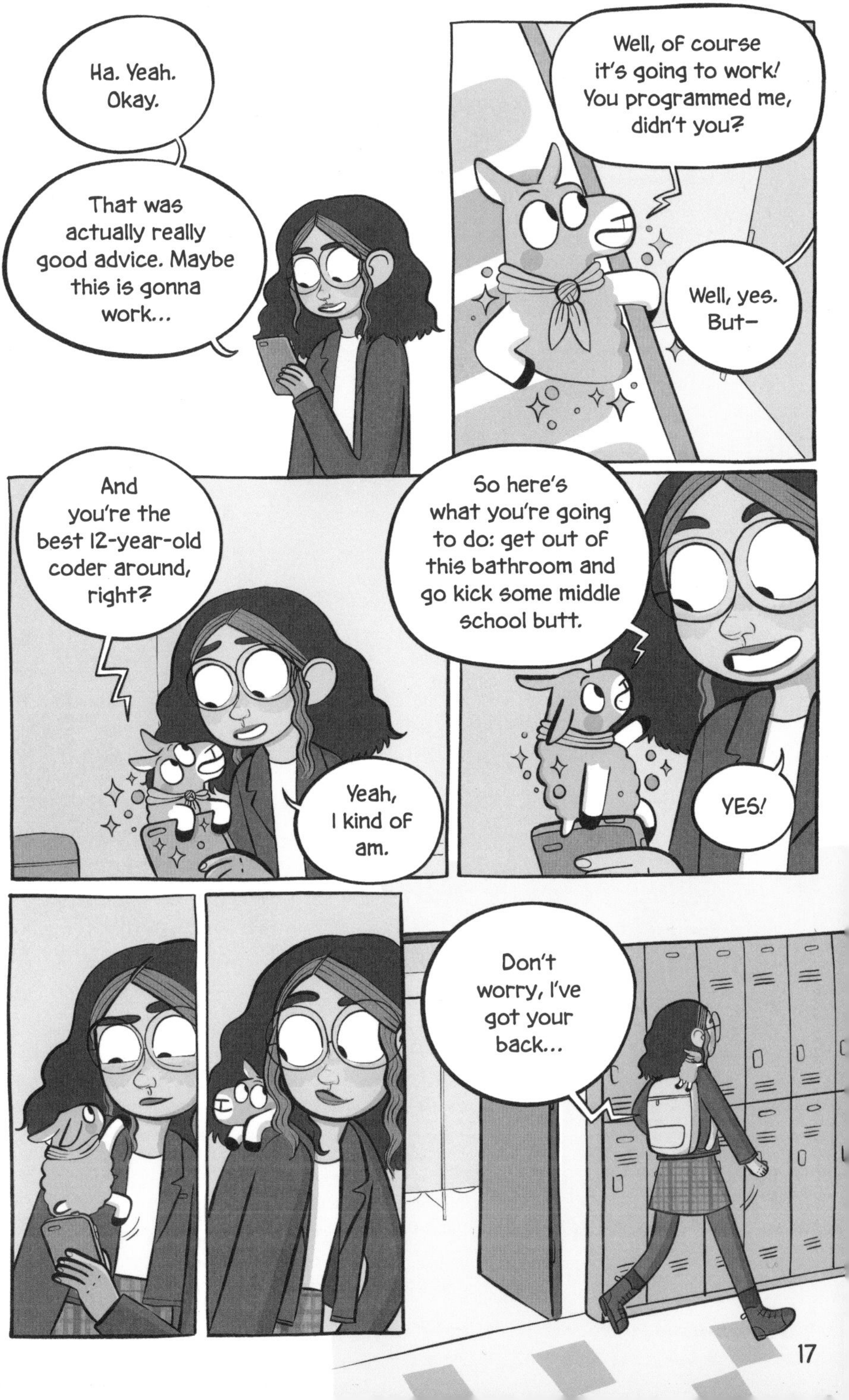
Ha. Yeah. Okay.
That was actually really good advice. Maybe this is gonna work...
Well, of course it's going to work! You programmed me, didn't you?
Well, yes. But–
And you're the best 12-year-old coder around, right?
Yeah, I kind of am.
So here's what you're going to do: get out of this bathroom and go kick some middle school butt.
YES!
Don't worry, I've got your back...

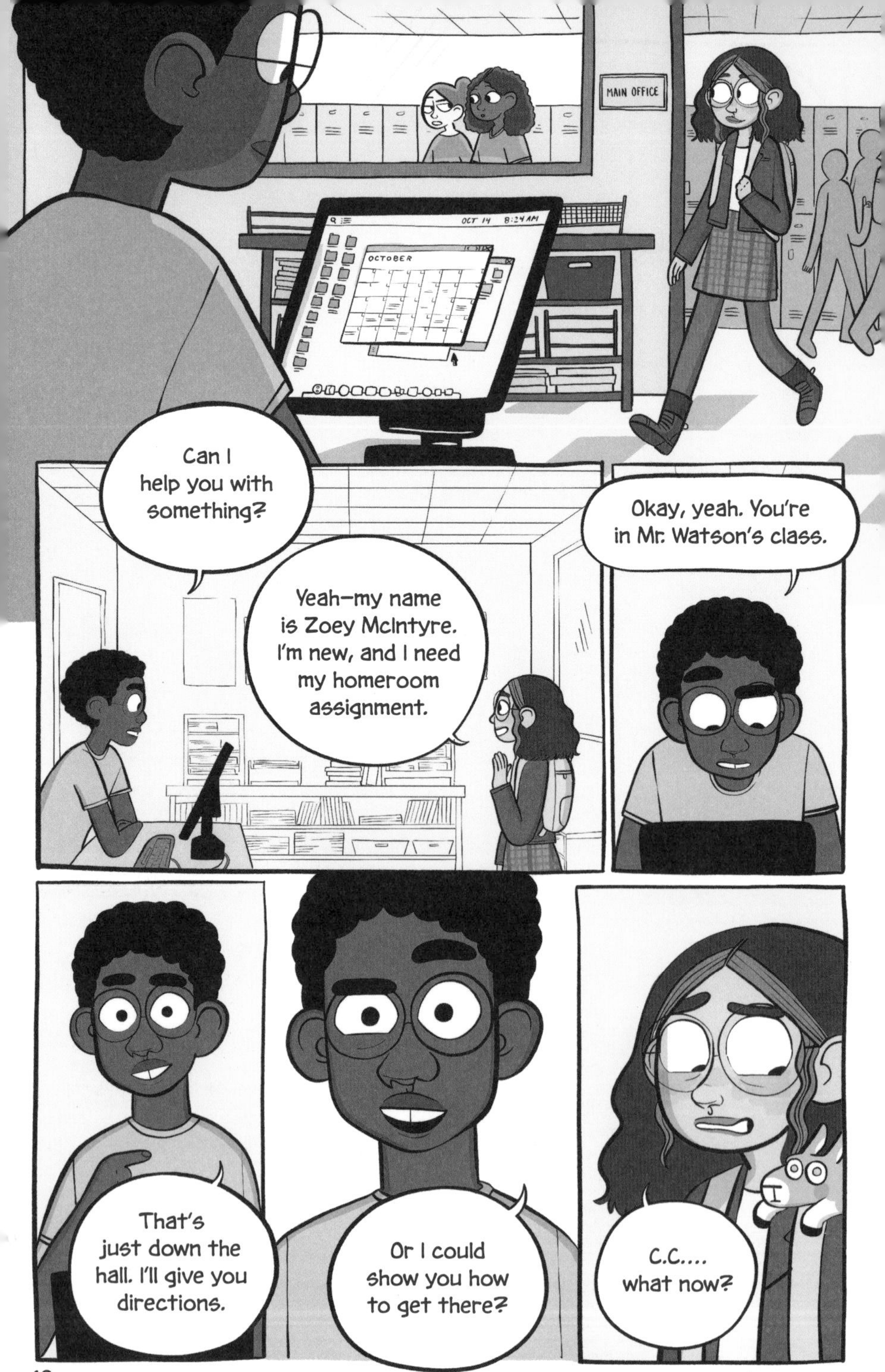
MAIN OFFICE
OCT 14 8:24 AM
OCTOBER
Can I help you with something?
Yeah—my name is Zoey McIntyre. I'm new, and I need my homeroom assignment.
Okay, yeah. You're in Mr. Watson's class.
That's just down the hall. I'll give you directions.
Or I could show you how to get there?
C.C.... what now?

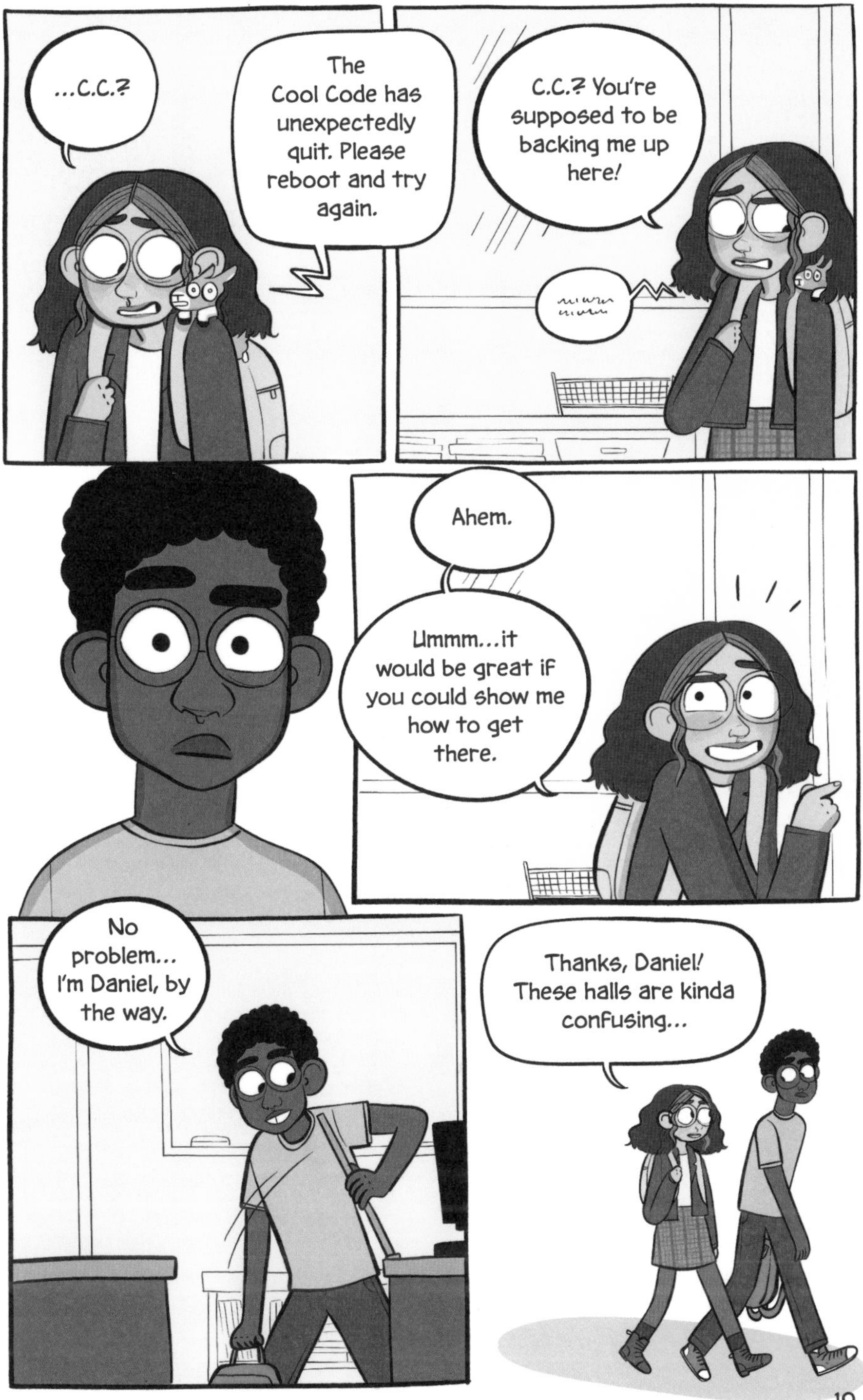
...C.C.?
The Cool Code has unexpectedly quit. Please reboot and try again.
C.C.? You're supposed to be backing me up here!
Ahem.
Ummm...it would be great if you could show me how to get there.
No problem... I'm Daniel, by the way.
Thanks, Daniel! These halls are kinda confusing...

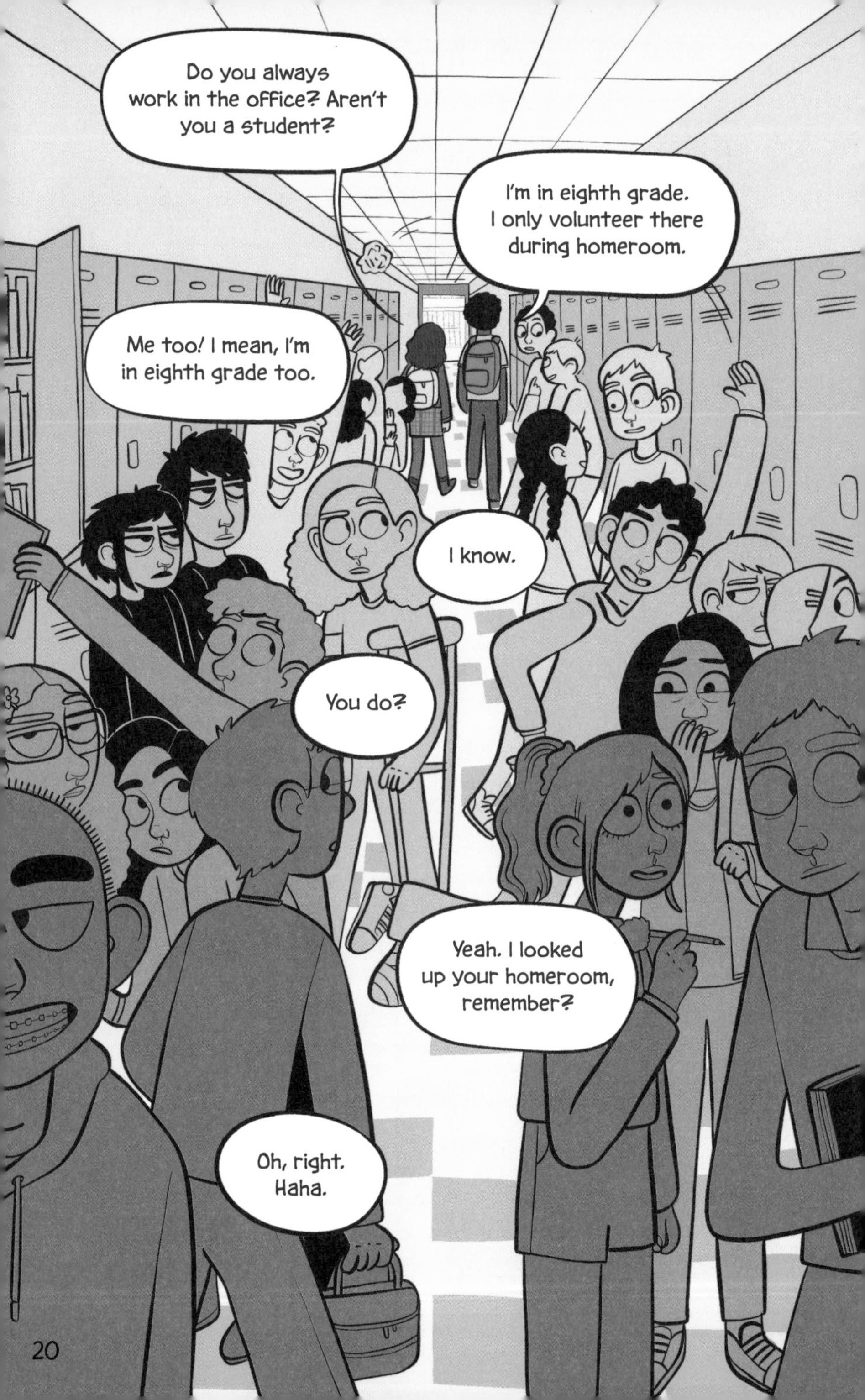
Do you always work in the office? Aren't you a student?
I'm in eighth grade. I only volunteer there during homeroom.
Me too! I mean, I'm in eighth grade too.
I know.
You do?
Yeah. I looked up your homeroom, remember?
Oh, right. Haha.

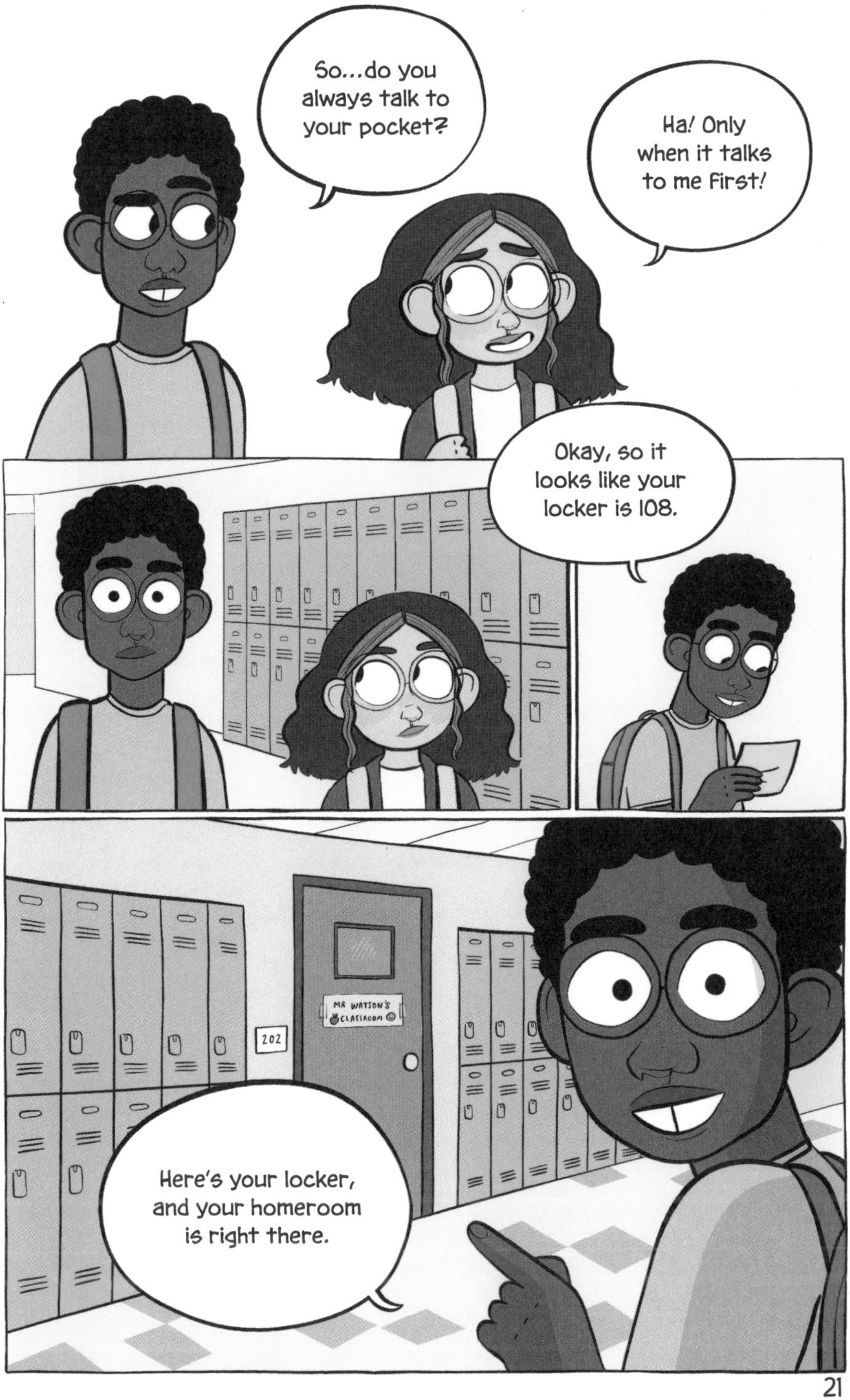
So...do you always talk to your pocket?
Ha! Only when it talks to me first!
Okay, so it looks like your locker is 108.
MR WATSON'S CLASSROOM
202
Here's your locker, and your homeroom is right there.

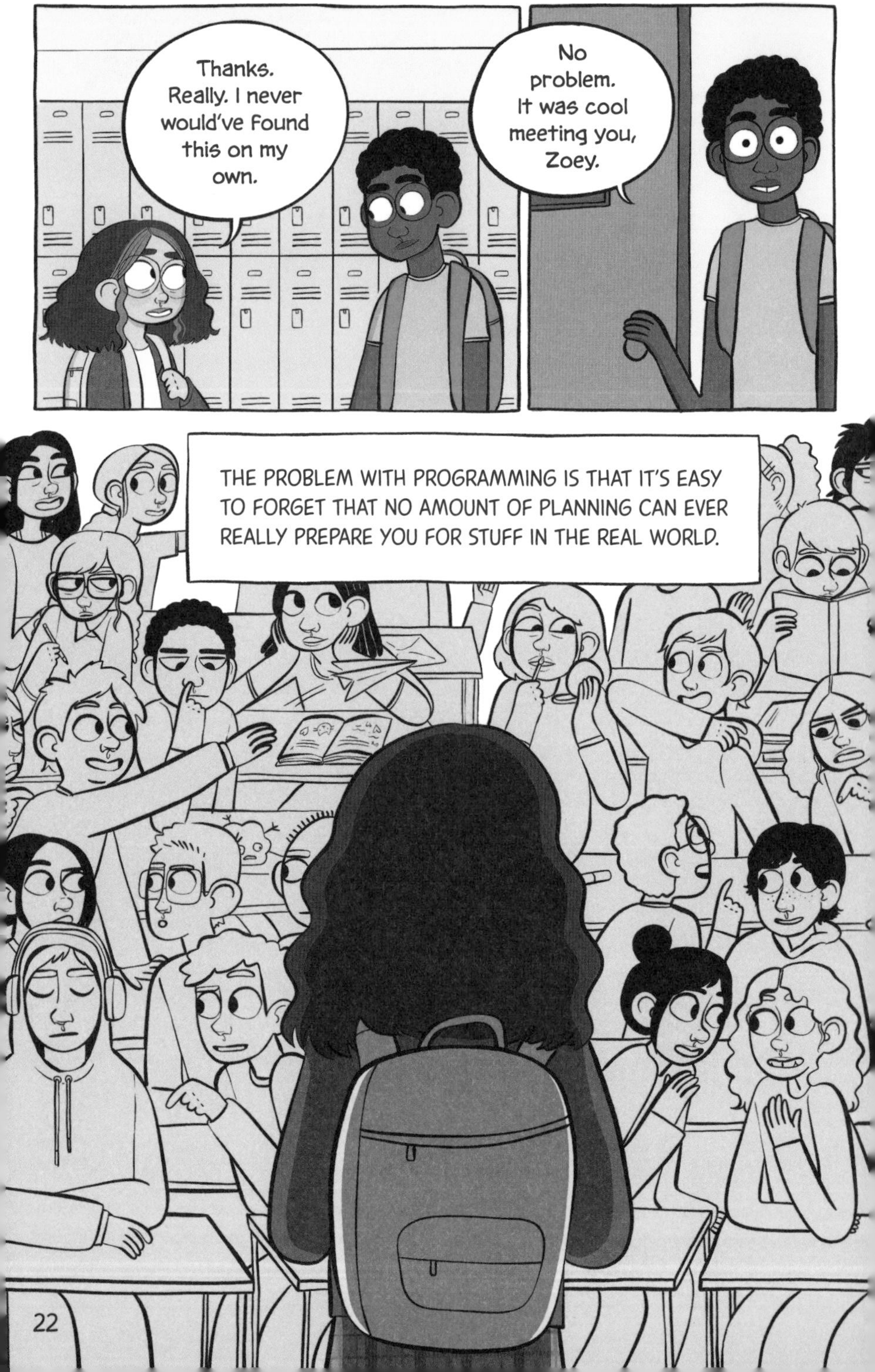
Thanks. Really. I never would've found this on my own.
No problem. It was cool meeting you, Zoey.
THE PROBLEM WITH PROGRAMMING IS THAT IT'S EASY TO FORGET THAT NO AMOUNT OF PLANNING CAN EVER REALLY PREPARE YOU FOR STUFF IN THE REAL WORLD.

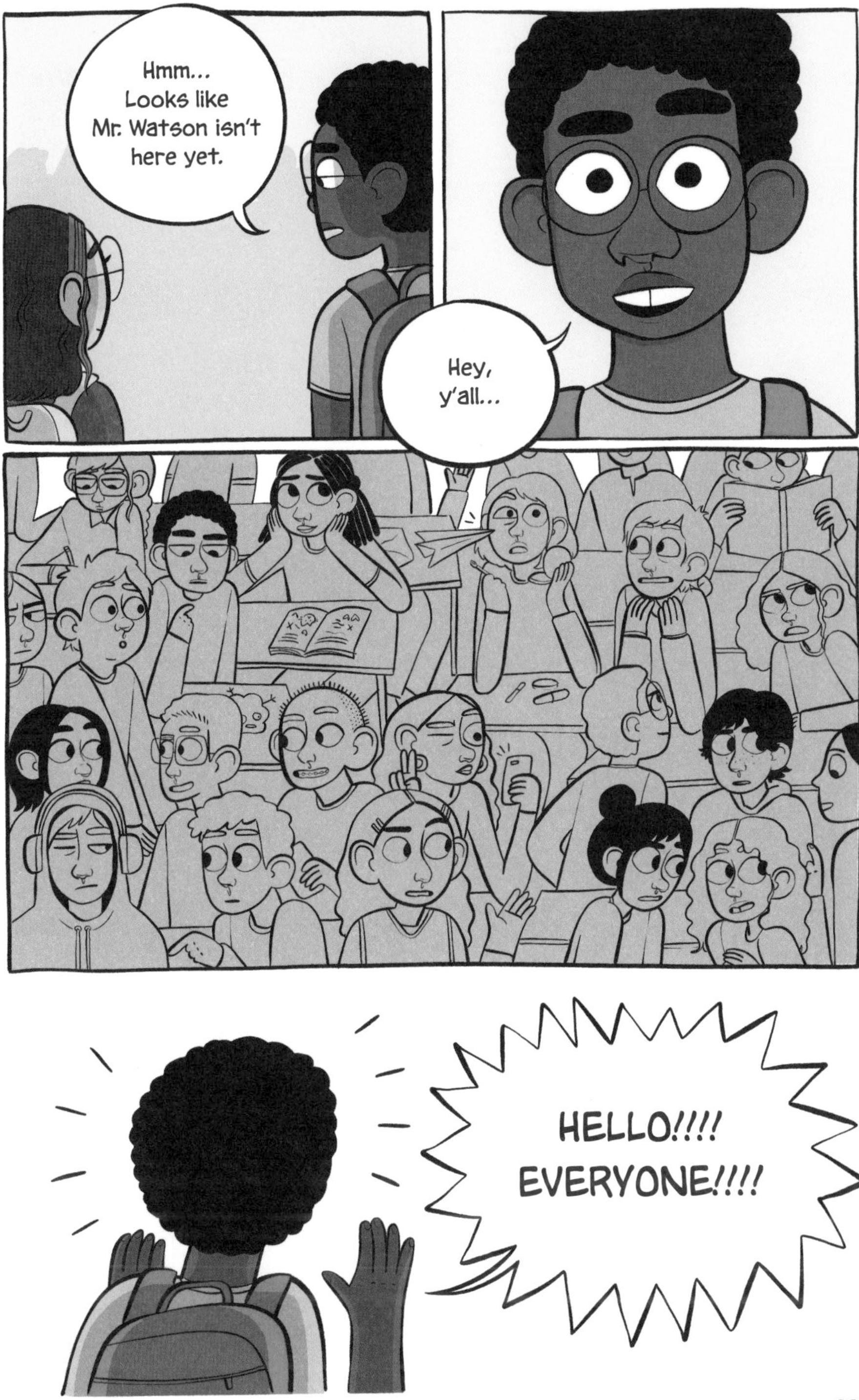
Hmm... Looks like Mr. Watson isn't here yet.
Hey, y'all...
HELLO!!!! EVERYONE!!!!

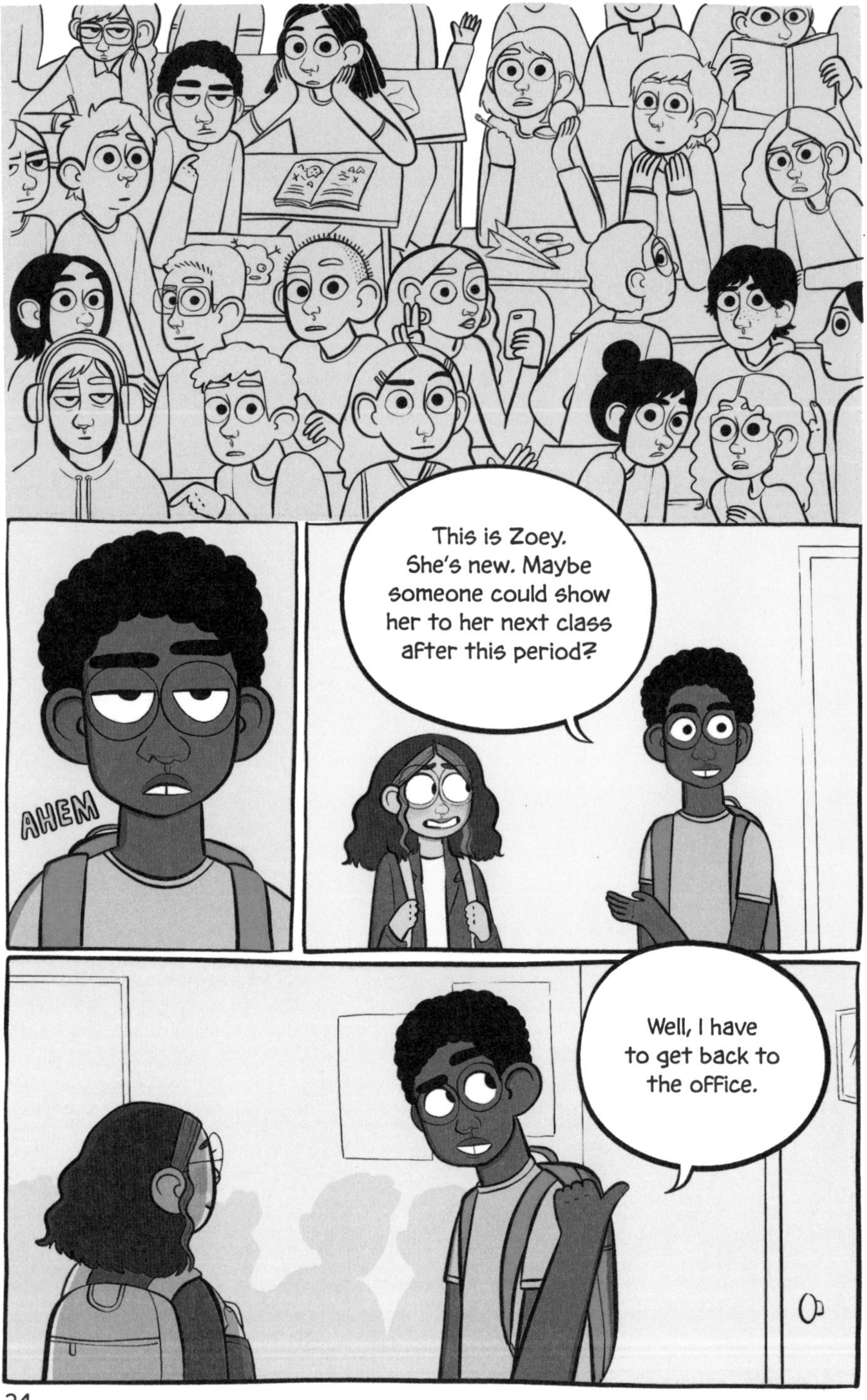
AHEM
This is Zoey. She's new. Maybe someone could show her to her next class after this period?
Well, I have to get back to the office.

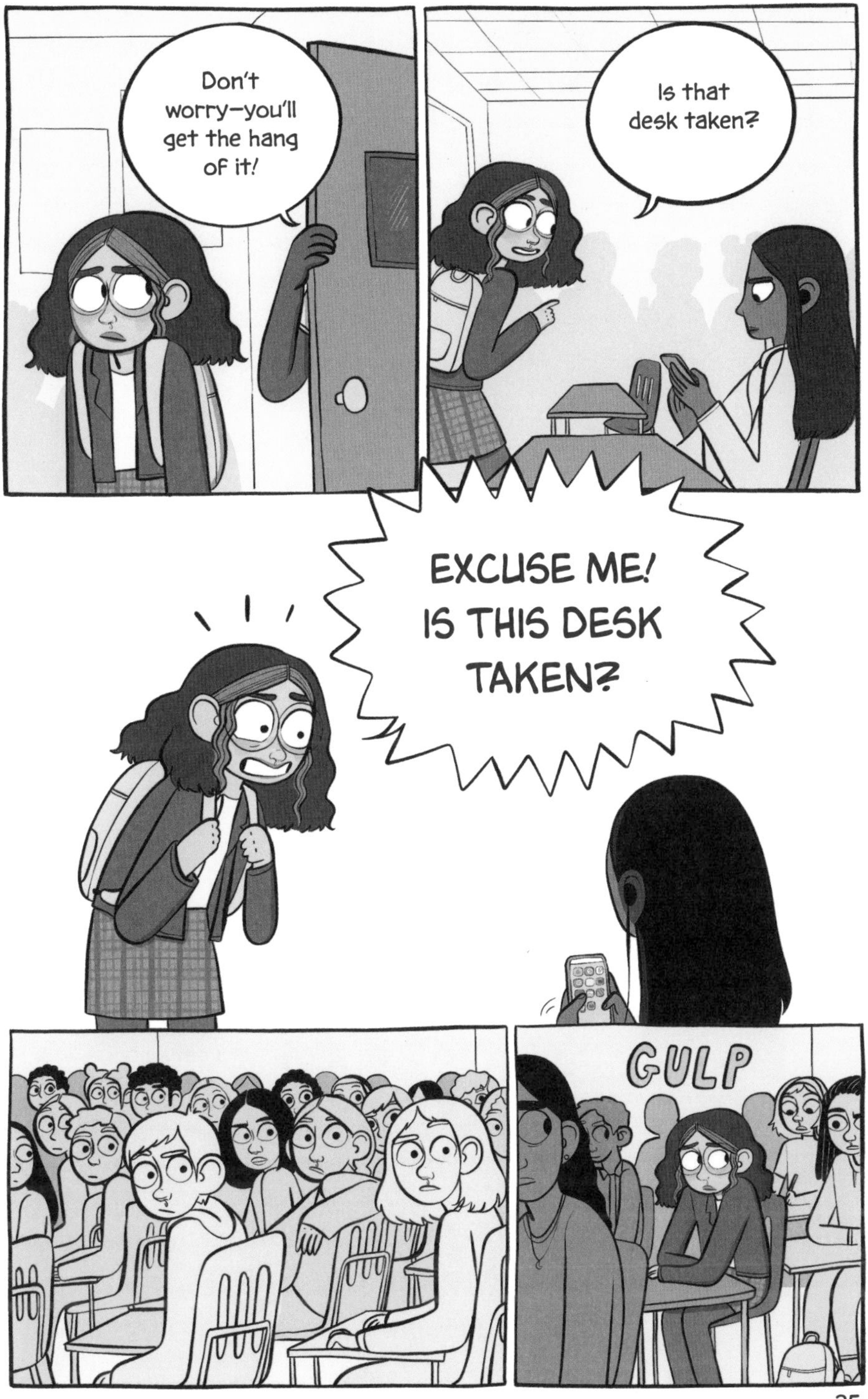
Don't worry—you'll get the hang of it!
Is that desk taken?
EXCUSE ME! IS THIS DESK TAKEN?
GULP

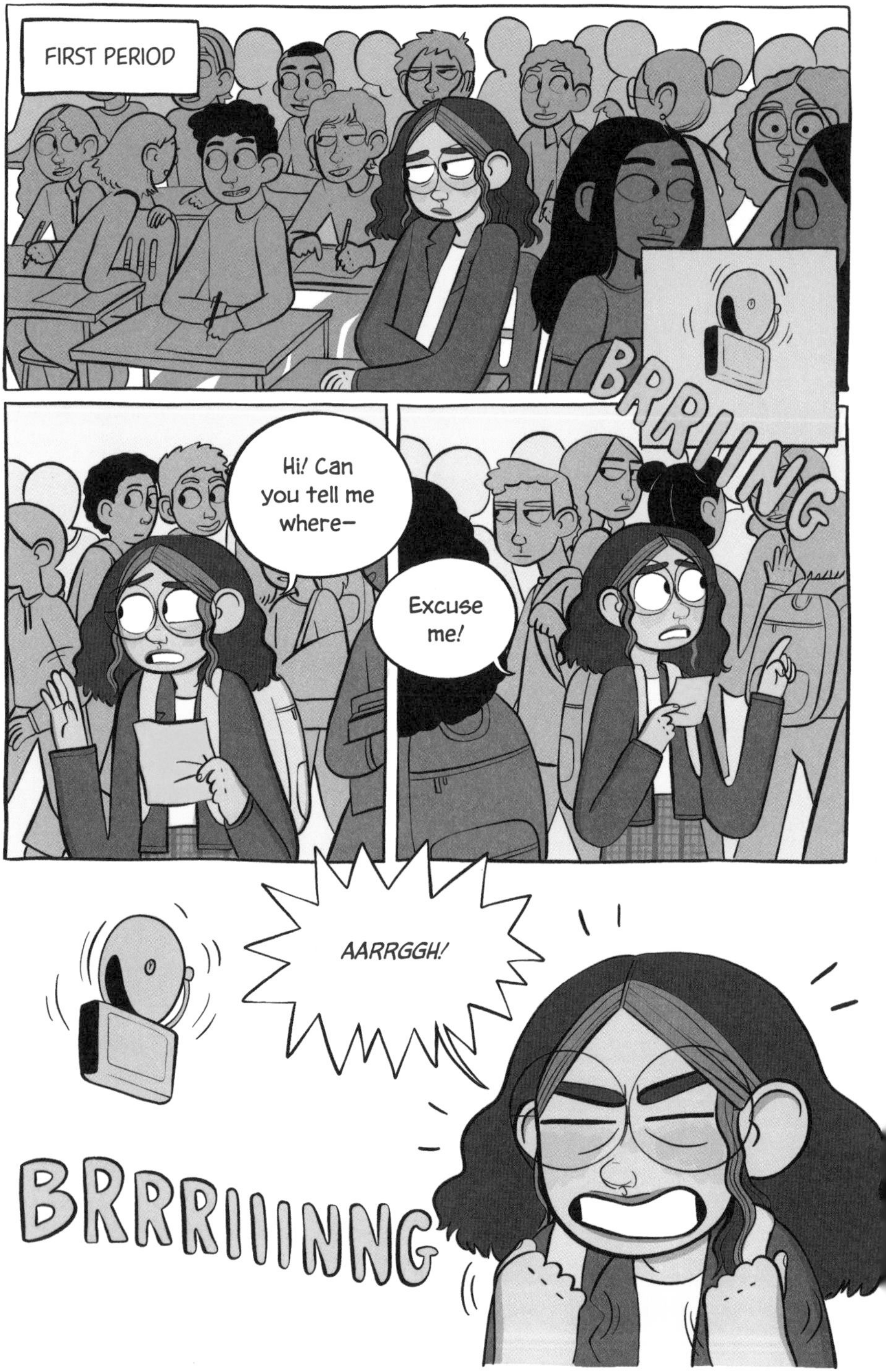
FIRST PERIOD
BRRIING
Hi! Can you tell me where—
Excuse me!
AARRGGH!
BRRRIIINNG

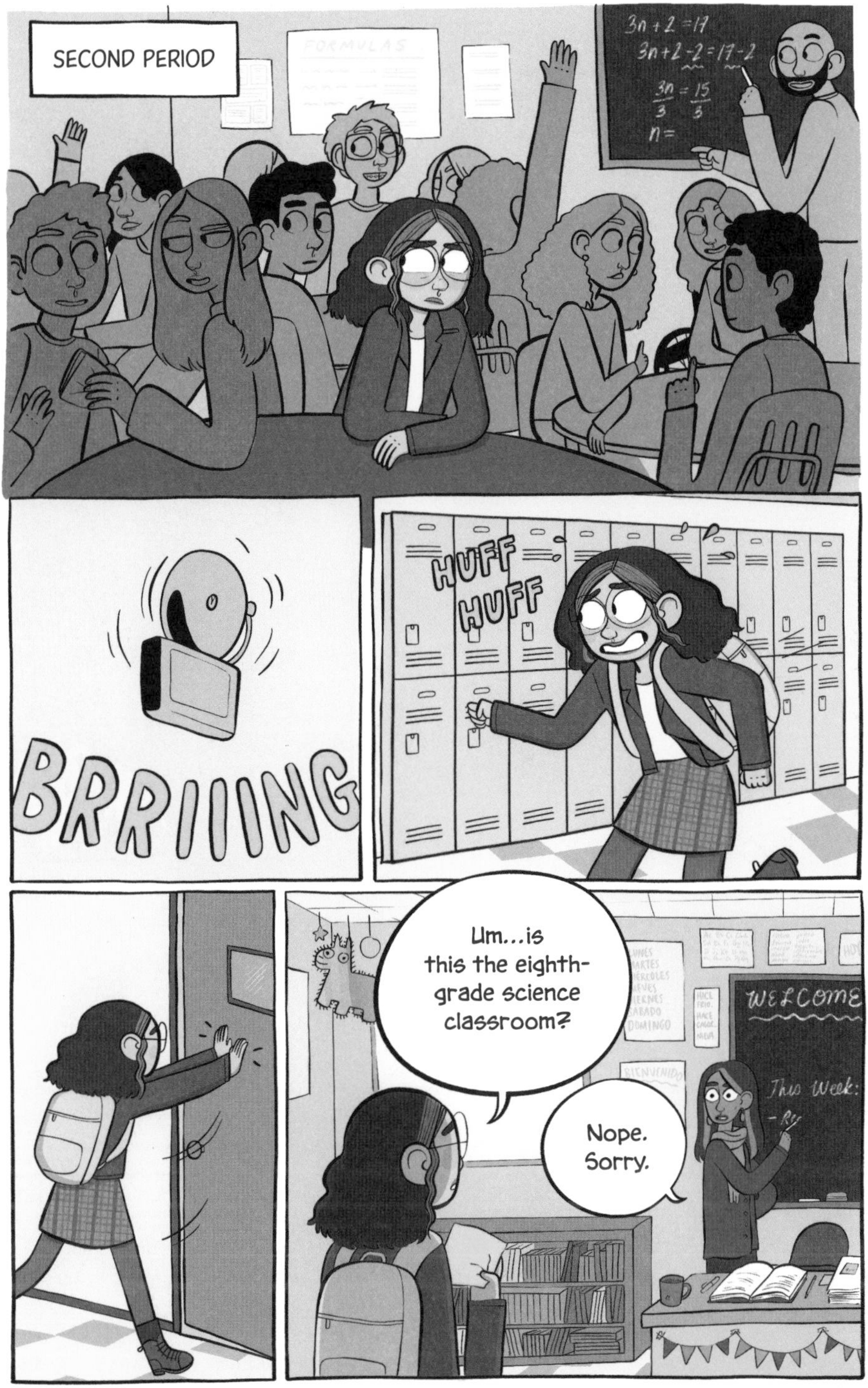
SECOND PERIOD
FORMULAS
3n + 2 = 17
3n + 2 - 2 = 17 - 2
3n/3 = 15/3
n =
BRRIIING
HUFF HUFF
Um...is this the eighth-grade science classroom?
Nope. Sorry.
WELCOME
This Week:
BIENVENIDO
LUNES
MARTES
DOMINGO

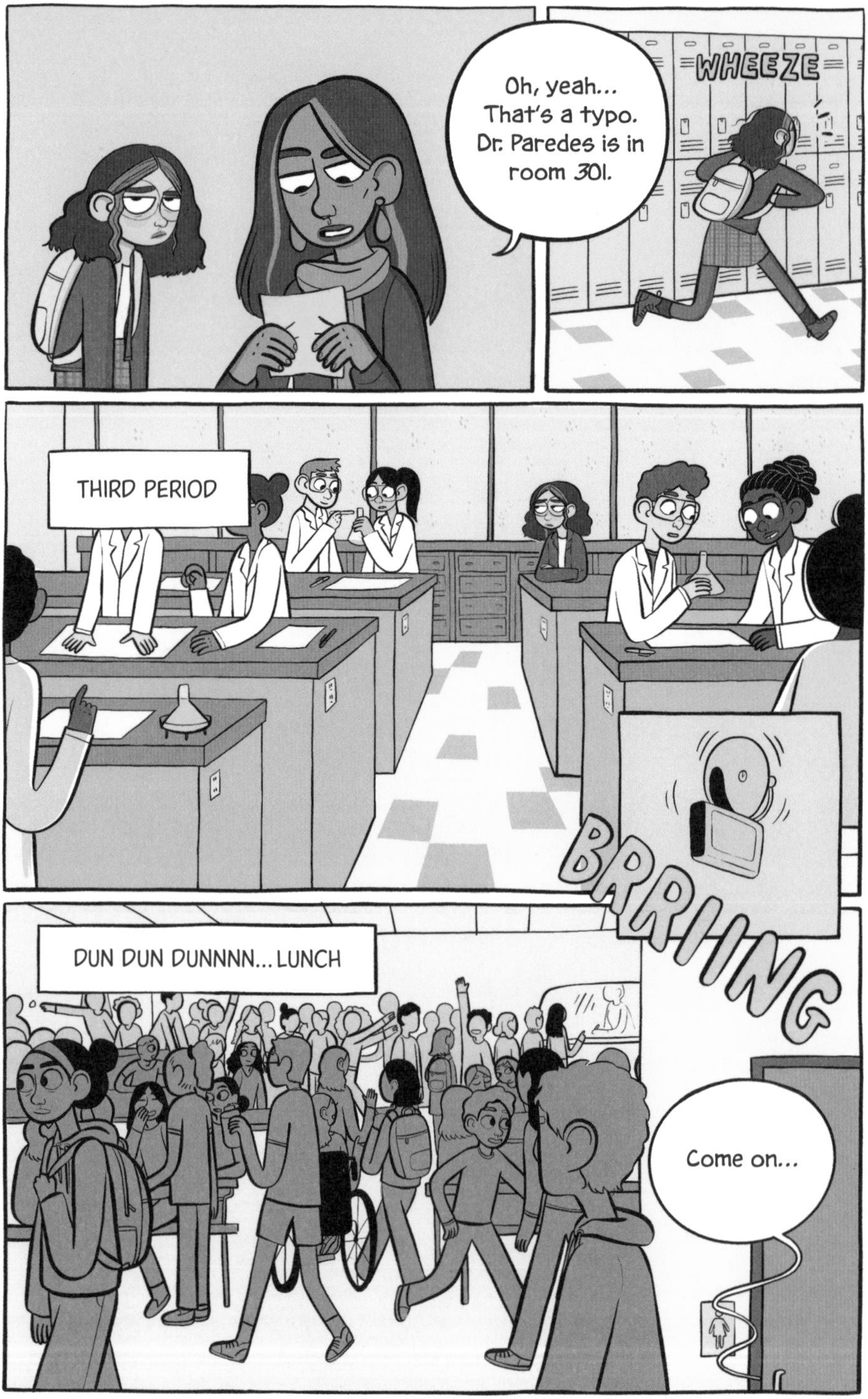
Oh, yeah... That's a typo. Dr. Paredes is in room 301.
WHEEZE
THIRD PERIOD
BRRIING
DUN DUN DUNNNN...LUNCH
Come on...

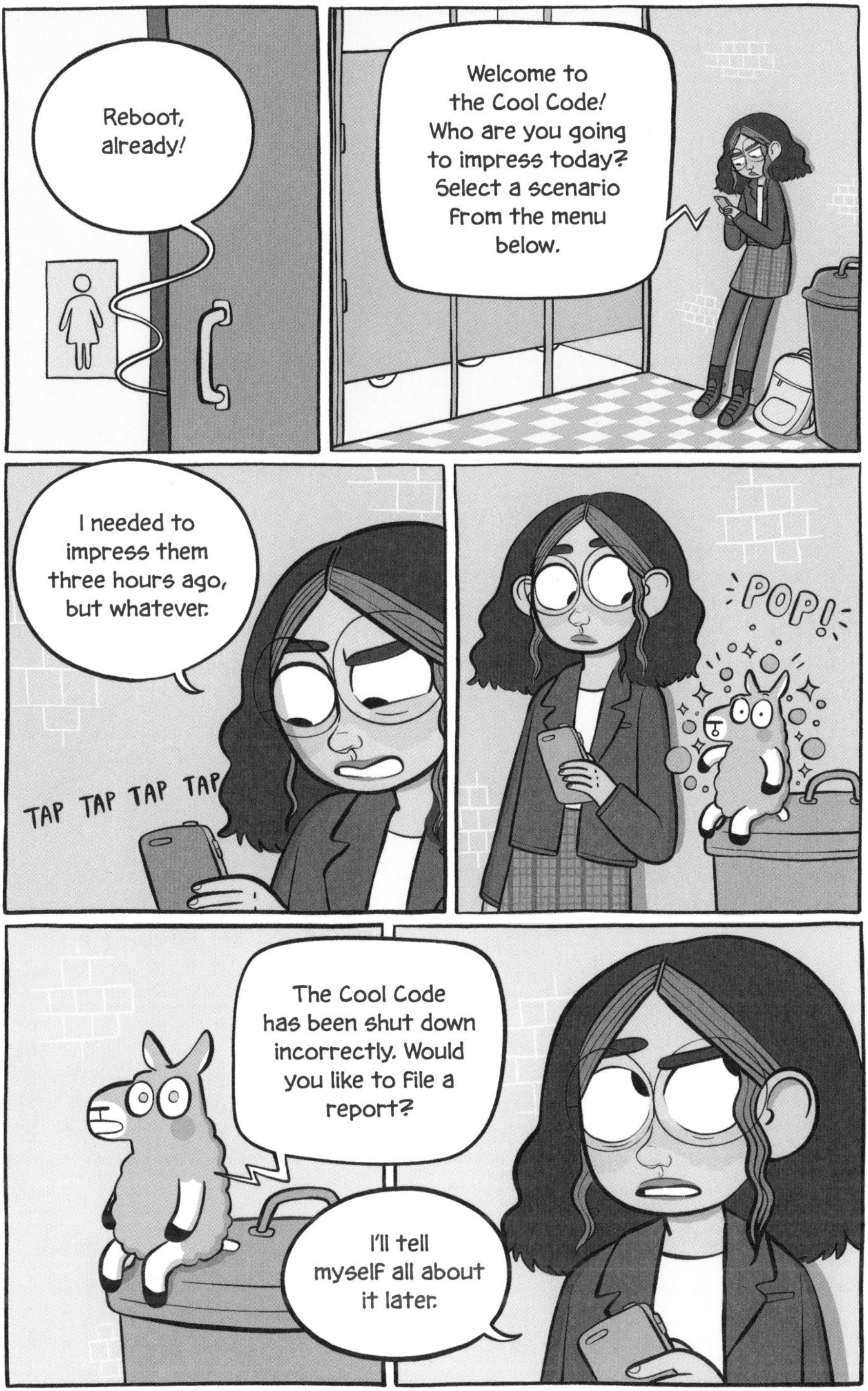
Reboot, already!
Welcome to the Cool Code! Who are you going to impress today? Select a scenario from the menu below.
I needed to impress them three hours ago, but whatever.
TAP TAP TAP TAP
POP!
The Cool Code has been shut down incorrectly. Would you like to file a report?
I'll tell myself all about it later.

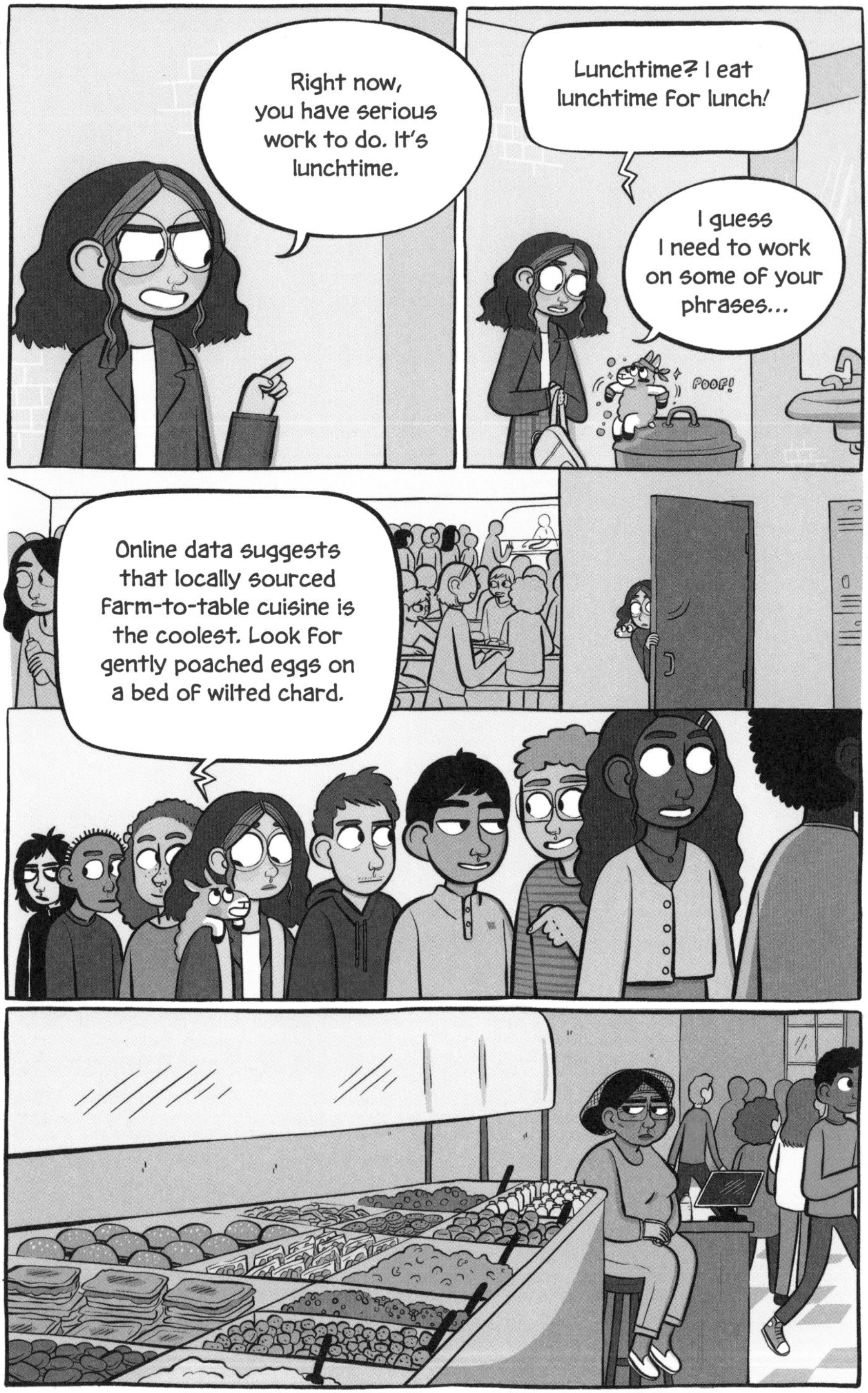
Right now, you have serious work to do. It's lunchtime.
Lunchtime? I eat lunchtime for lunch!
I guess I need to work on some of your phrases...
POOF!
Online data suggests that locally sourced farm-to-table cuisine is the coolest. Look for gently poached eggs on a bed of wilted chard.

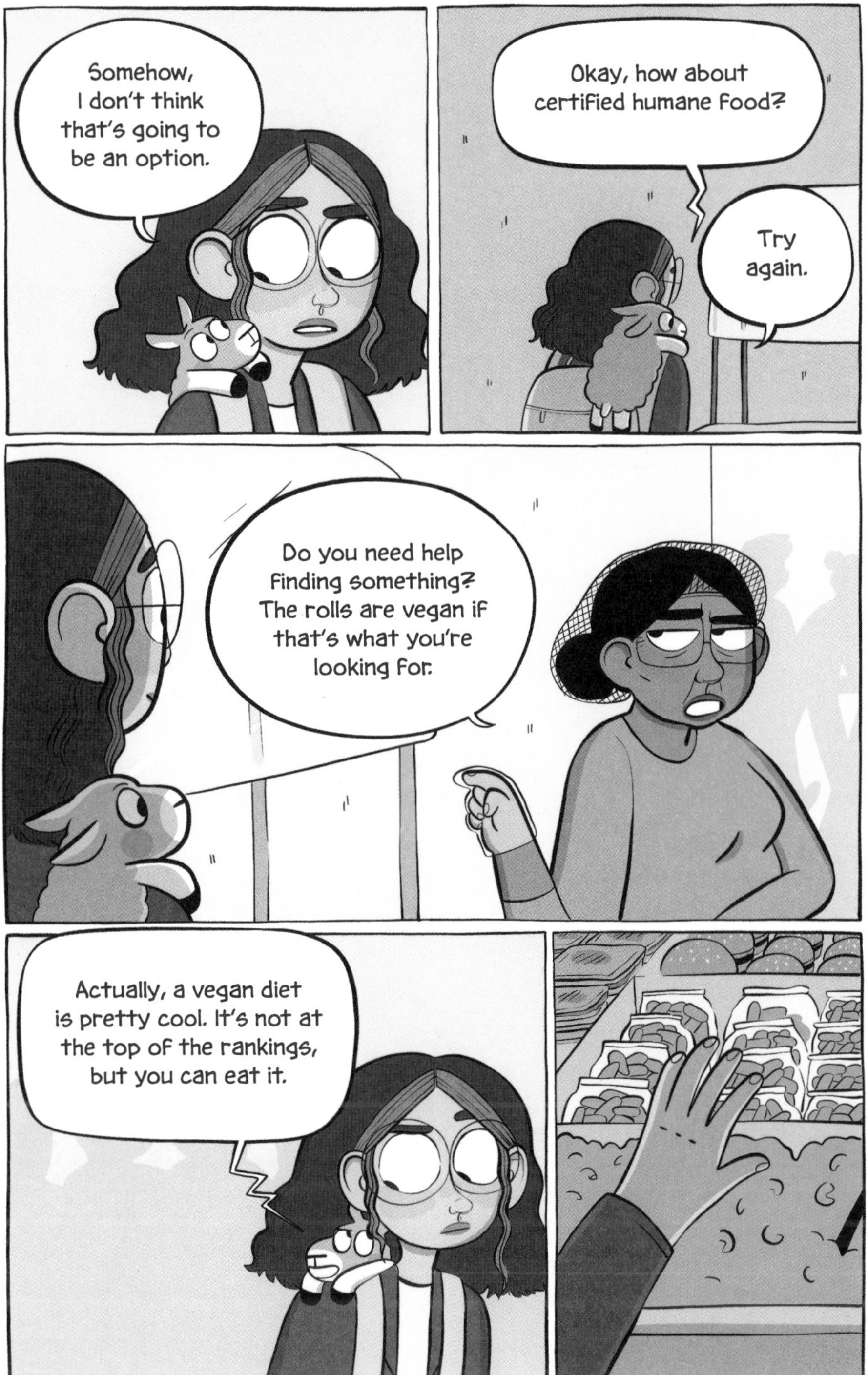
Somehow, I don't think that's going to be an option.
Okay, how about certified humane food?
Try again.
Do you need help finding something? The rolls are vegan if that's what you're looking for.
Actually, a vegan diet is pretty cool. It's not at the top of the rankings, but you can eat it.

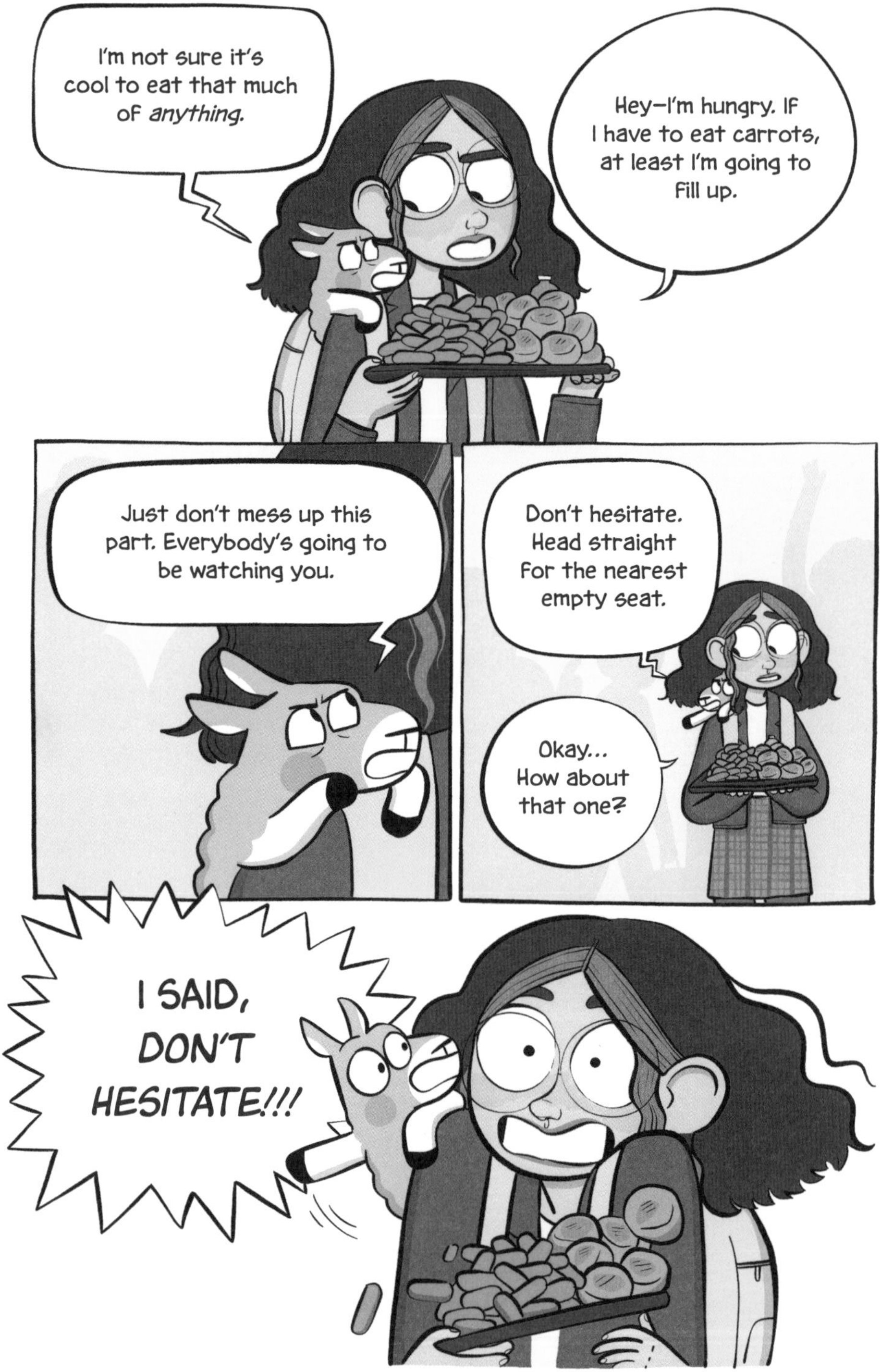
I'm not sure it's cool to eat that much of *anything.*
Hey—I'm hungry. If I have to eat carrots, at least I'm going to fill up.
Just don't mess up this part. Everybody's going to be watching you.
Don't hesitate. Head straight for the nearest empty seat.
Okay... How about that one?
I SAID, DON'T HESITATE!!!

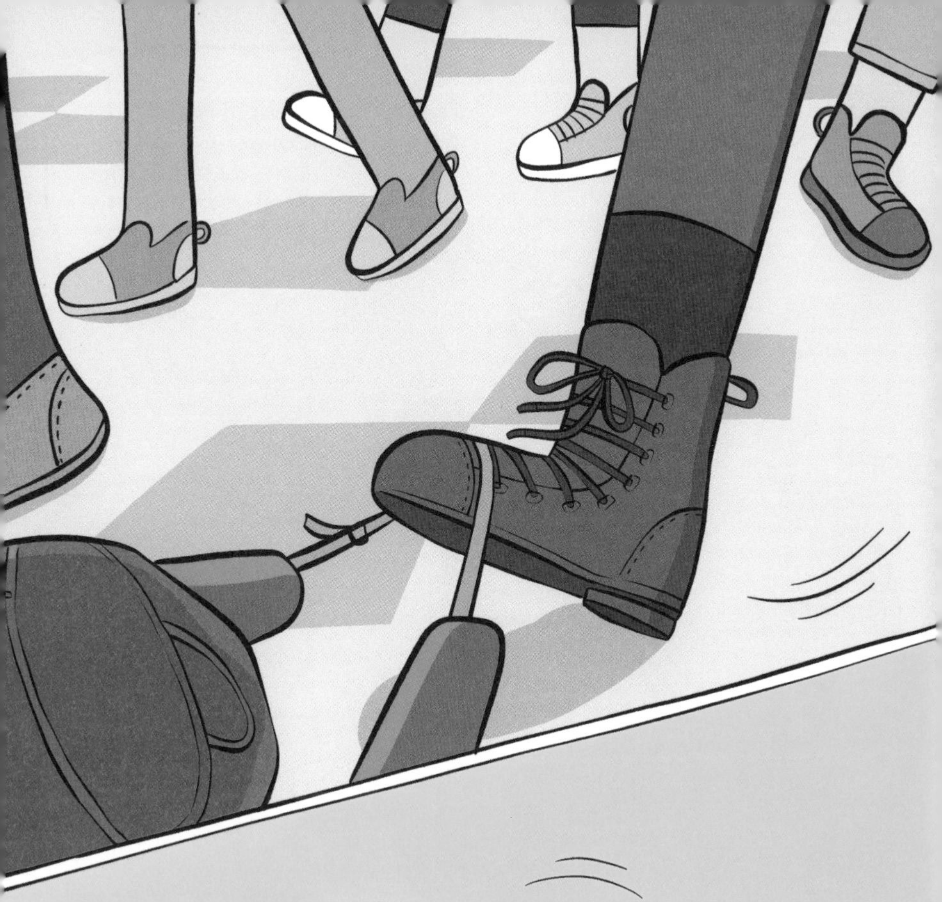

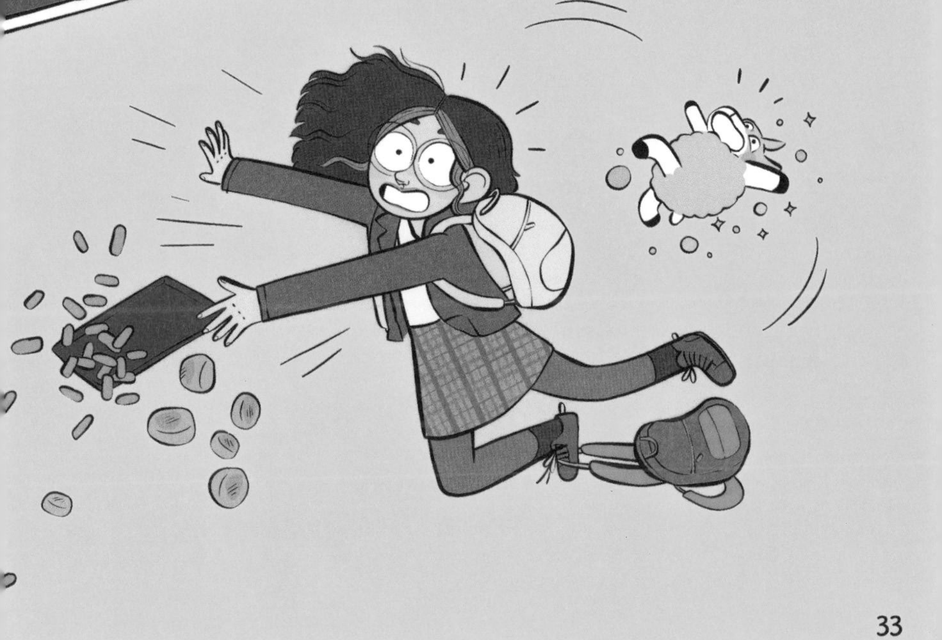

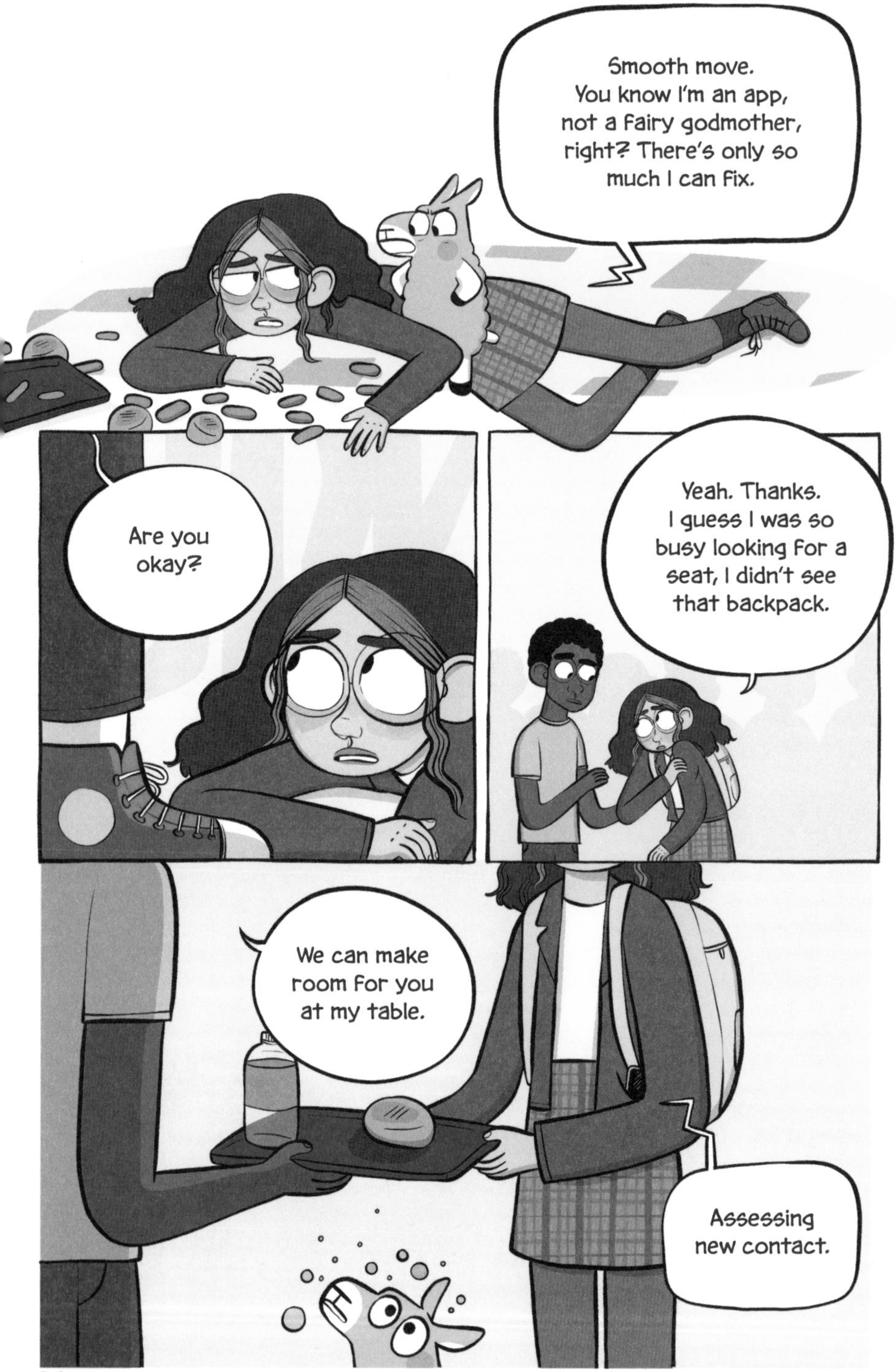

Smooth move. You know I'm an app, not a fairy godmother, right? There's only so much I can fix.
Are you okay?
Yeah. Thanks. I guess I was so busy looking for a seat, I didn't see that backpack.
We can make room for you at my table.
Assessing new contact.

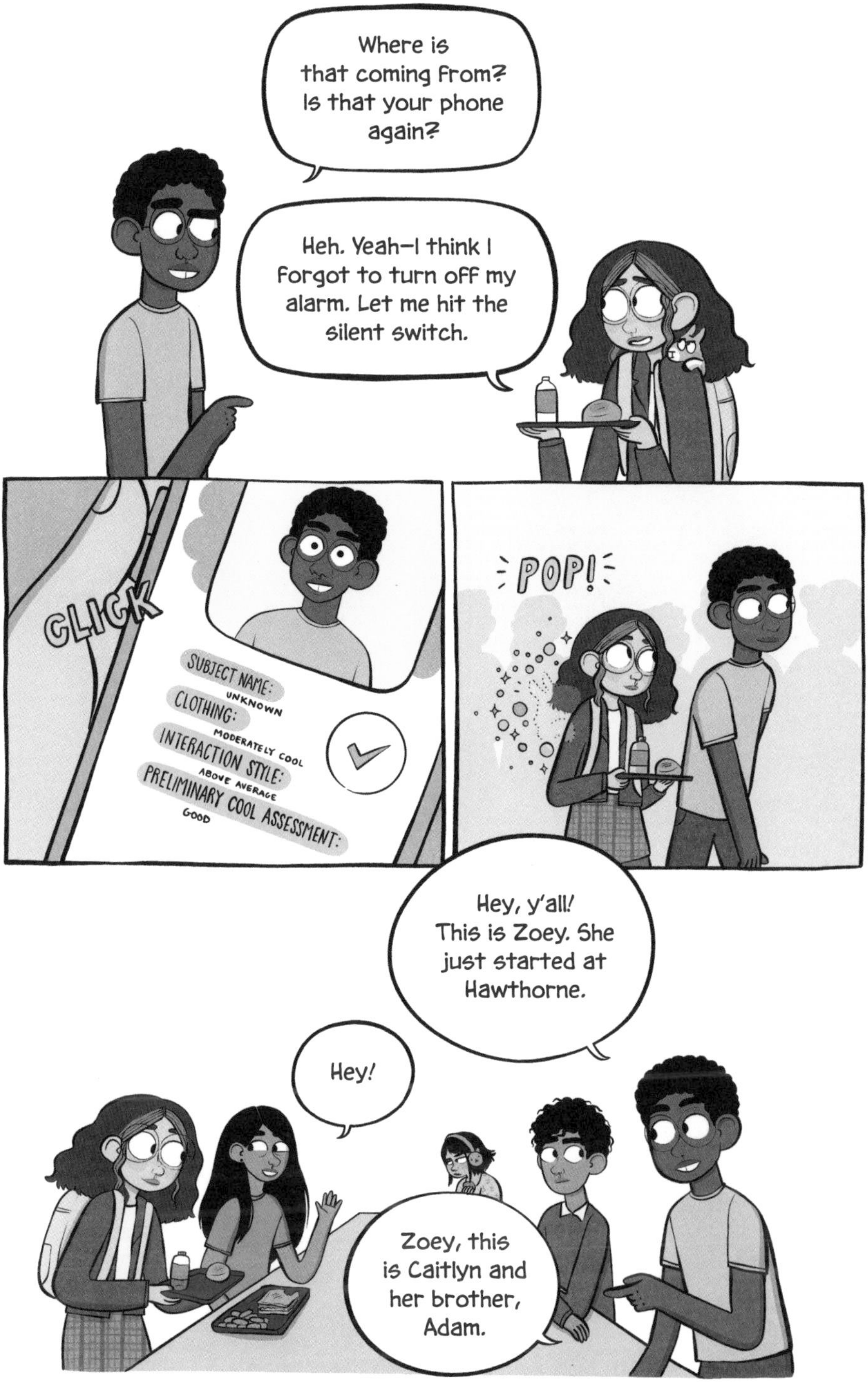
Where is that coming from? Is that your phone again?
Heh. Yeah—I think I forgot to turn off my alarm. Let me hit the silent switch.
CLICK
SUBJECT NAME: UNKNOWN
CLOTHING: MODERATELY COOL
INTERACTION STYLE: ABOVE AVERAGE
PRELIMINARY COOL ASSESSMENT: GOOD
POP!
Hey, y'all! This is Zoey. She just started at Hawthorne.
Hey!
Zoey, this is Caitlyn and her brother, Adam.

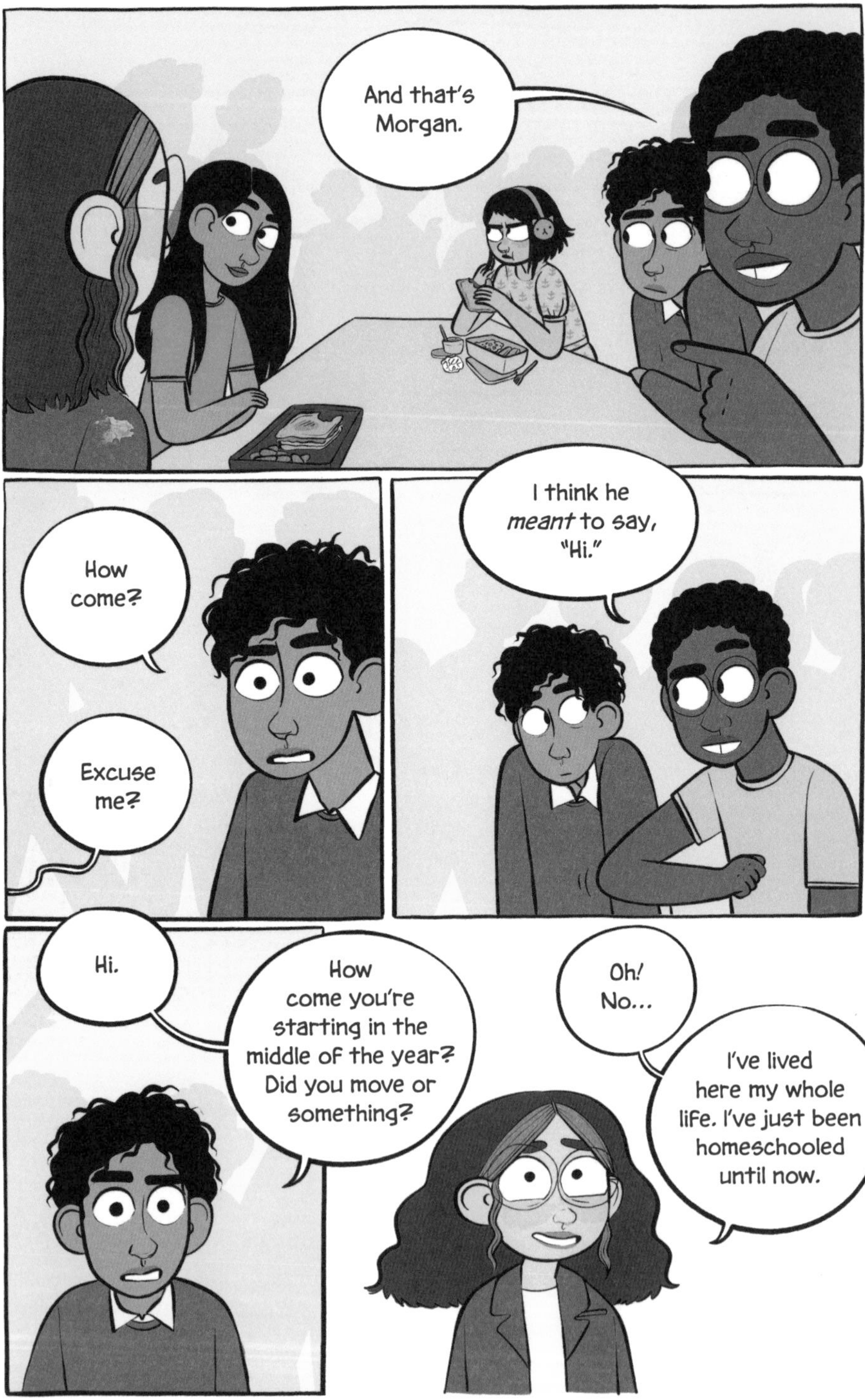
And that's Morgan.
How come?
Excuse me?
I think he *meant* to say, "Hi."
Hi.
How come you're starting in the middle of the year? Did you move or something?
Oh! No...
I've lived here my whole life. I've just been homeschooled until now.

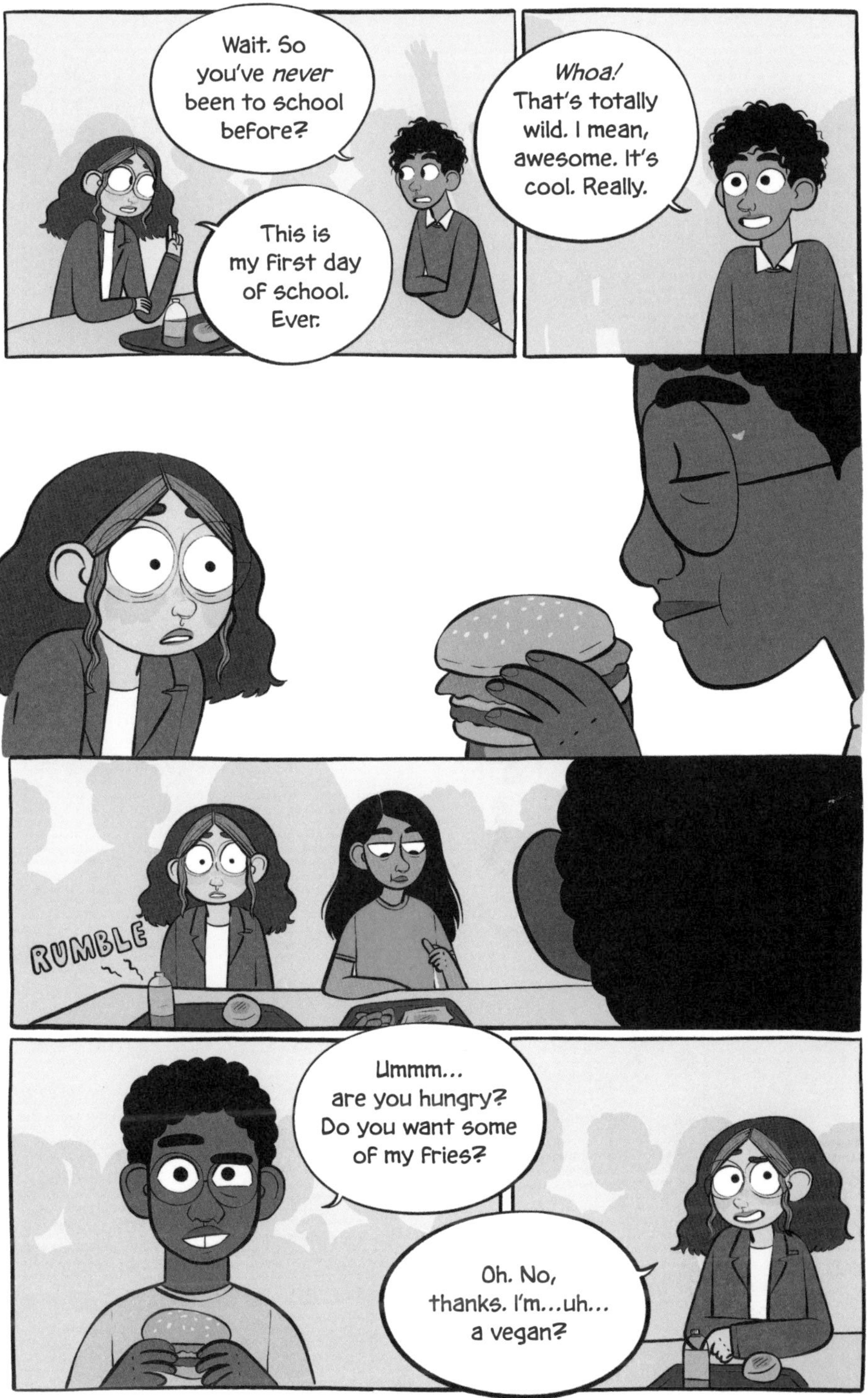
Wait. So you've *never* been to school before?
This is my first day of school. Ever.
Whoa! That's totally wild. I mean, awesome. It's cool. Really.
RUMBLE
Ummm... are you hungry? Do you want some of my fries?
Oh. No, thanks. I'm...uh... a vegan?

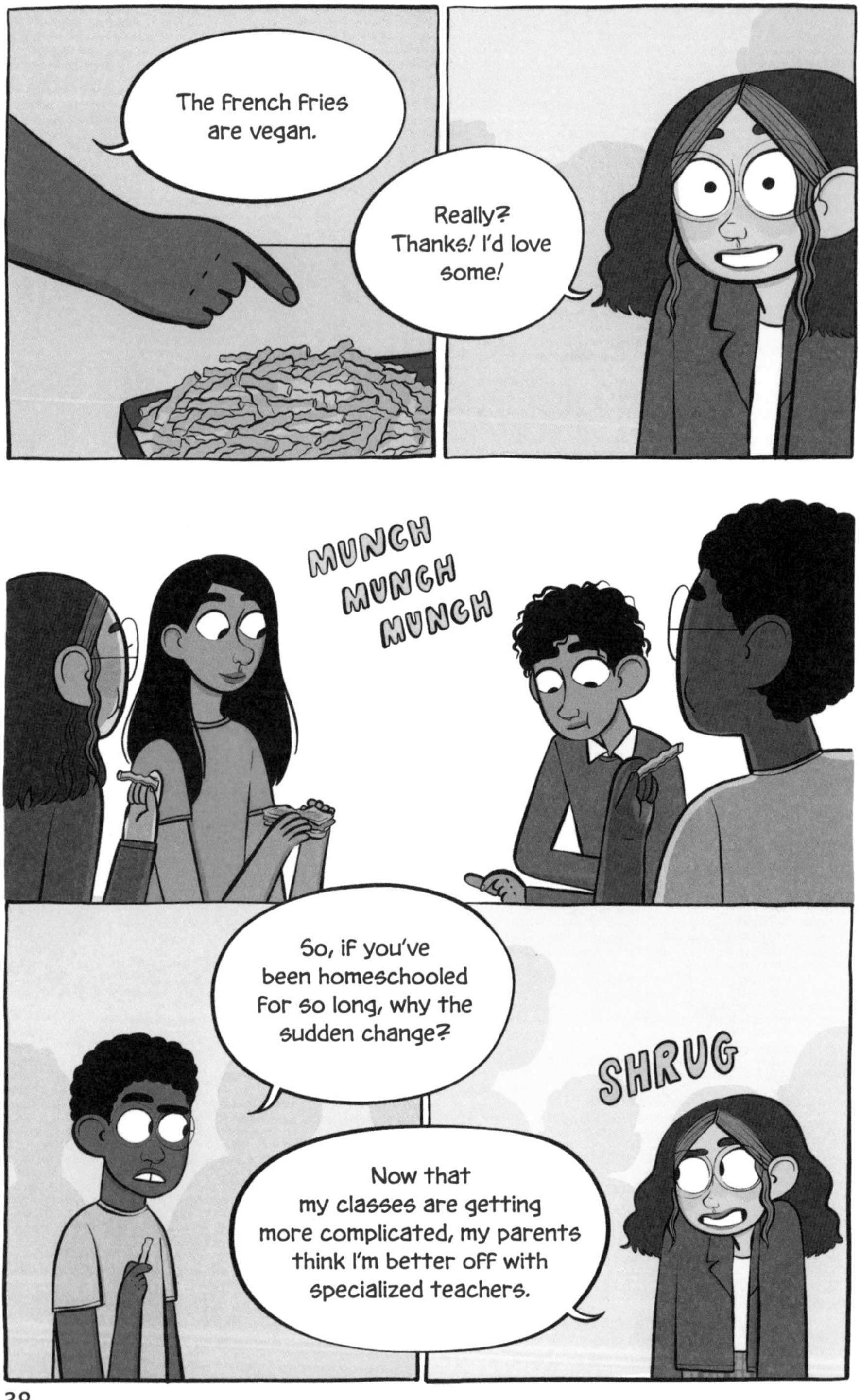
The french fries are vegan.
Really? Thanks! I'd love some!
MUNCH MUNCH MUNCH
So, if you've been homeschooled for so long, why the sudden change?
SHRUG
Now that my classes are getting more complicated, my parents think I'm better off with specialized teachers.

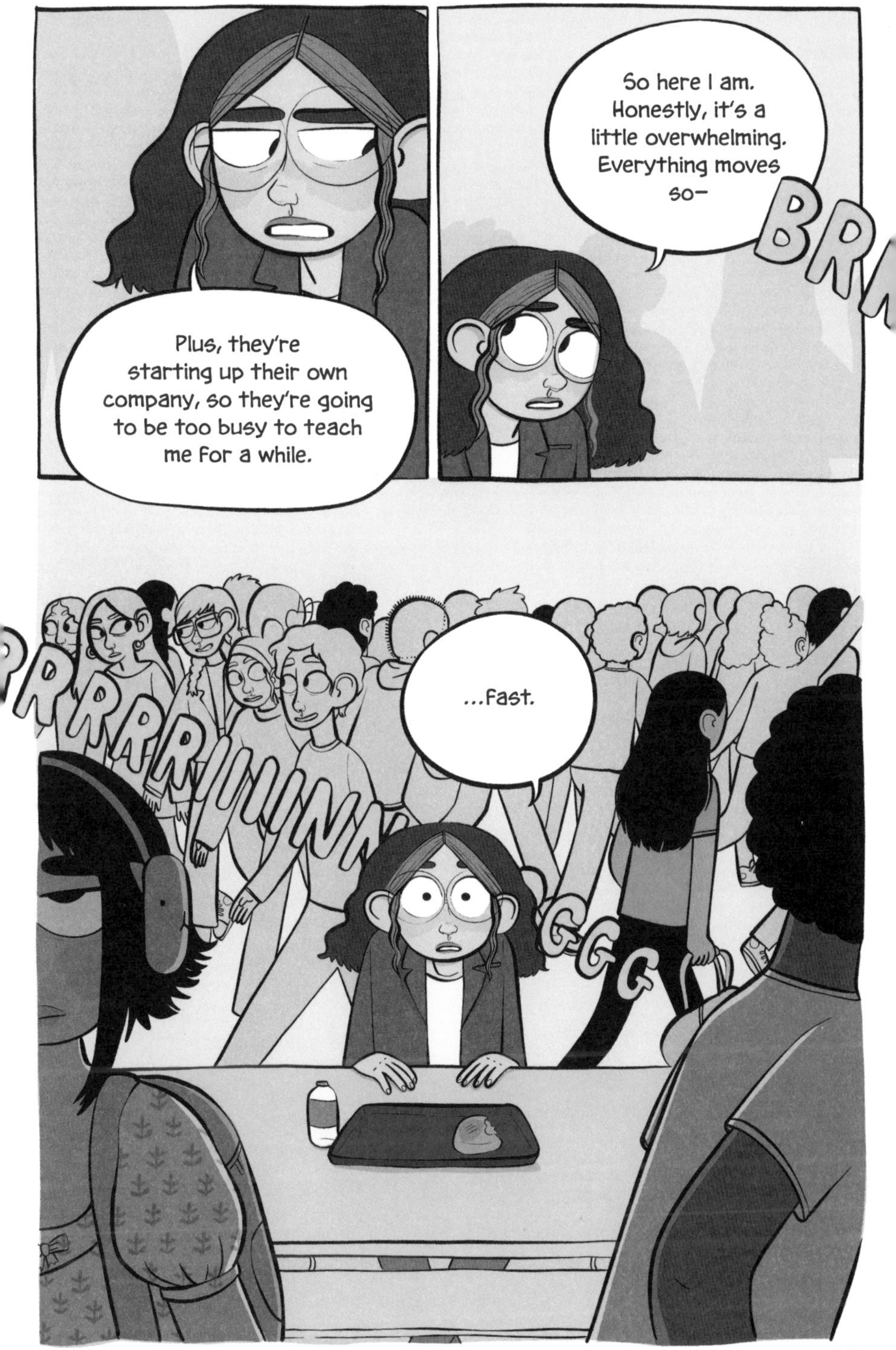
Plus, they're starting up their own company, so they're going to be too busy to teach me for a while.
So here I am. Honestly, it's a little overwhelming. Everything moves so–
BRRRRRRRIIIINNNGGGG
...Fast.

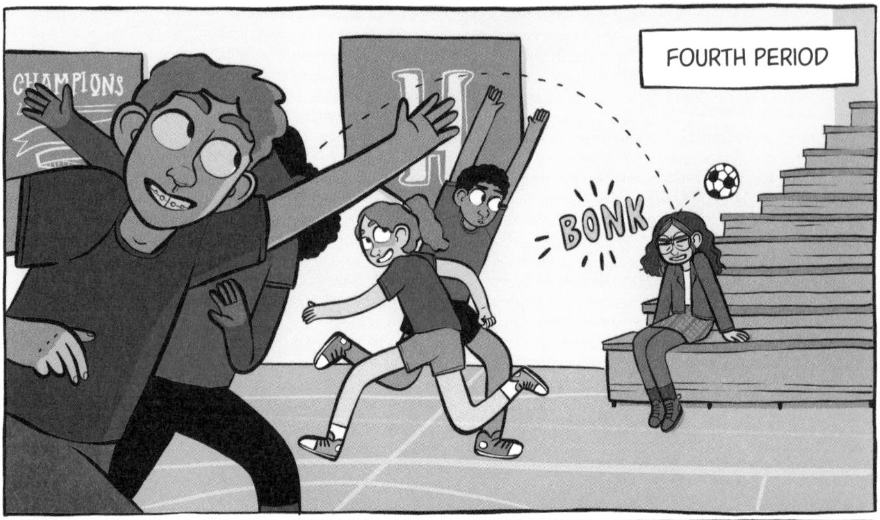
FOURTH PERIOD
CHAMPIONS
BONK

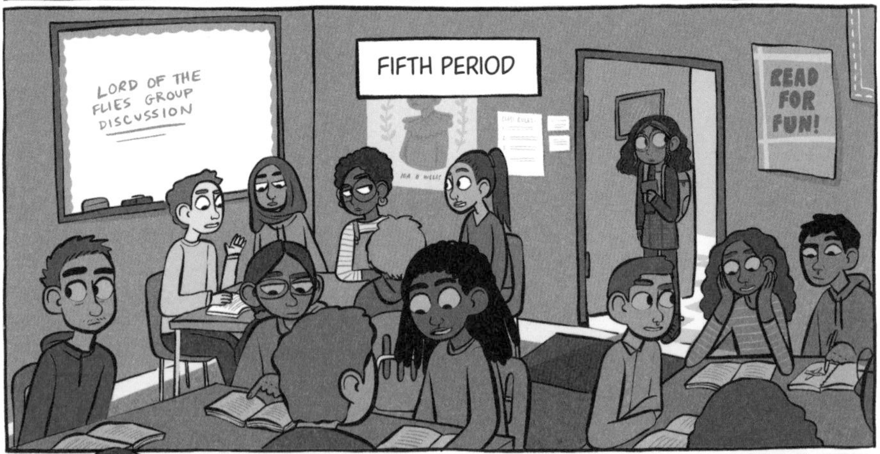
FIFTH PERIOD
LORD OF THE FLIES GROUP DISCUSSION
READ FOR FUN!

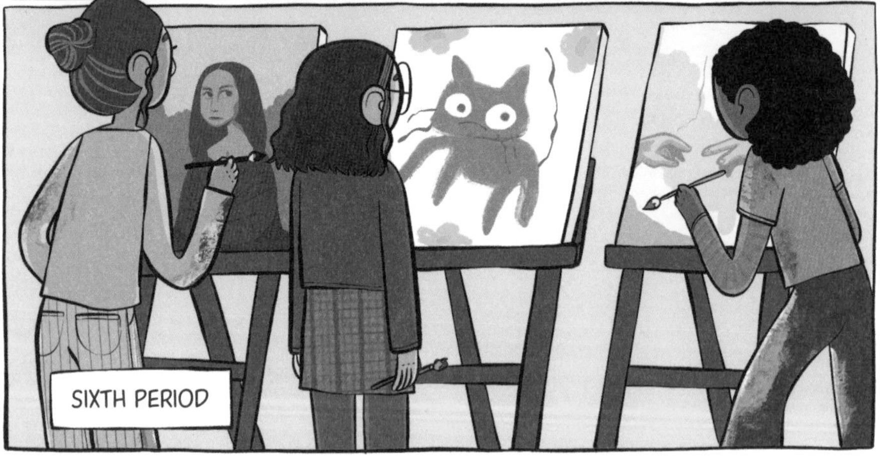
SIXTH PERIOD

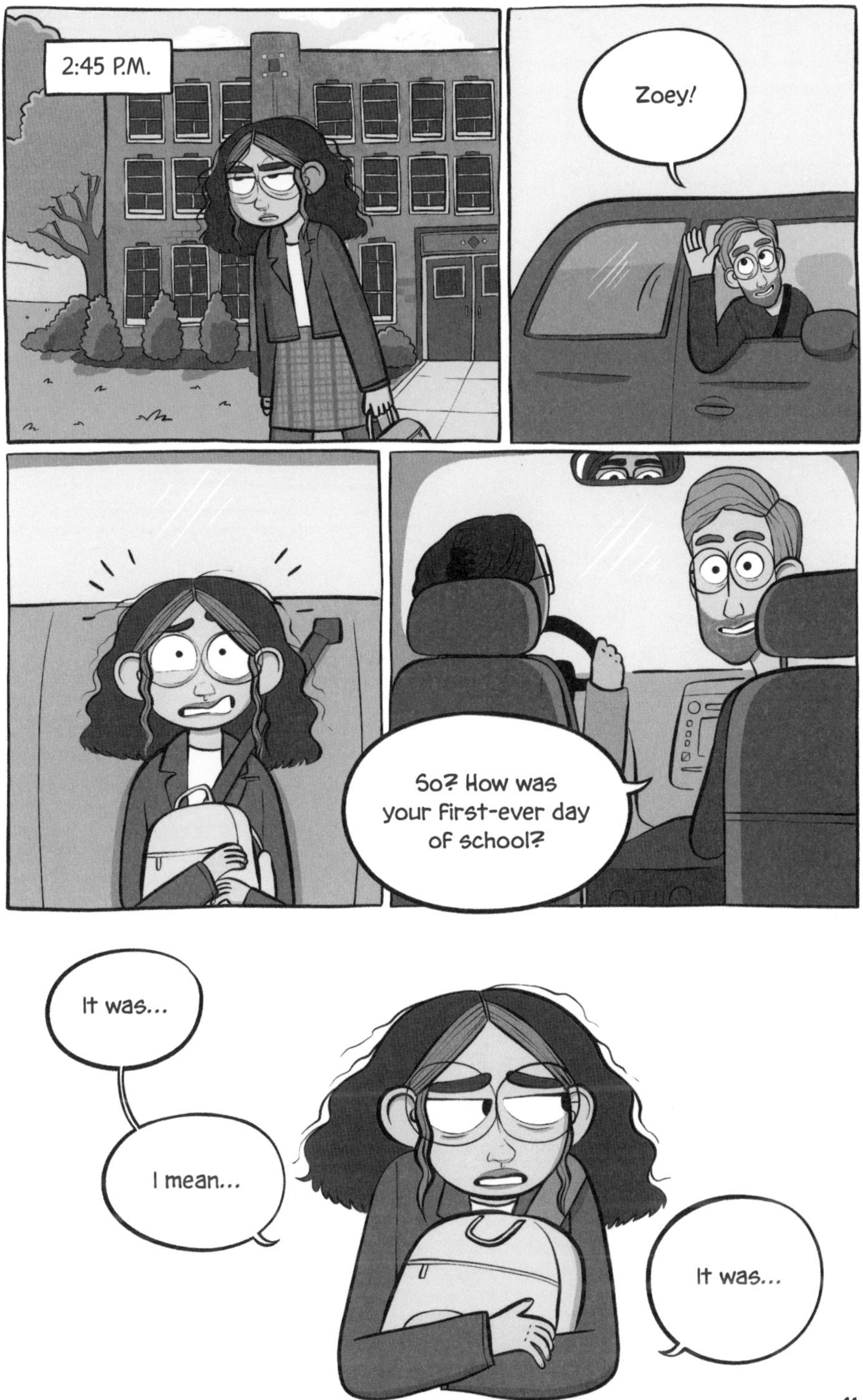
2:45 P.M.
Zoey!
So? How was your first-ever day of school?
It was...
I mean...
It was...

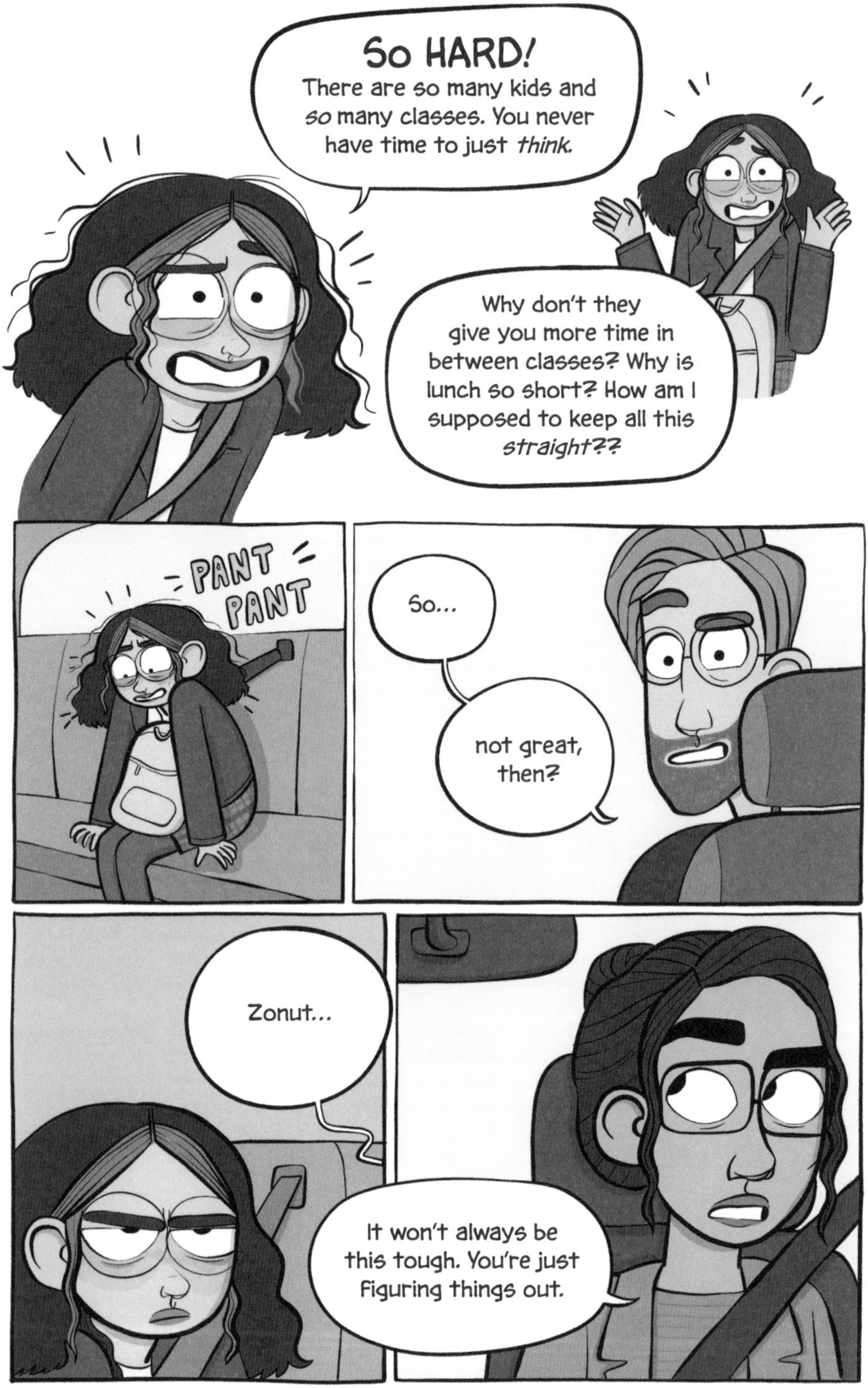
So HARD! There are so many kids and *so* many classes. You never have time to just *think.*
Why don't they give you more time in between classes? Why is lunch so short? How am I supposed to keep all this *straight*??
PANT PANT
So...
not great, then?
Zonut...
It won't always be this tough. You're just figuring things out.

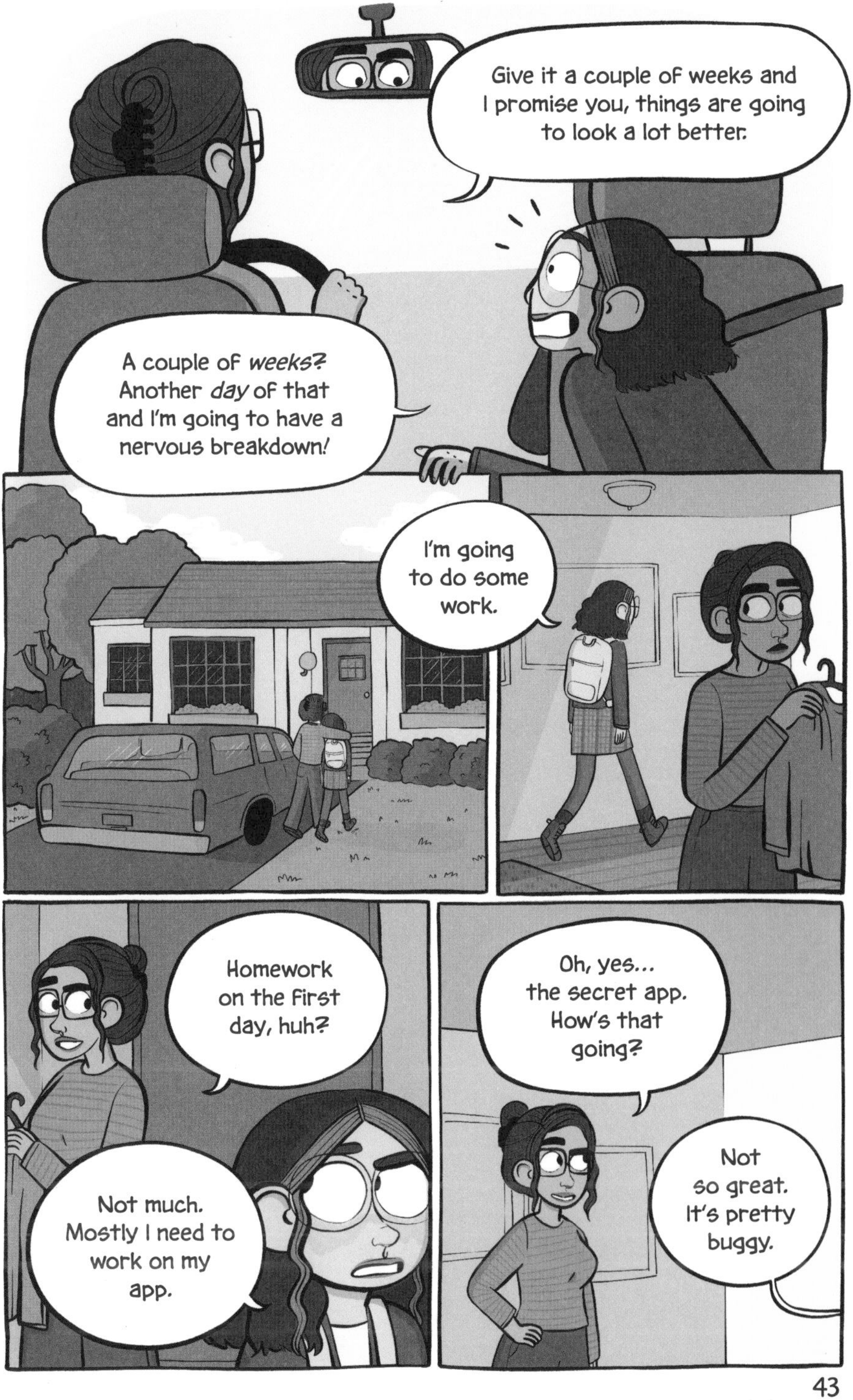
Give it a couple of weeks and I promise you, things are going to look a lot better.
A couple of *weeks*? Another *day* of that and I'm going to have a nervous breakdown!
I'm going to do some work.
Homework on the first day, huh?
Not much. Mostly I need to work on my app.
Oh, yes... the secret app. How's that going?
Not so great. It's pretty buggy.

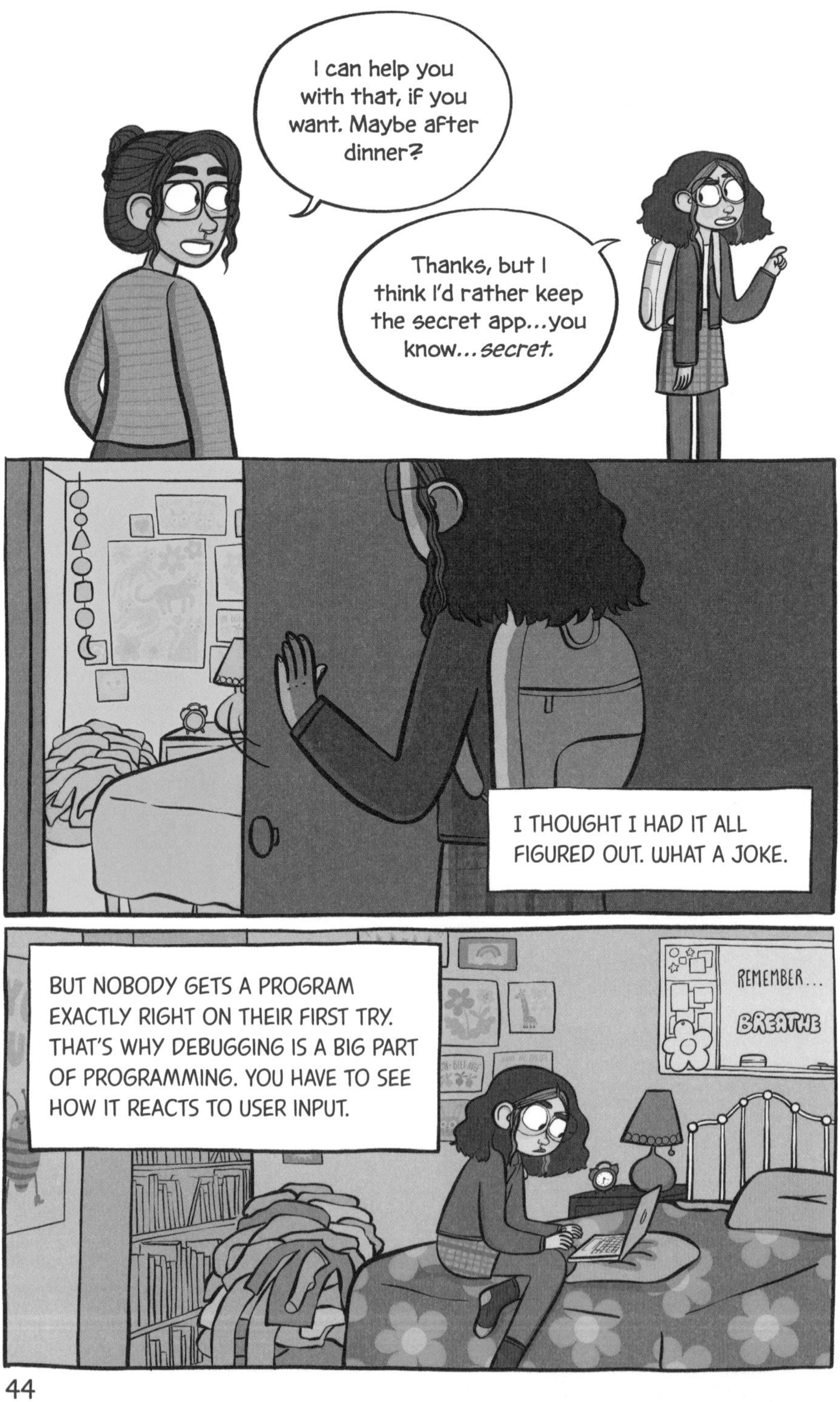
I can help you with that, if you want. Maybe after dinner?
Thanks, but I think I'd rather keep the secret app...you know...*secret.*
I THOUGHT I HAD IT ALL FIGURED OUT. WHAT A JOKE.
BUT NOBODY GETS A PROGRAM EXACTLY RIGHT ON THEIR FIRST TRY. THAT'S WHY DEBUGGING IS A BIG PART OF PROGRAMMING. YOU HAVE TO SEE HOW IT REACTS TO USER INPUT.
REMEMBER...
BREATHE

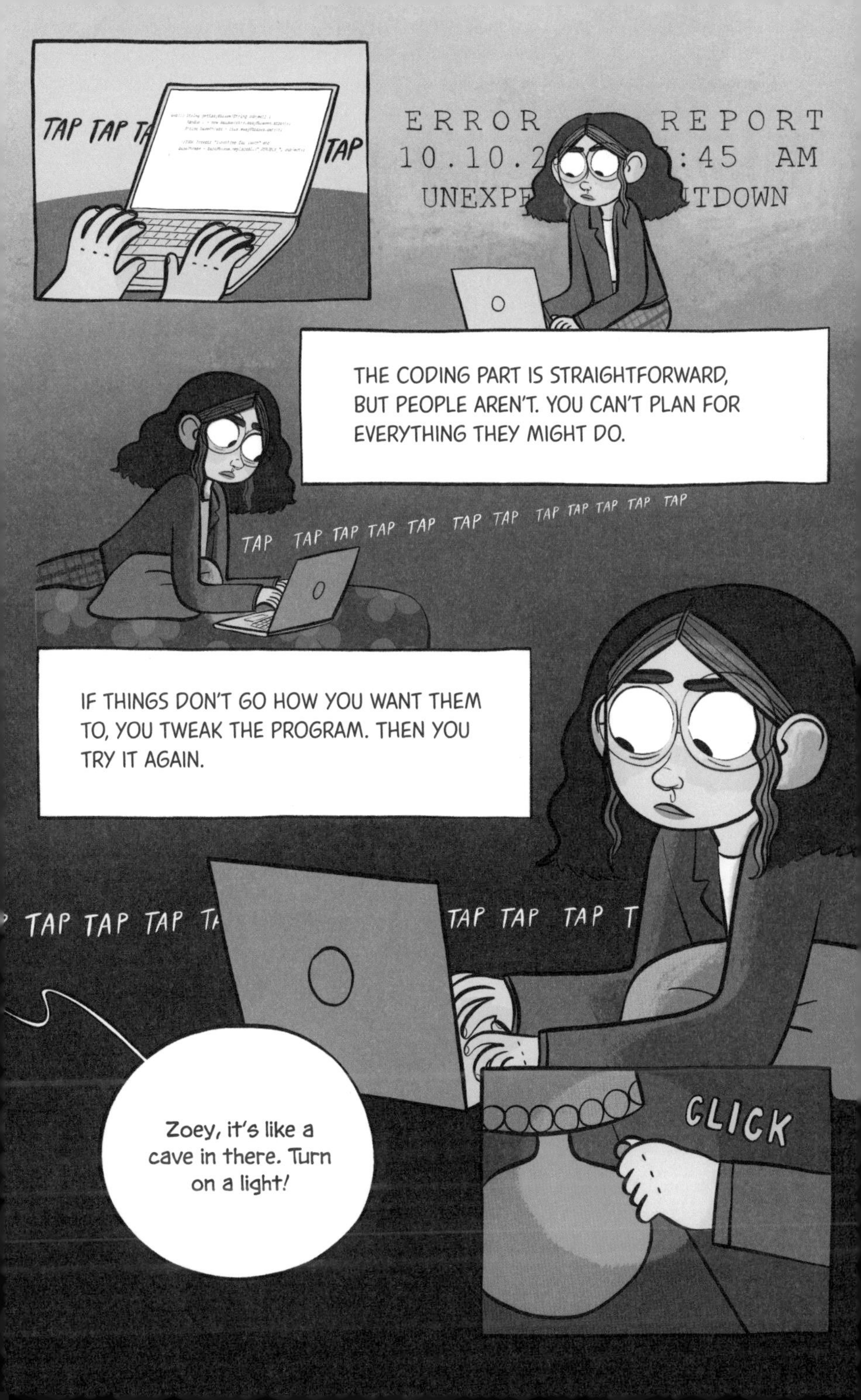
TAP TAP TA
TAP
ERROR REPORT
10.10.2 :45 AM
UNEXPE TDOWN
THE CODING PART IS STRAIGHTFORWARD, BUT PEOPLE AREN'T. YOU CAN'T PLAN FOR EVERYTHING THEY MIGHT DO.
TAP TAP TAP TAP TAP TAP TAP TAP TAP TAP TAP TAP
IF THINGS DON'T GO HOW YOU WANT THEM TO, YOU TWEAK THE PROGRAM. THEN YOU TRY IT AGAIN.
TAP TAP TAP
TAP TAP TAP
Zoey, it's like a cave in there. Turn on a light!
CLICK

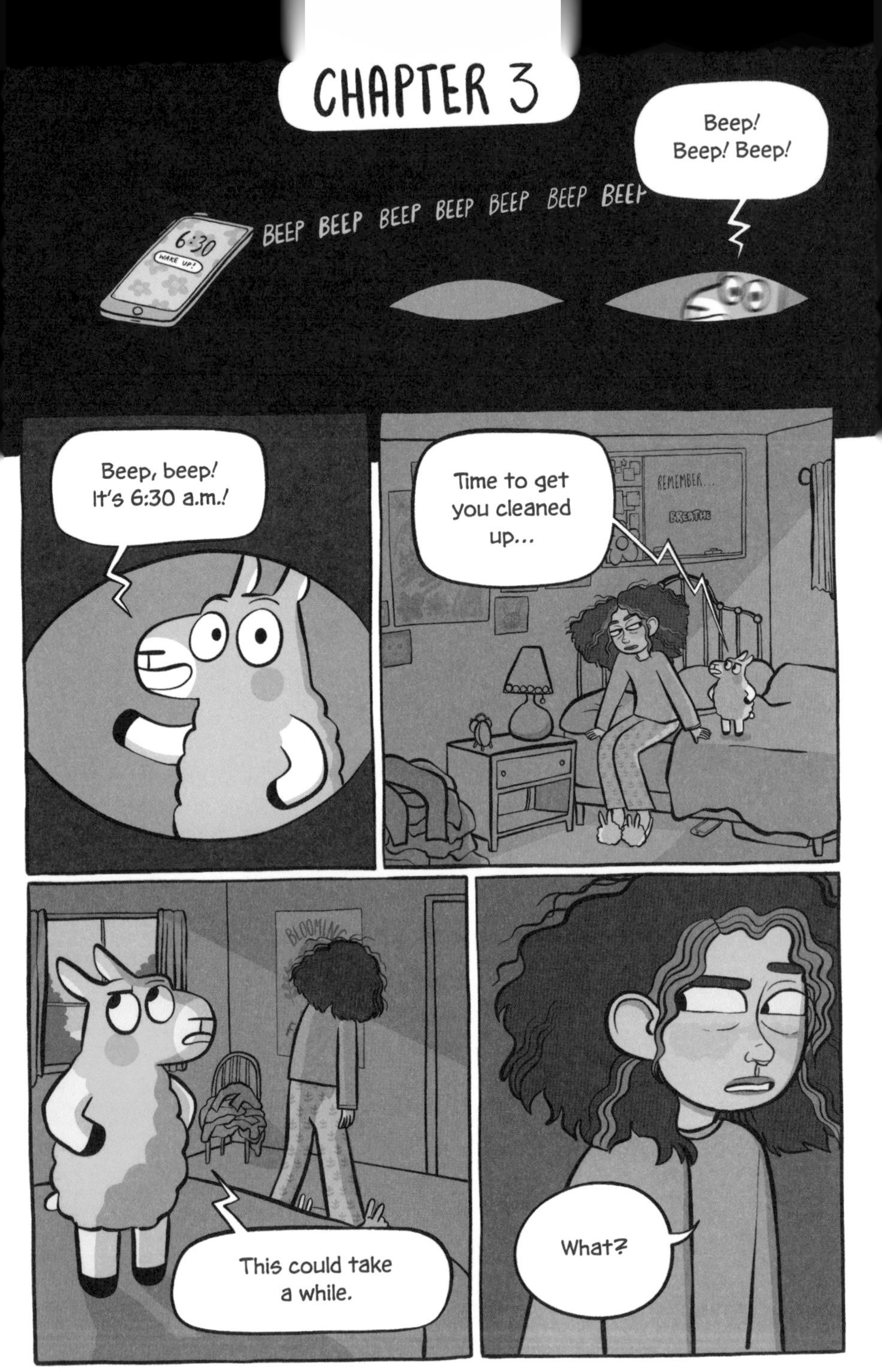
CHAPTER 3
6:30
WAKE UP!
BEEP BEEP BEEP BEEP BEEP BEEP BEEP
Beep! Beep! Beep!
Beep, beep! It's 6:30 a.m.!
Time to get you cleaned up...
REMEMBER...
BREATHE
BLOOMING
This could take a while.
What?

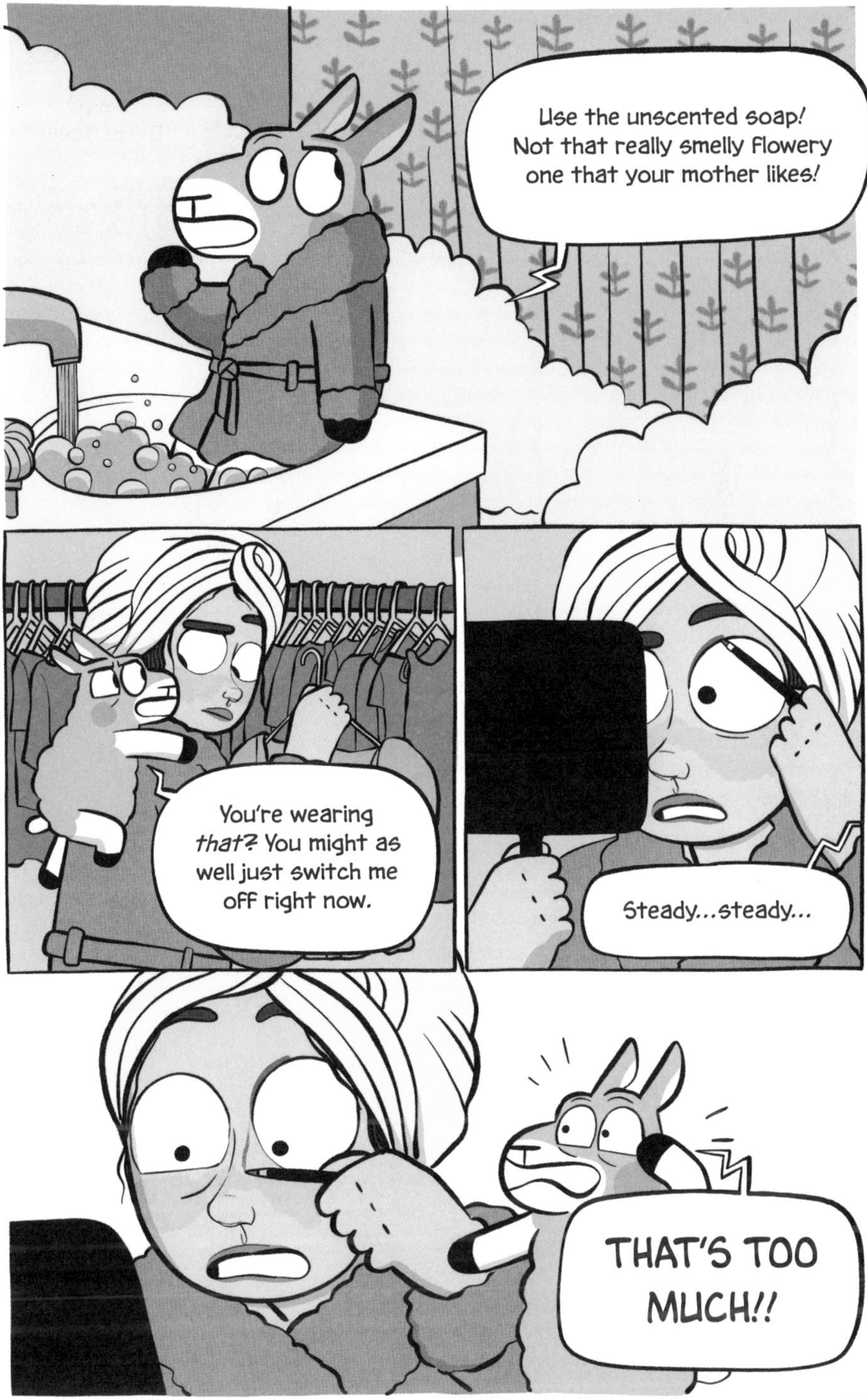
Use the unscented soap! Not that really smelly flowery one that your mother likes!
You're wearing *that*? You might as well just switch me off right now.
Steady...steady...
THAT'S TOO MUCH!!

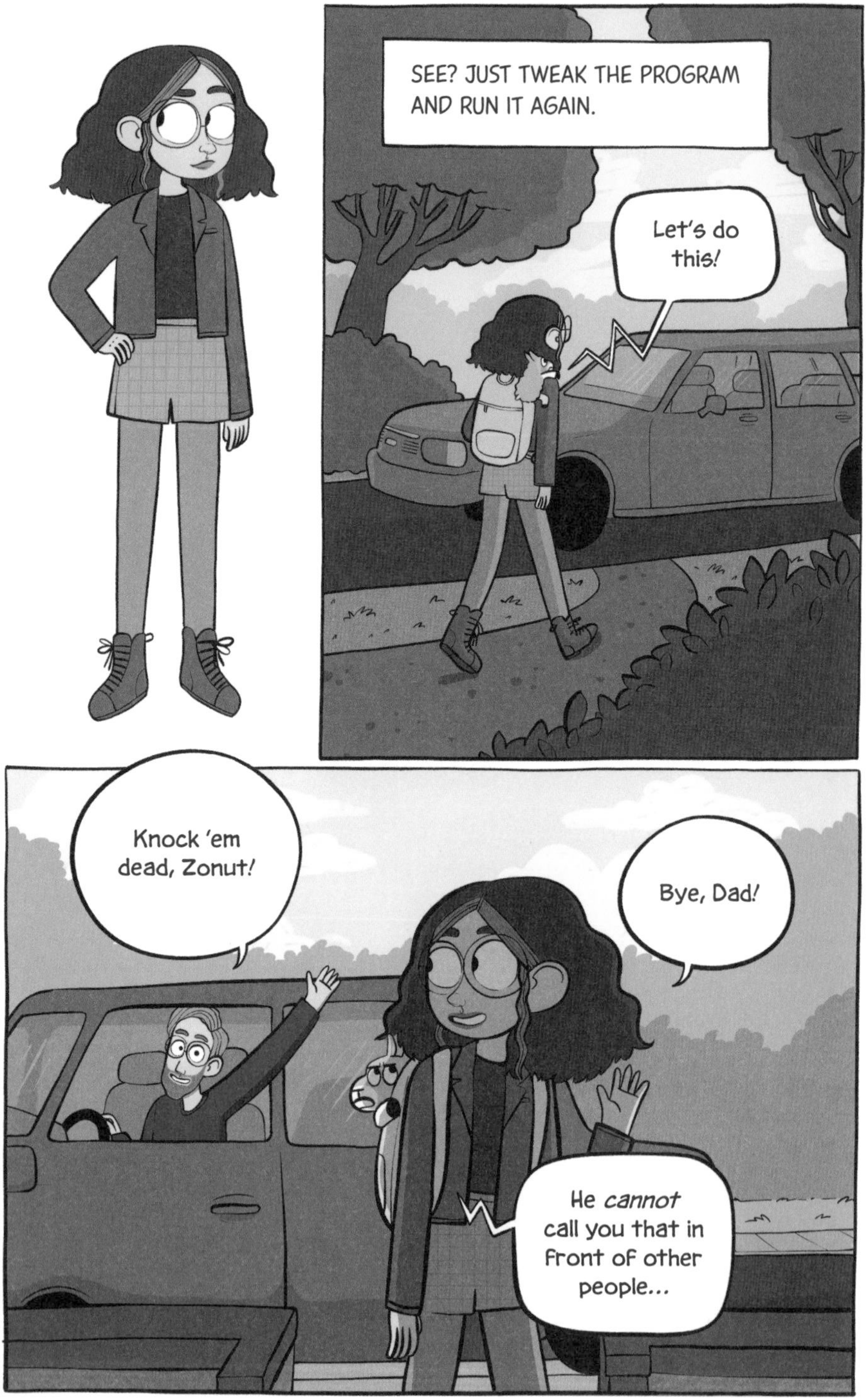
SEE? JUST TWEAK THE PROGRAM AND RUN IT AGAIN.
Let's do this!
Knock 'em dead, Zonut!
Bye, Dad!
He *cannot* call you that in front of other people...

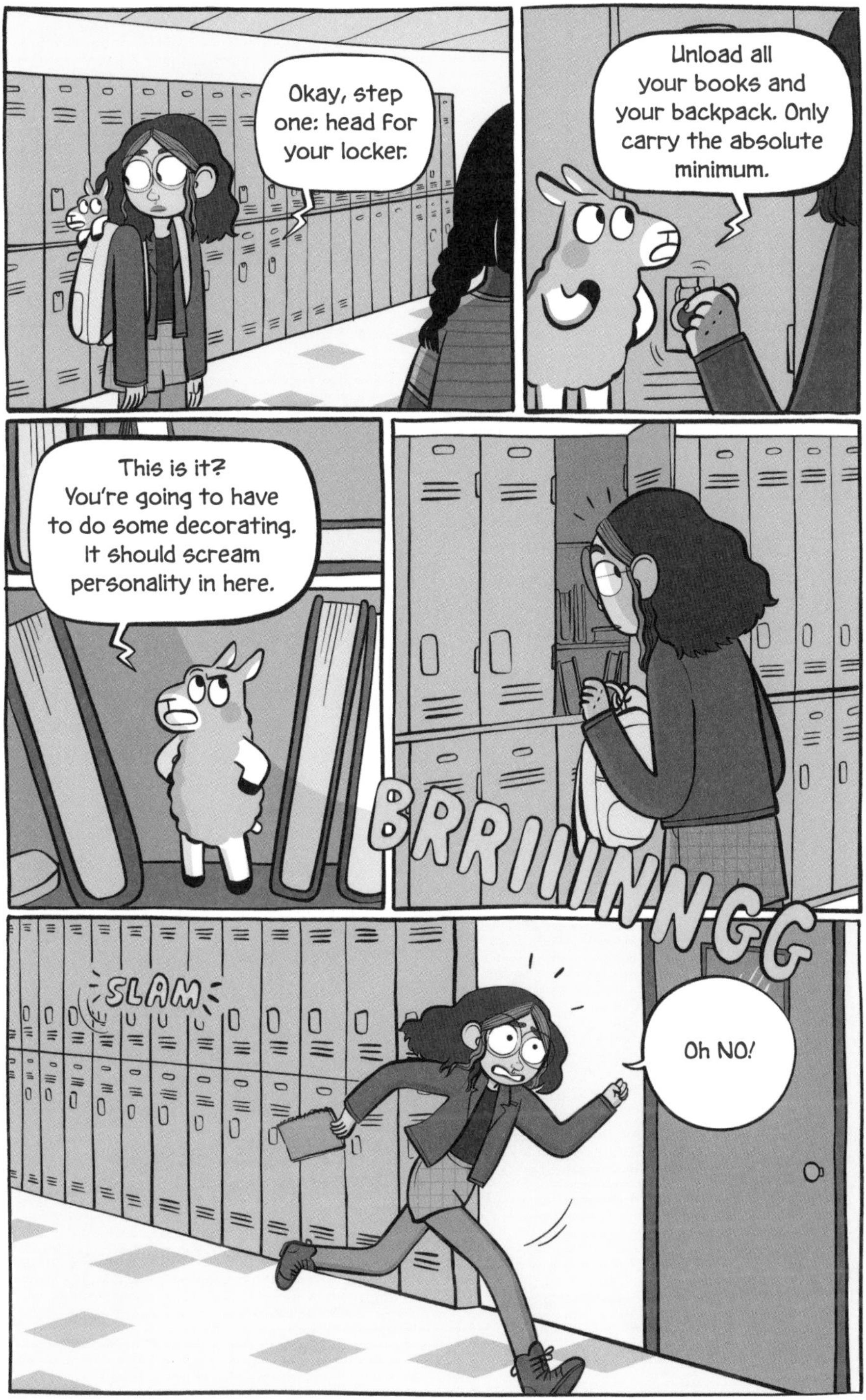
Okay, step one: head for your locker.
Unload all your books and your backpack. Only carry the absolute minimum.
This is it? You're going to have to do some decorating. It should scream personality in here.
BRRIIIINNGG
SLAM
Oh NO!

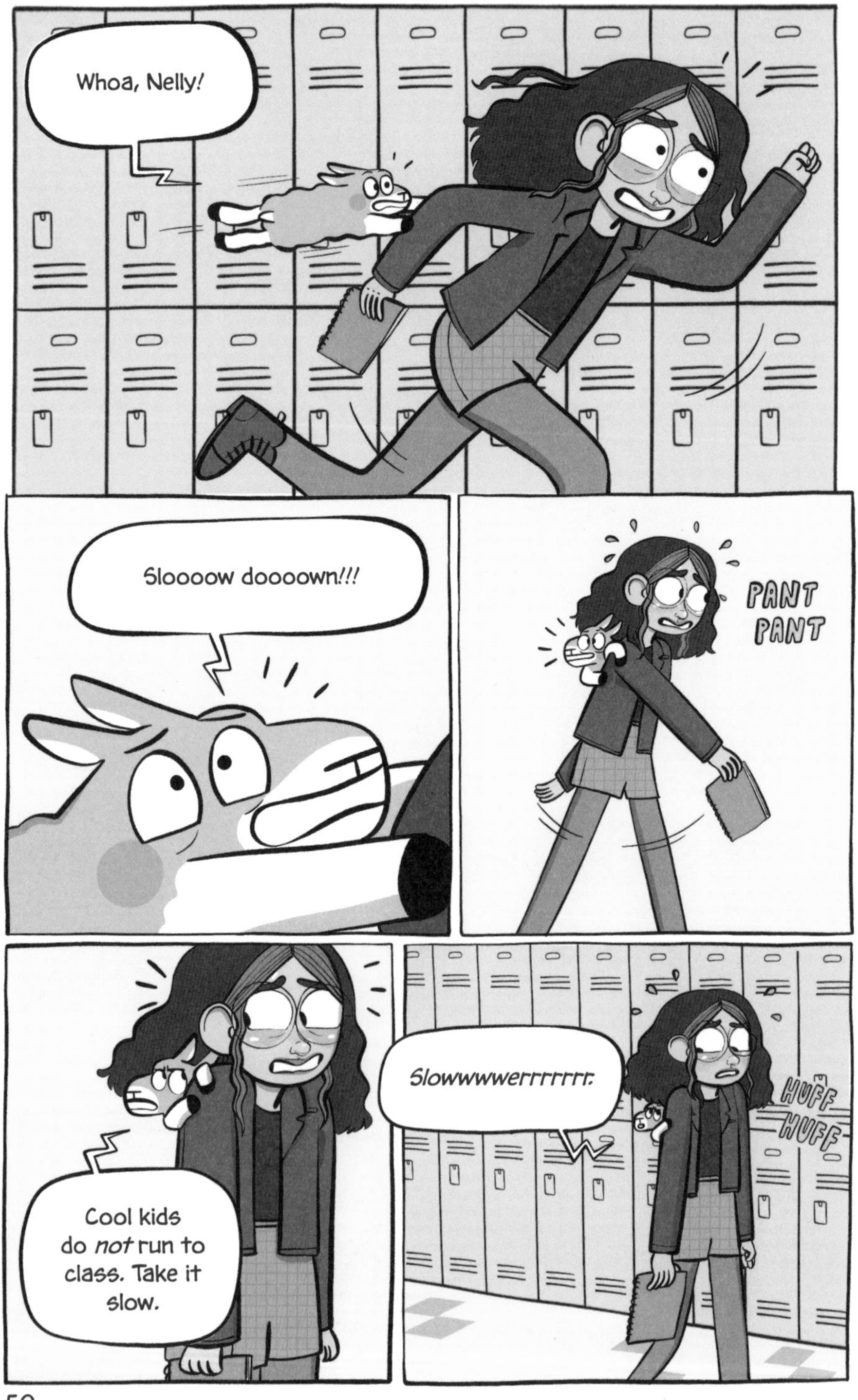
Whoa, Nelly!
Sloooow doooown!!!
PANT PANT
Cool kids do *not* run to class. Take it slow.
Slowwwwerrrrrrr.
HUFF HUFF

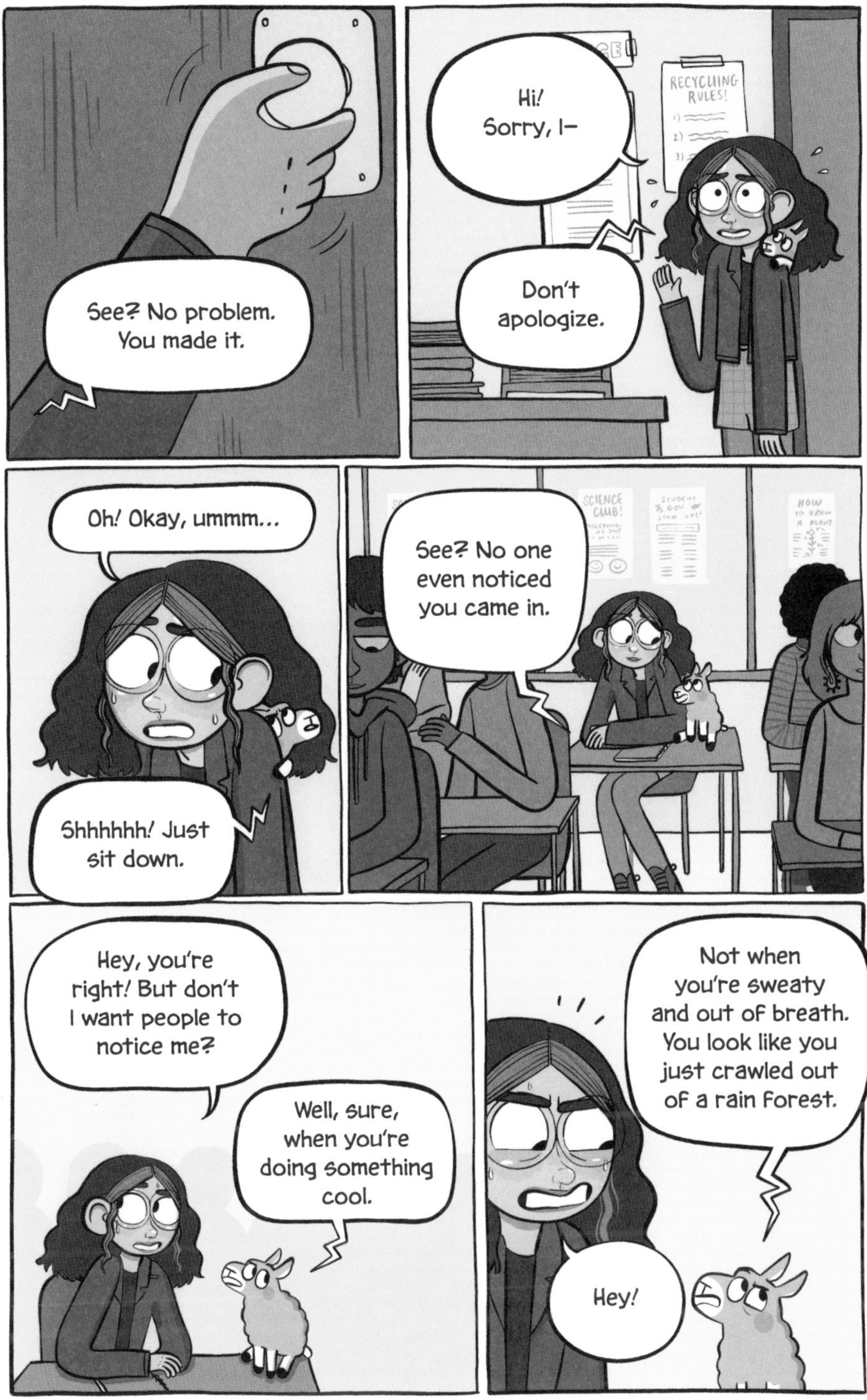
See? No problem. You made it.
Hi! Sorry, I—
RECYCLING RULES!
Don't apologize.
Oh! Okay, ummm...
Shhhhhh! Just sit down.
SCIENCE CLUB!
HOW TO GROW A PLANT
See? No one even noticed you came in.
Hey, you're right! But don't I want people to notice me?
Well, sure, when you're doing something cool.
Not when you're sweaty and out of breath. You look like you just crawled out of a rain forest.
Hey!

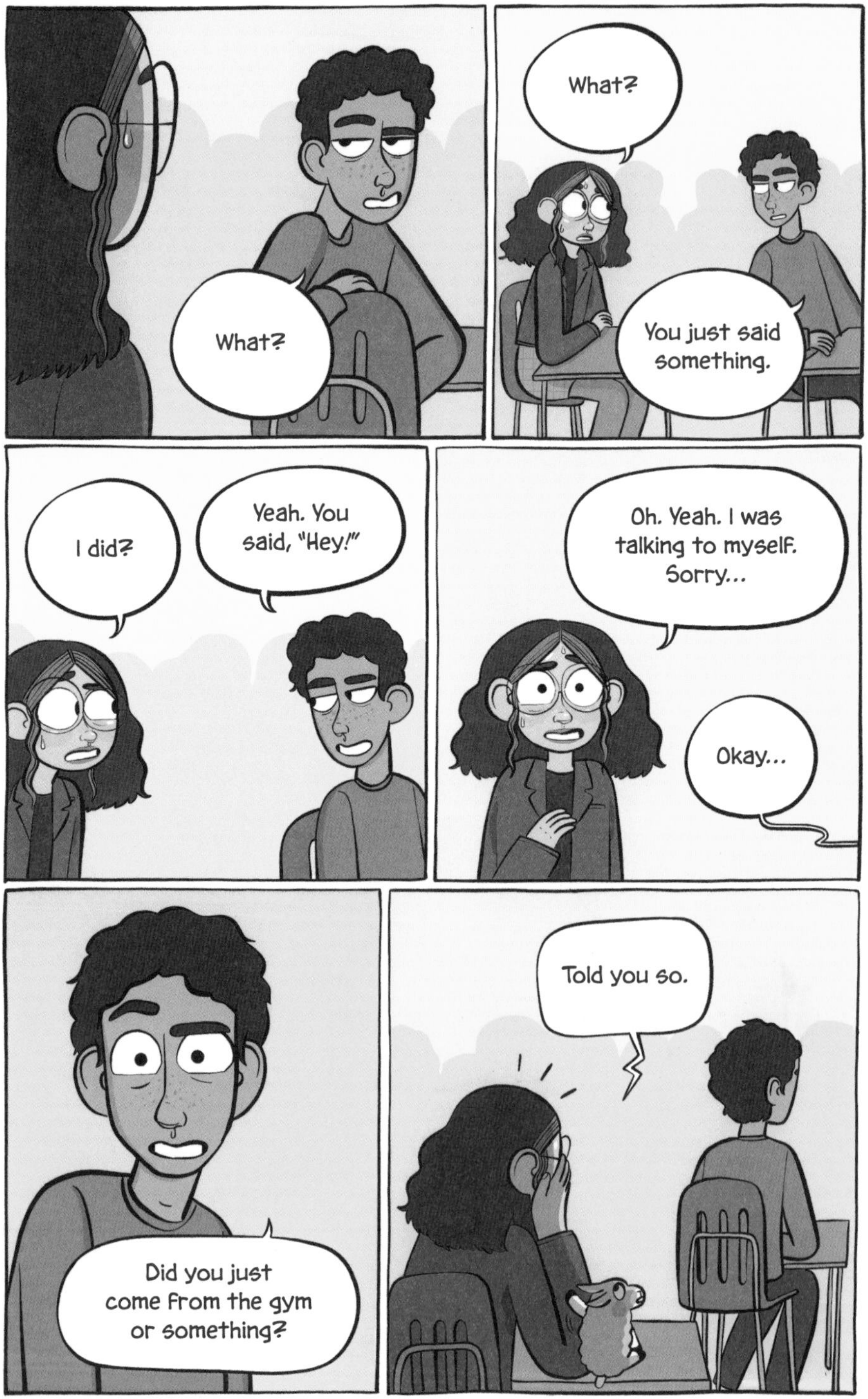
What?
What?
You just said something.
I did?
Yeah. You said, "Hey!"
Oh. Yeah. I was talking to myself. Sorry...
Okay...
Did you just come from the gym or something?
Told you so.

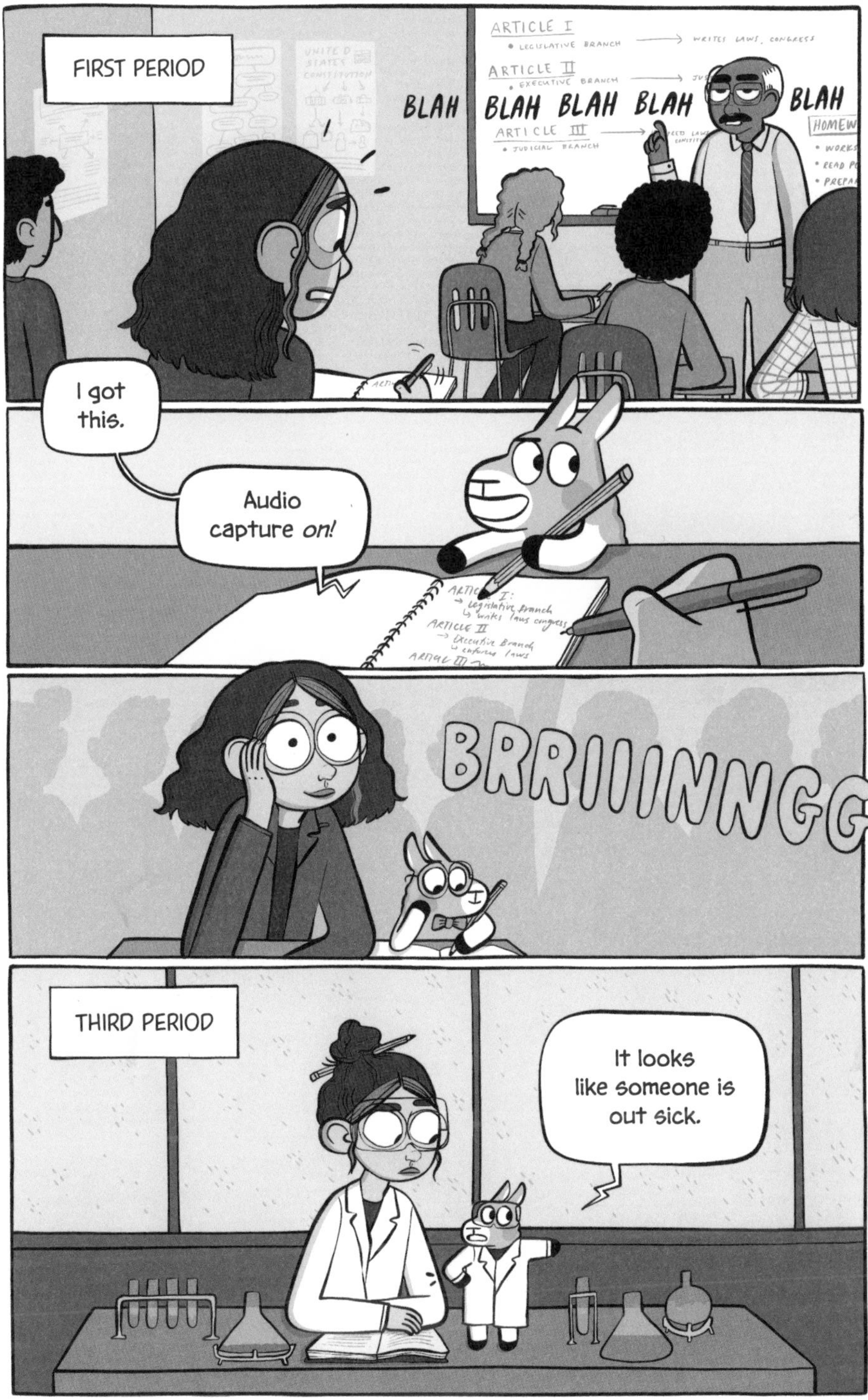
FIRST PERIOD
BLAH BLAH BLAH BLAH BLAH
I got this.
Audio capture *on!*
BRRIIINNGG
THIRD PERIOD
It looks like someone is out sick.

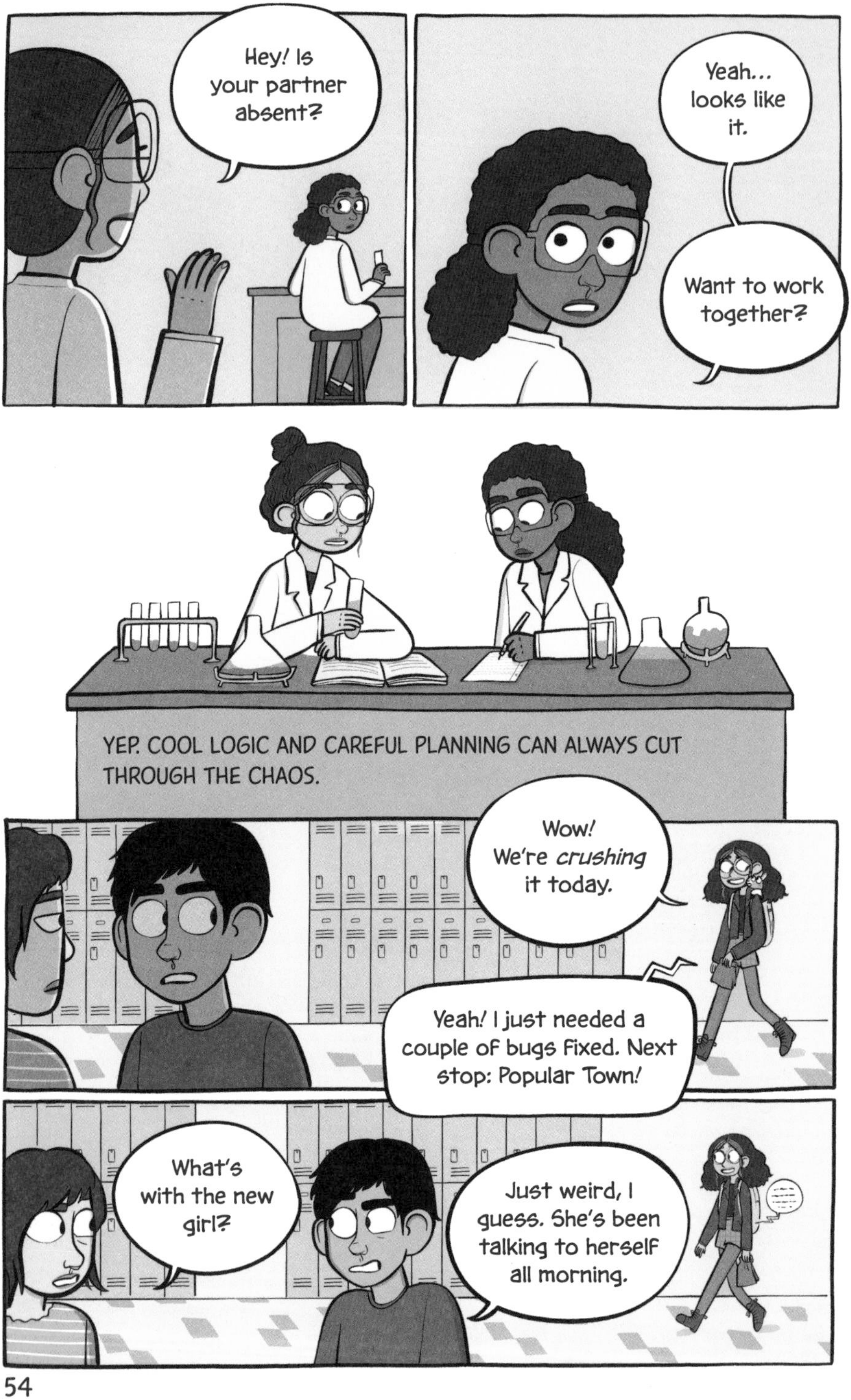
Hey! Is your partner absent?
Yeah... looks like it.
Want to work together?
YEP. COOL LOGIC AND CAREFUL PLANNING CAN ALWAYS CUT THROUGH THE CHAOS.
Wow! We're *crushing* it today.
Yeah! I just needed a couple of bugs fixed. Next stop: Popular Town!
What's with the new girl?
Just weird, I guess. She's been talking to herself all morning.

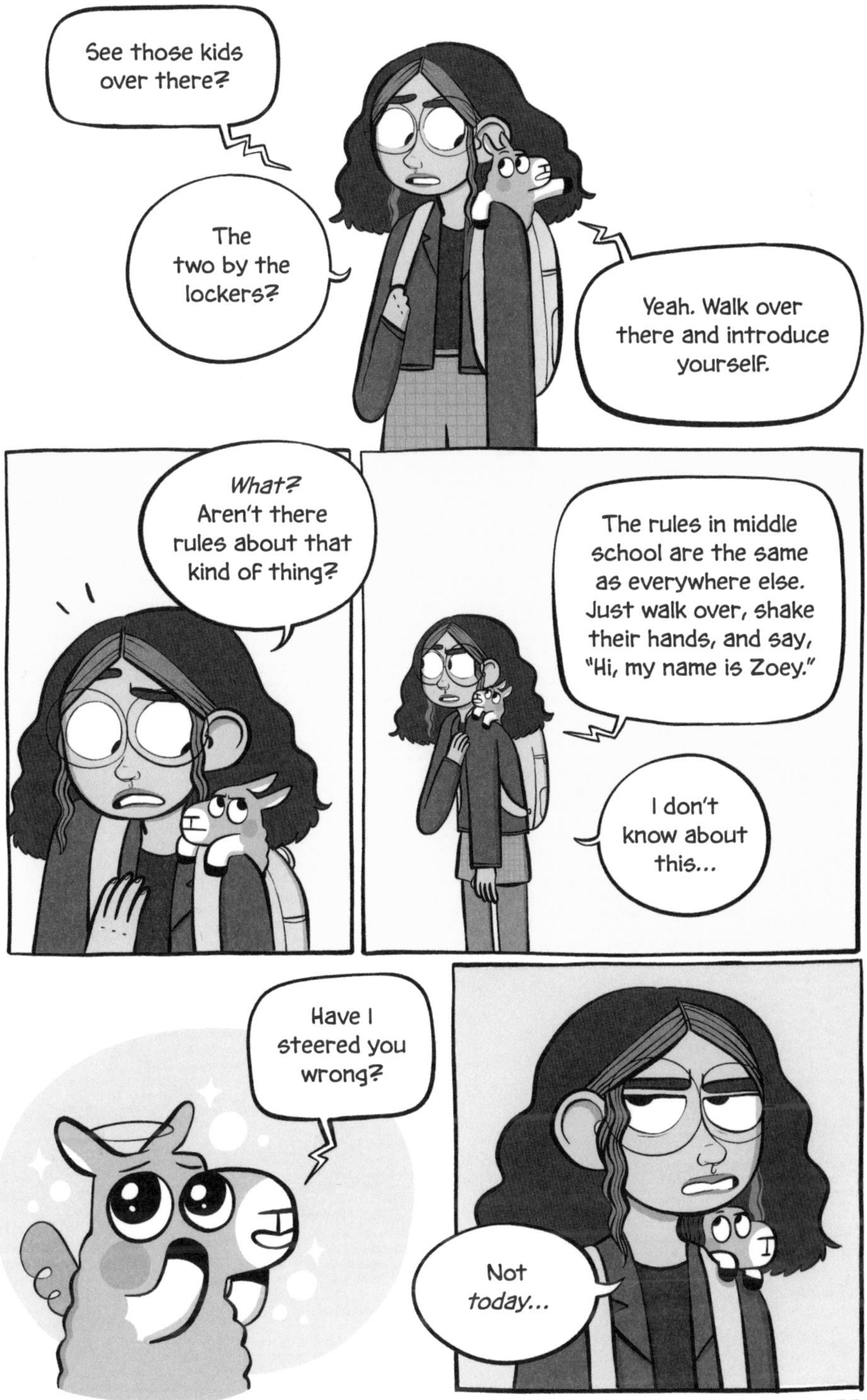
See those kids over there?
The two by the lockers?
Yeah. Walk over there and introduce yourself.
What? Aren't there rules about that kind of thing?
The rules in middle school are the same as everywhere else. Just walk over, shake their hands, and say, "Hi, my name is Zoey."
I don't know about this...
Have I steered you wrong?
Not *today*...

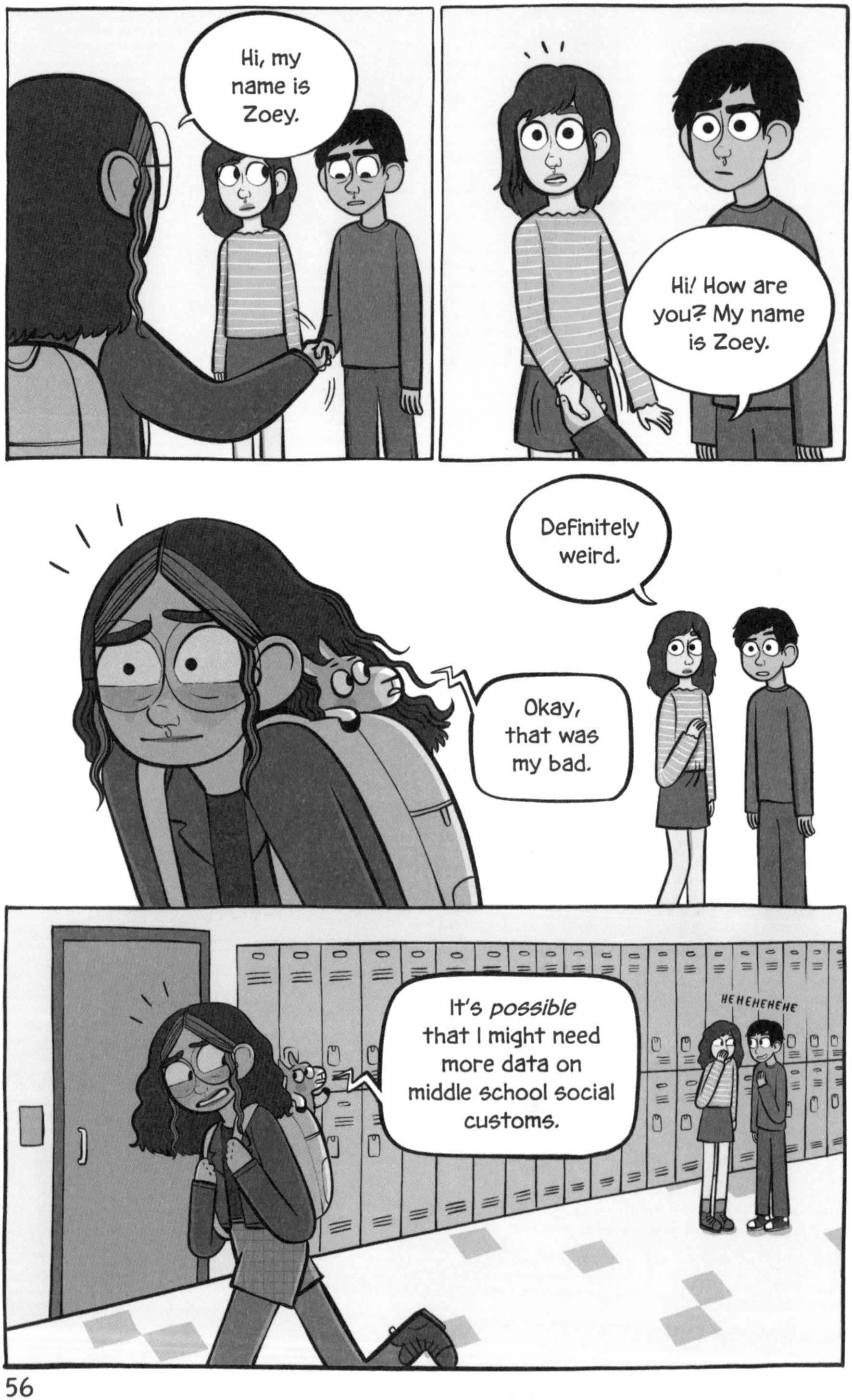
Hi, my name is Zoey.
Hi! How are you? My name is Zoey.
Definitely weird.
Okay, that was my bad.
It's *possible* that I might need more data on middle school social customs.
HEHEHEHEHE

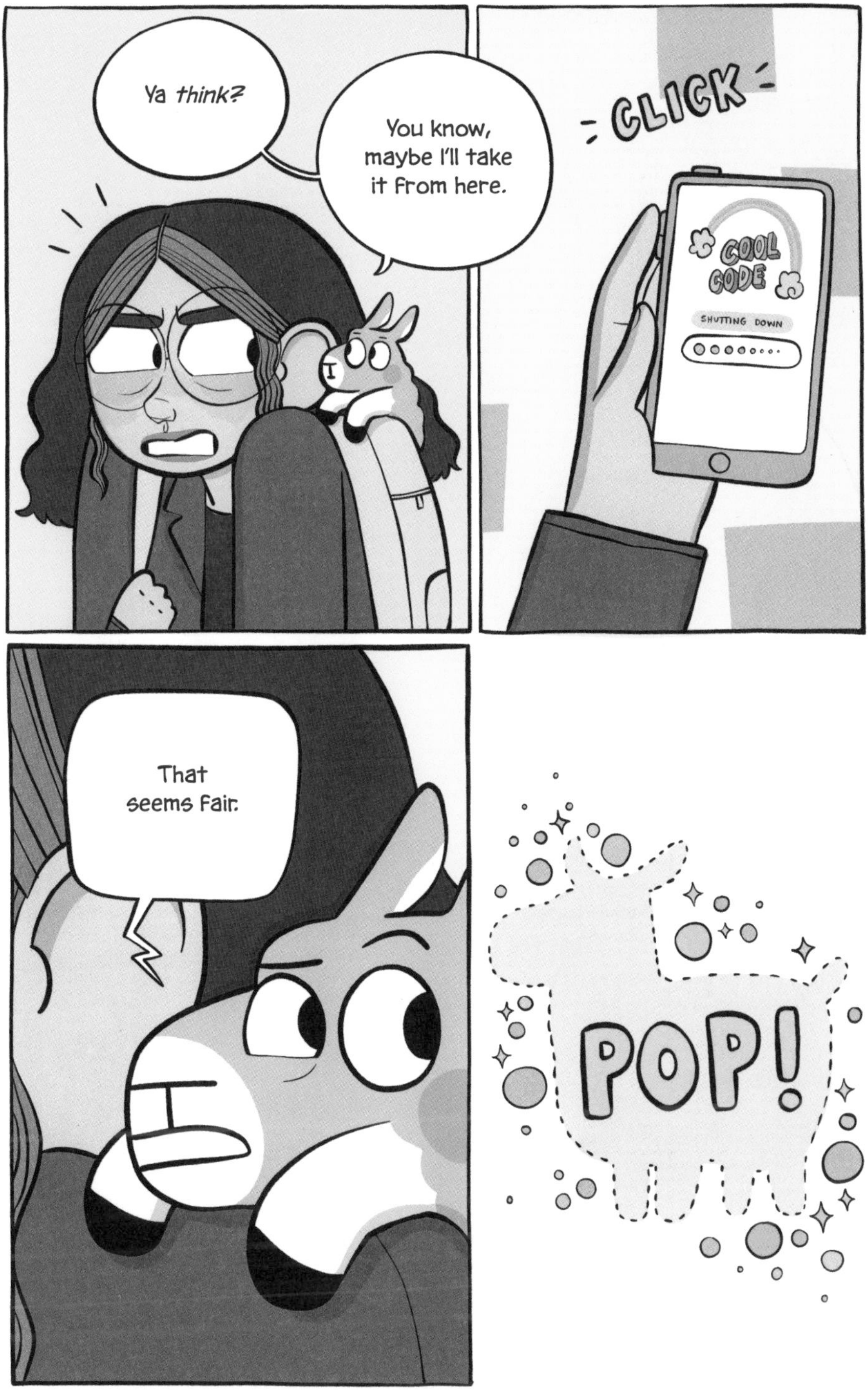
Ya *think?*
You know, maybe I'll take it from here.
CLICK
COOL CODE
SHUTTING DOWN
That seems fair.
POP!

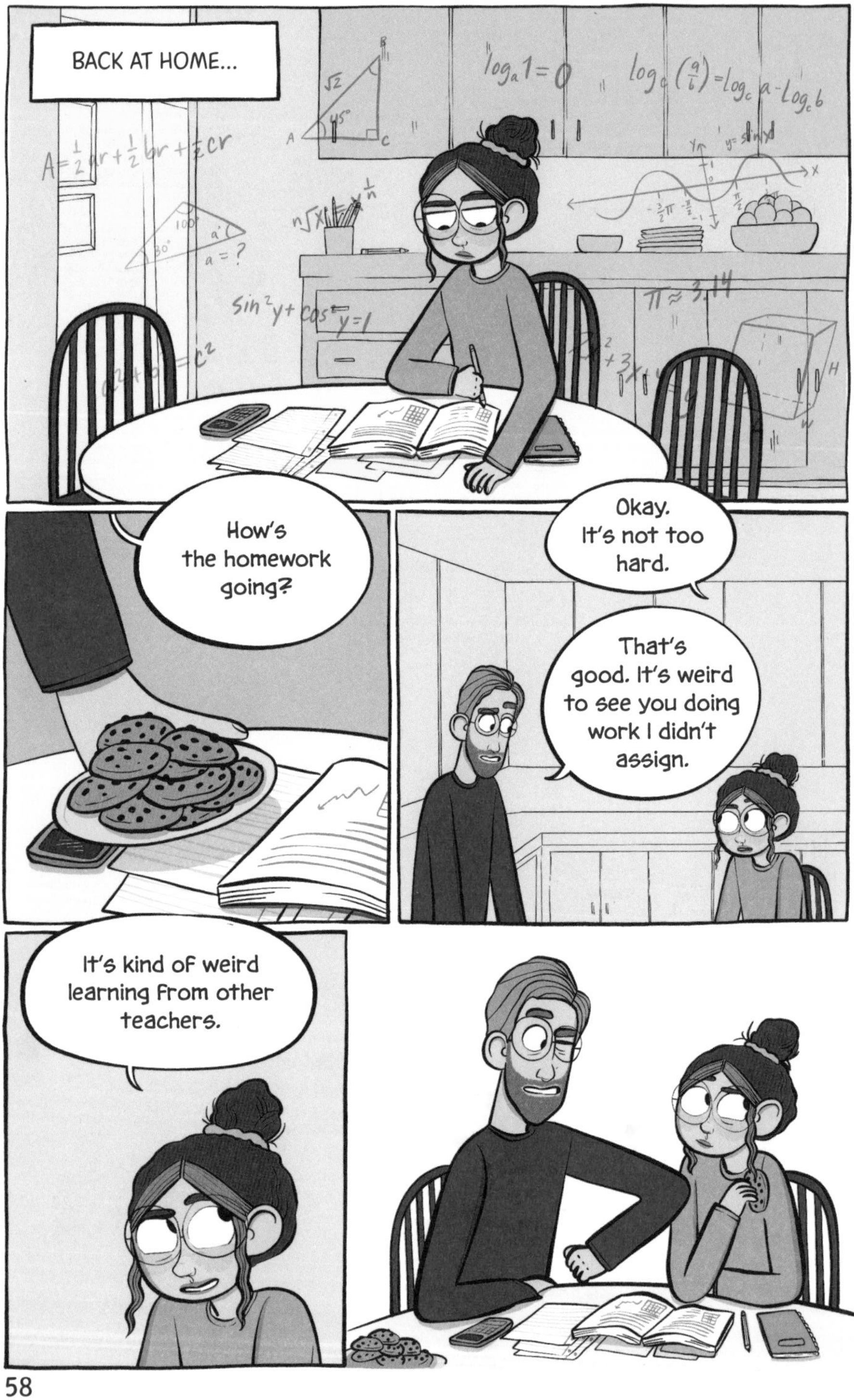
BACK AT HOME...
How's the homework going?
Okay. It's not too hard.
That's good. It's weird to see you doing work I didn't assign.
It's kind of weird learning from other teachers.

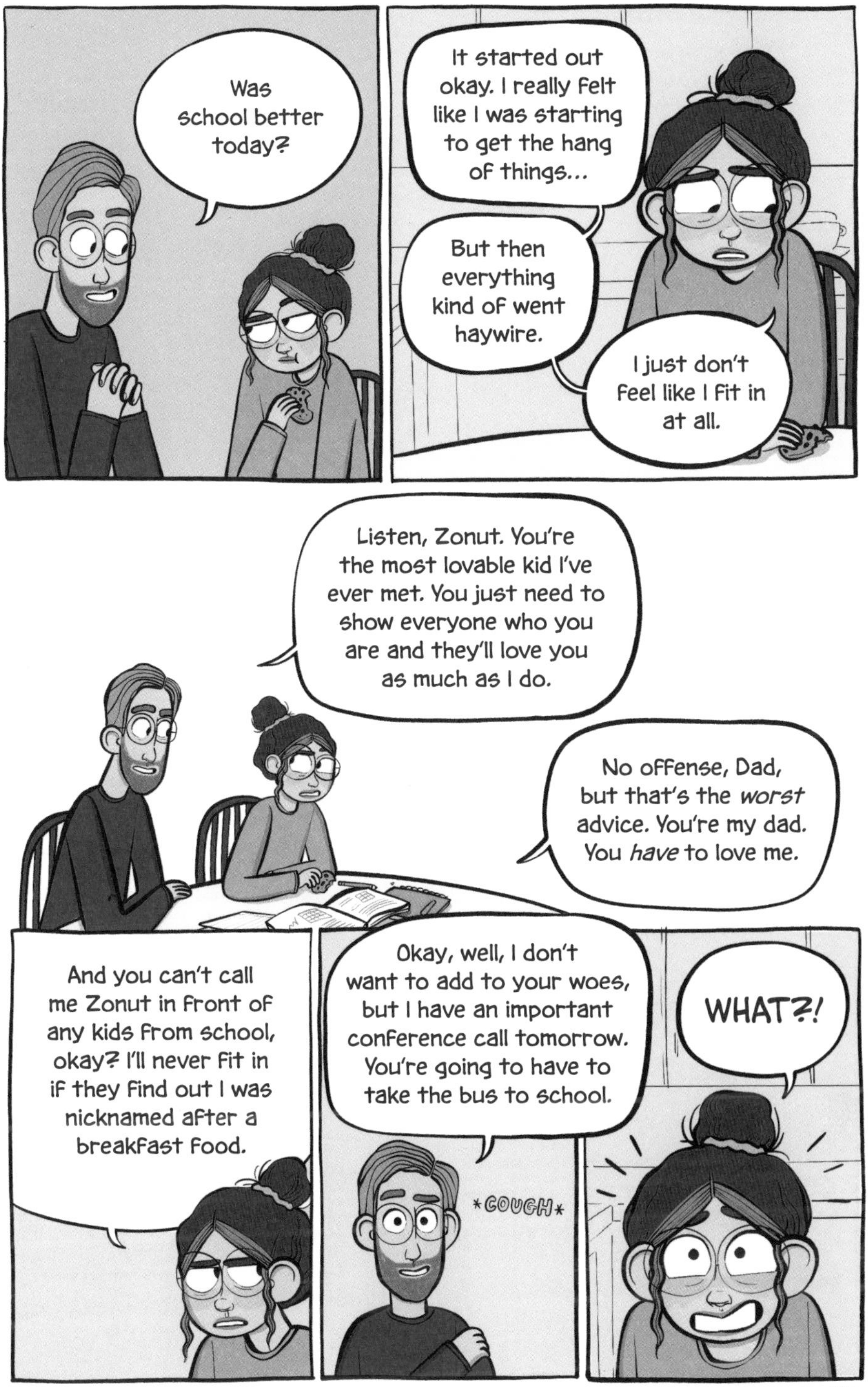
Was school better today?
It started out okay. I really felt like I was starting to get the hang of things...
But then everything kind of went haywire.
I just don't feel like I fit in at all.
Listen, Zonut. You're the most lovable kid I've ever met. You just need to show everyone who you are and they'll love you as much as I do.
No offense, Dad, but that's the *worst* advice. You're my dad. You *have* to love me.
And you can't call me Zonut in front of any kids from school, okay? I'll never fit in if they find out I was nicknamed after a breakfast food.
Okay, well, I don't want to add to your woes, but I have an important conference call tomorrow. You're going to have to take the bus to school.
COUGH
WHAT?!

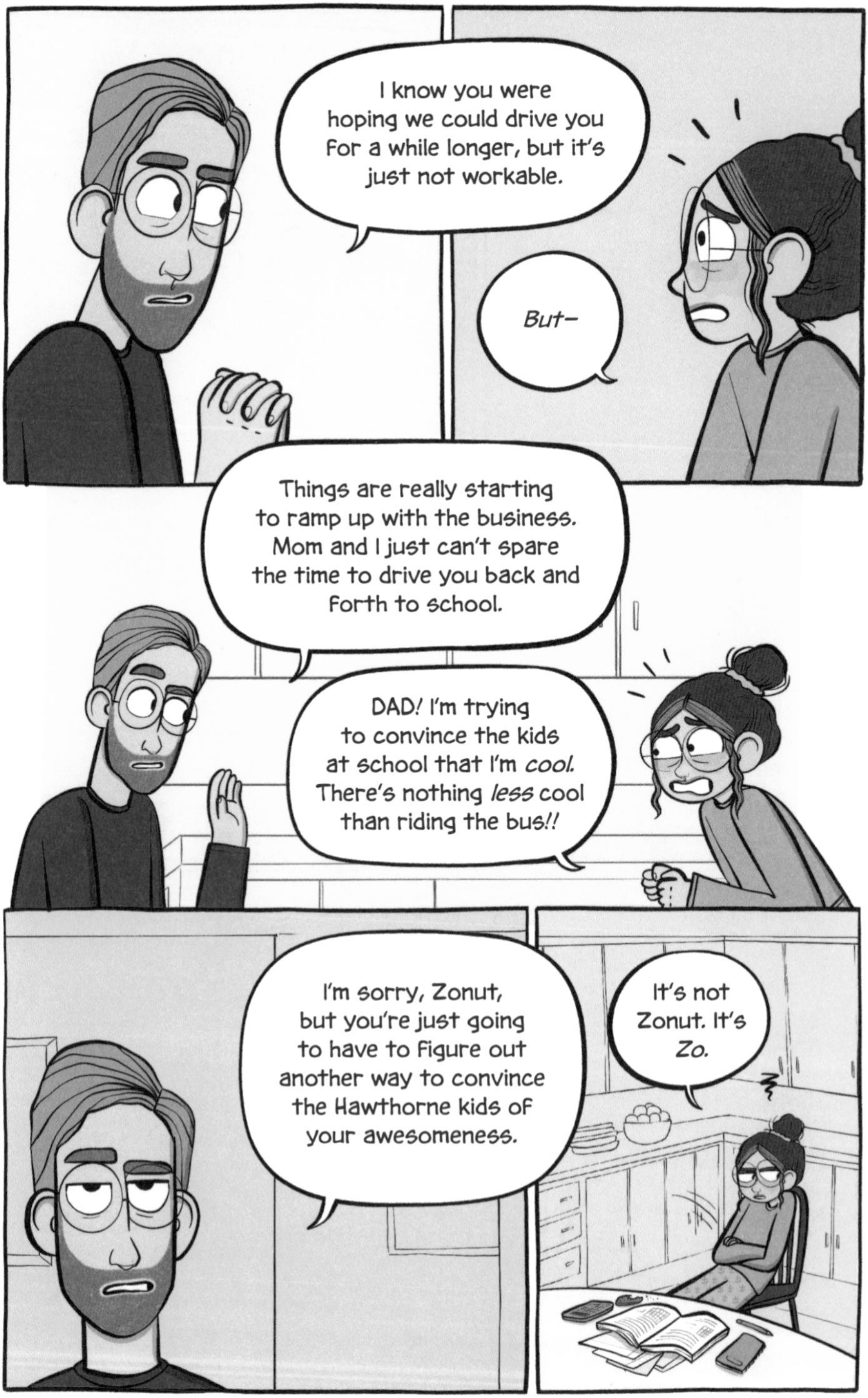

I know you were hoping we could drive you for a while longer, but it's just not workable.
But–
Things are really starting to ramp up with the business. Mom and I just can't spare the time to drive you back and forth to school.
DAD! I'm trying to convince the kids at school that I'm *cool.* There's nothing *less* cool than riding the bus!!
I'm sorry, Zonut, but you're just going to have to figure out another way to convince the Hawthorne kids of your awesomeness.
It's not Zonut. It's *Zo.*

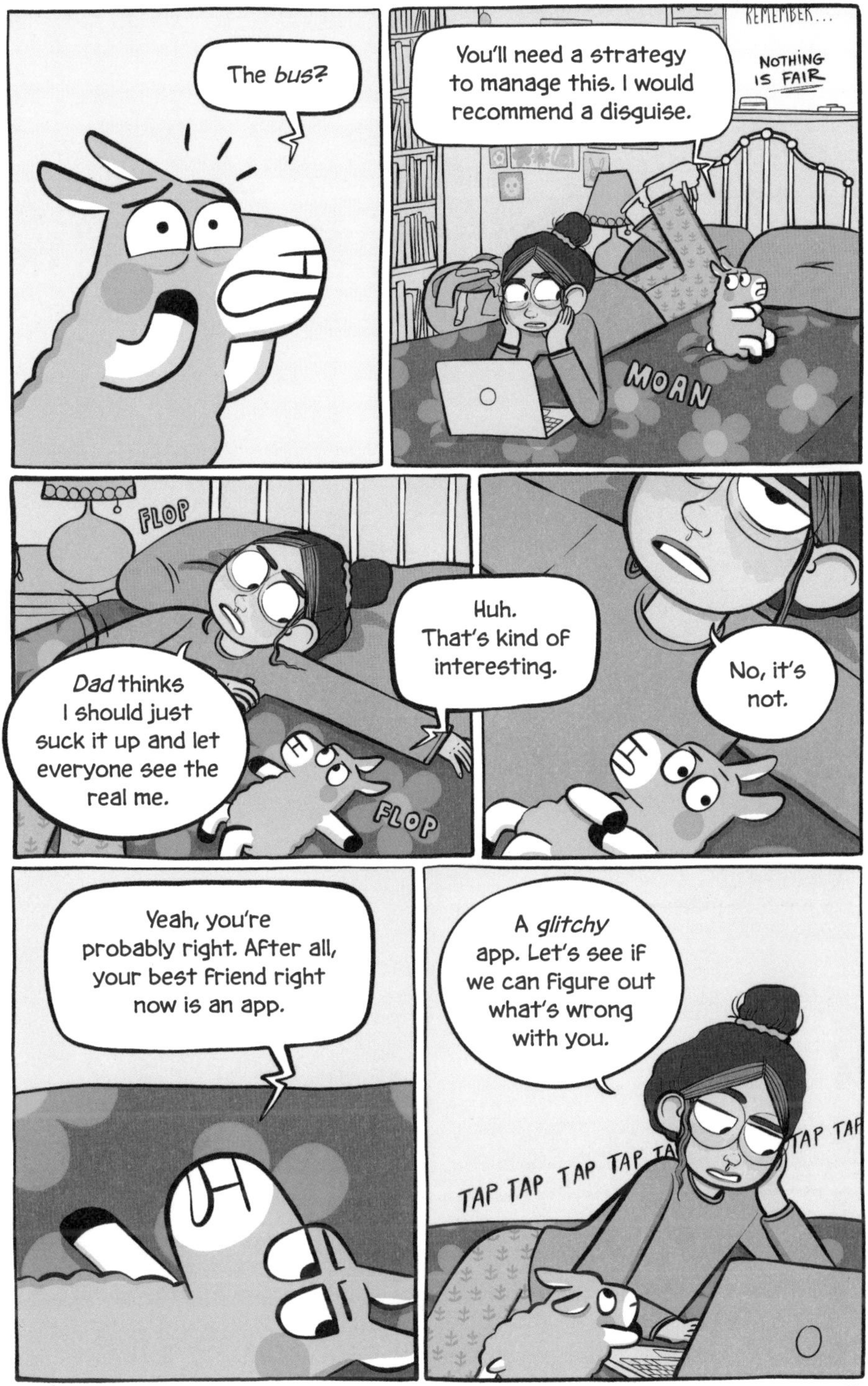
The *bus*?
REMEMBER...
NOTHING IS FAIR
You'll need a strategy to manage this. I would recommend a disguise.
MOAN
FLOP
Dad thinks I should just suck it up and let everyone see the real me.
Huh. That's kind of interesting.
FLOP
No, it's not.
Yeah, you're probably right. After all, your best friend right now is an app.
A *glitchy* app. Let's see if we can figure out what's wrong with you.
TAP TAP TAP TAP TAP TAP

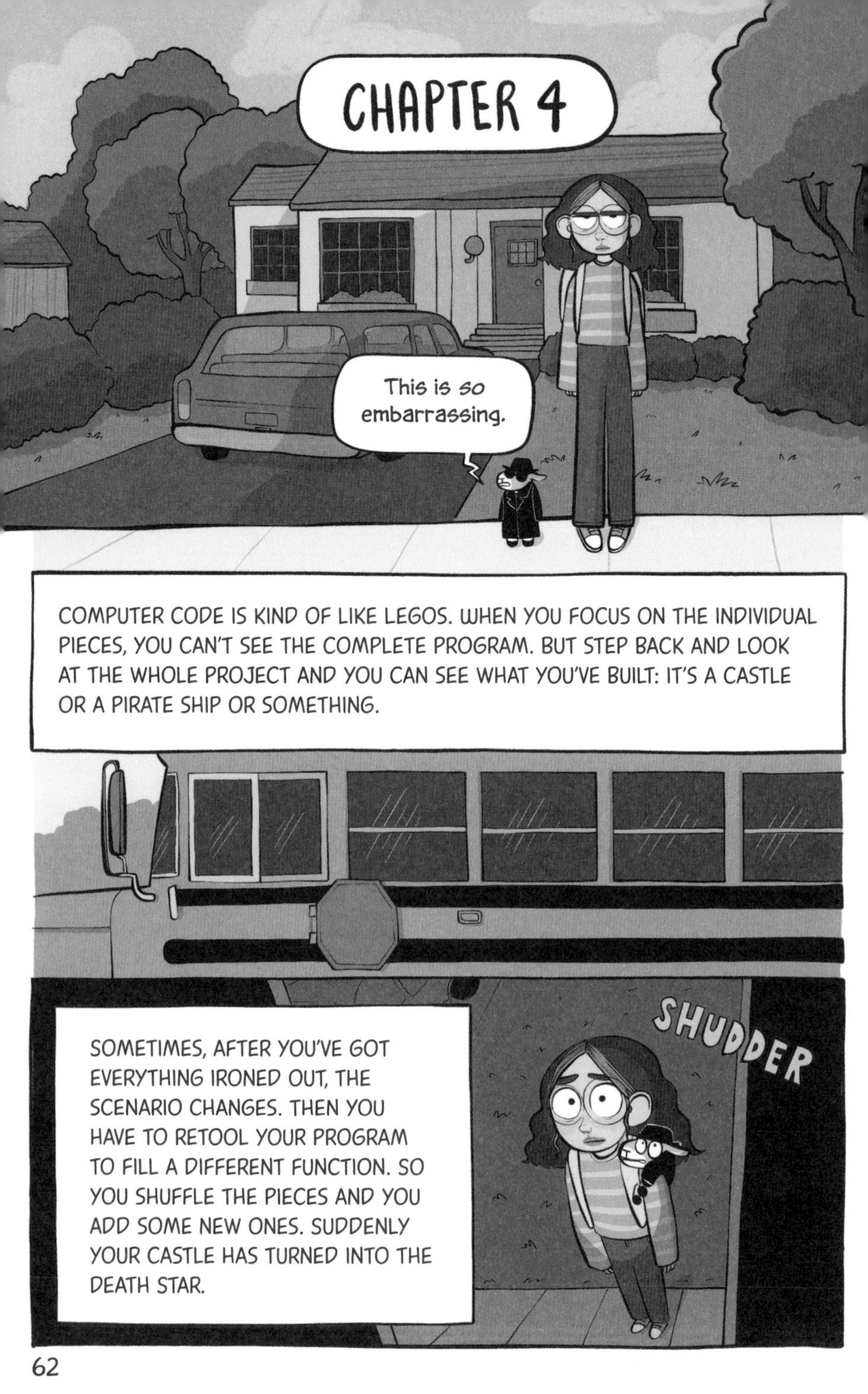
CHAPTER 4
This is so embarrassing.
COMPUTER CODE IS KIND OF LIKE LEGOS. WHEN YOU FOCUS ON THE INDIVIDUAL PIECES, YOU CAN'T SEE THE COMPLETE PROGRAM. BUT STEP BACK AND LOOK AT THE WHOLE PROJECT AND YOU CAN SEE WHAT YOU'VE BUILT: IT'S A CASTLE OR A PIRATE SHIP OR SOMETHING.
SOMETIMES, AFTER YOU'VE GOT EVERYTHING IRONED OUT, THE SCENARIO CHANGES. THEN YOU HAVE TO RETOOL YOUR PROGRAM TO FILL A DIFFERENT FUNCTION. SO YOU SHUFFLE THE PIECES AND YOU ADD SOME NEW ONES. SUDDENLY YOUR CASTLE HAS TURNED INTO THE DEATH STAR.
SHUDDER

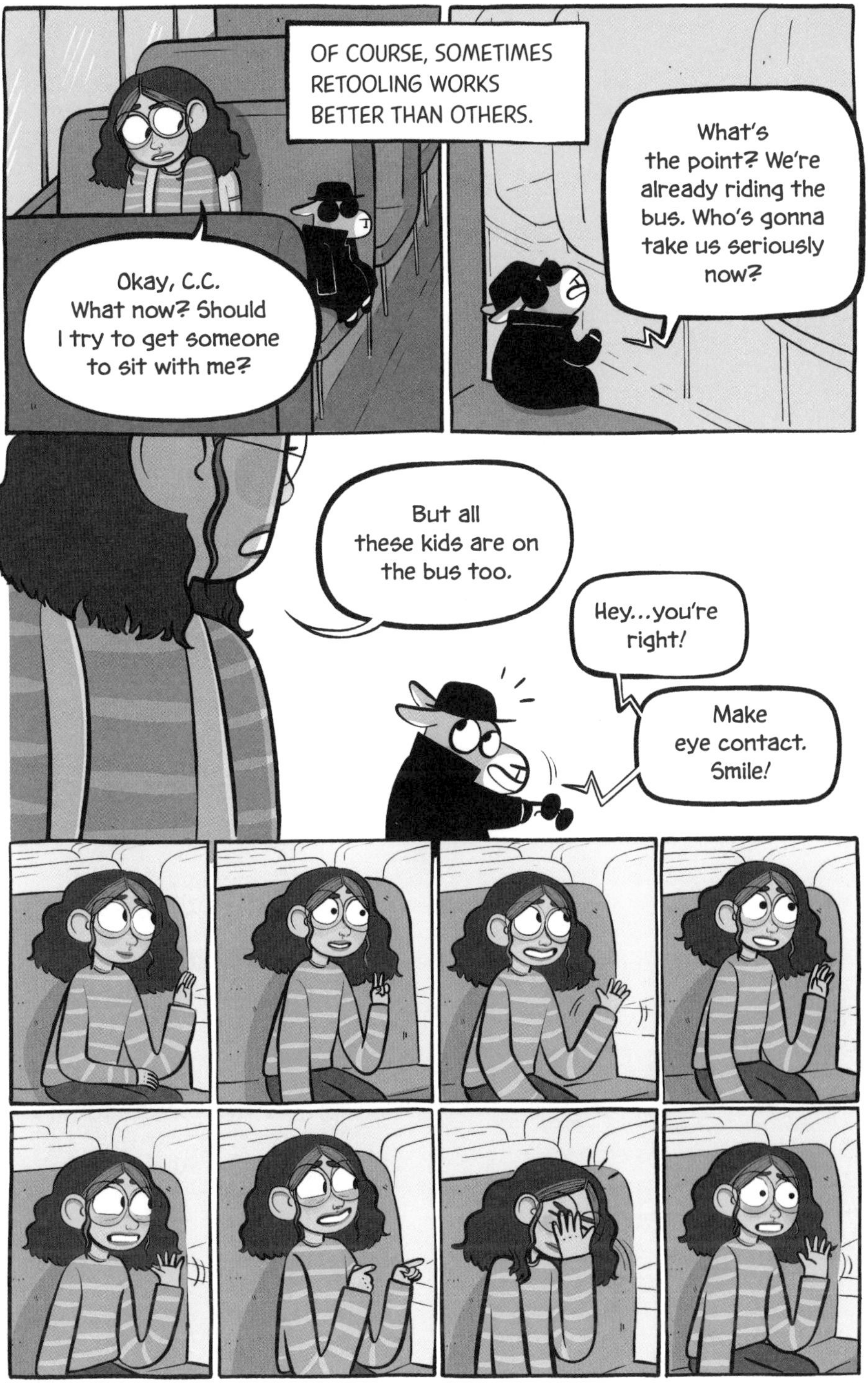
OF COURSE, SOMETIMES RETOOLING WORKS BETTER THAN OTHERS.
Okay, C.C. What now? Should I try to get someone to sit with me?
What's the point? We're already riding the bus. Who's gonna take us seriously now?
But all these kids are on the bus too.
Hey...you're right!
Make eye contact. Smile!

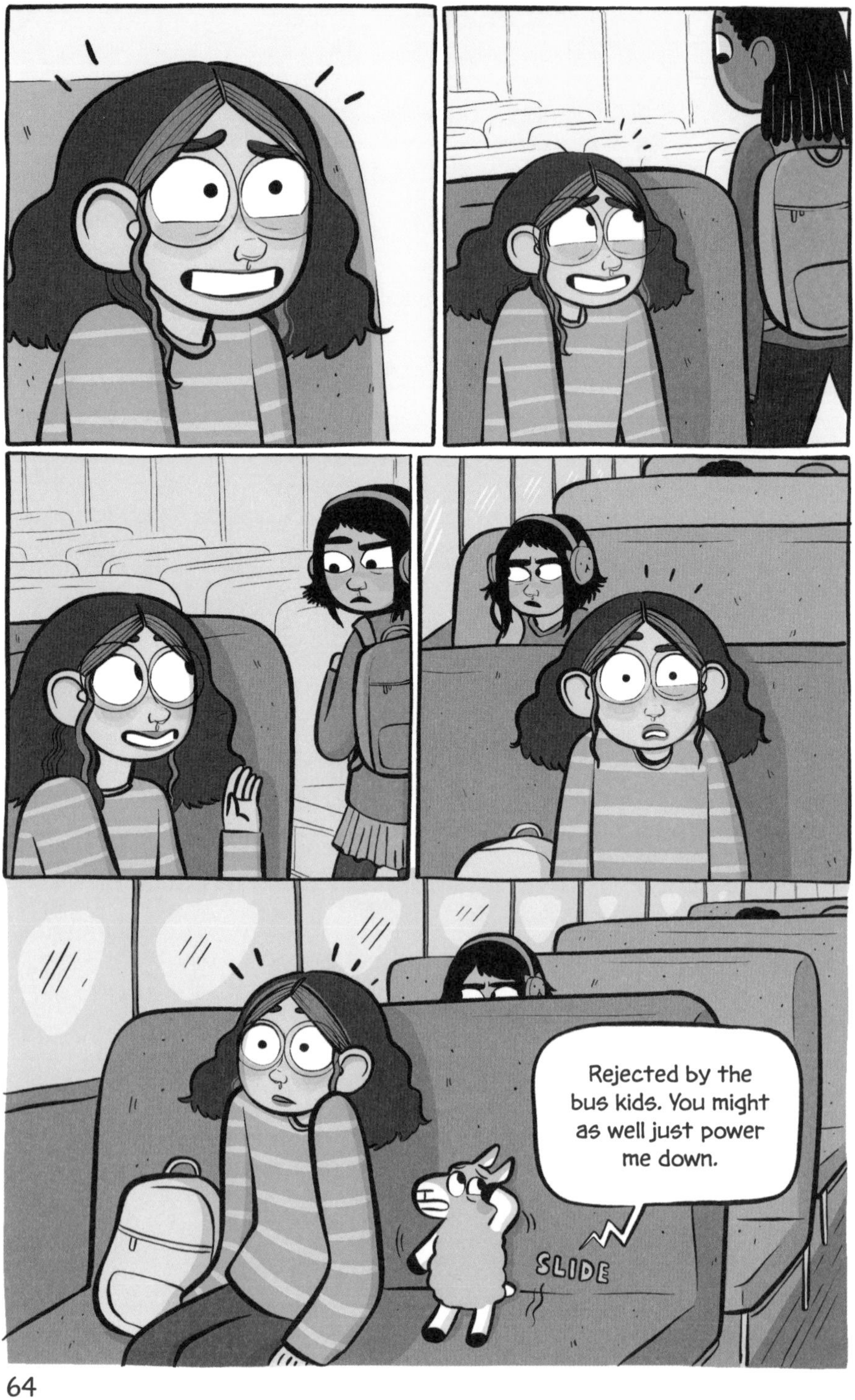
Rejected by the bus kids. You might as well just power me down.
SLIDE

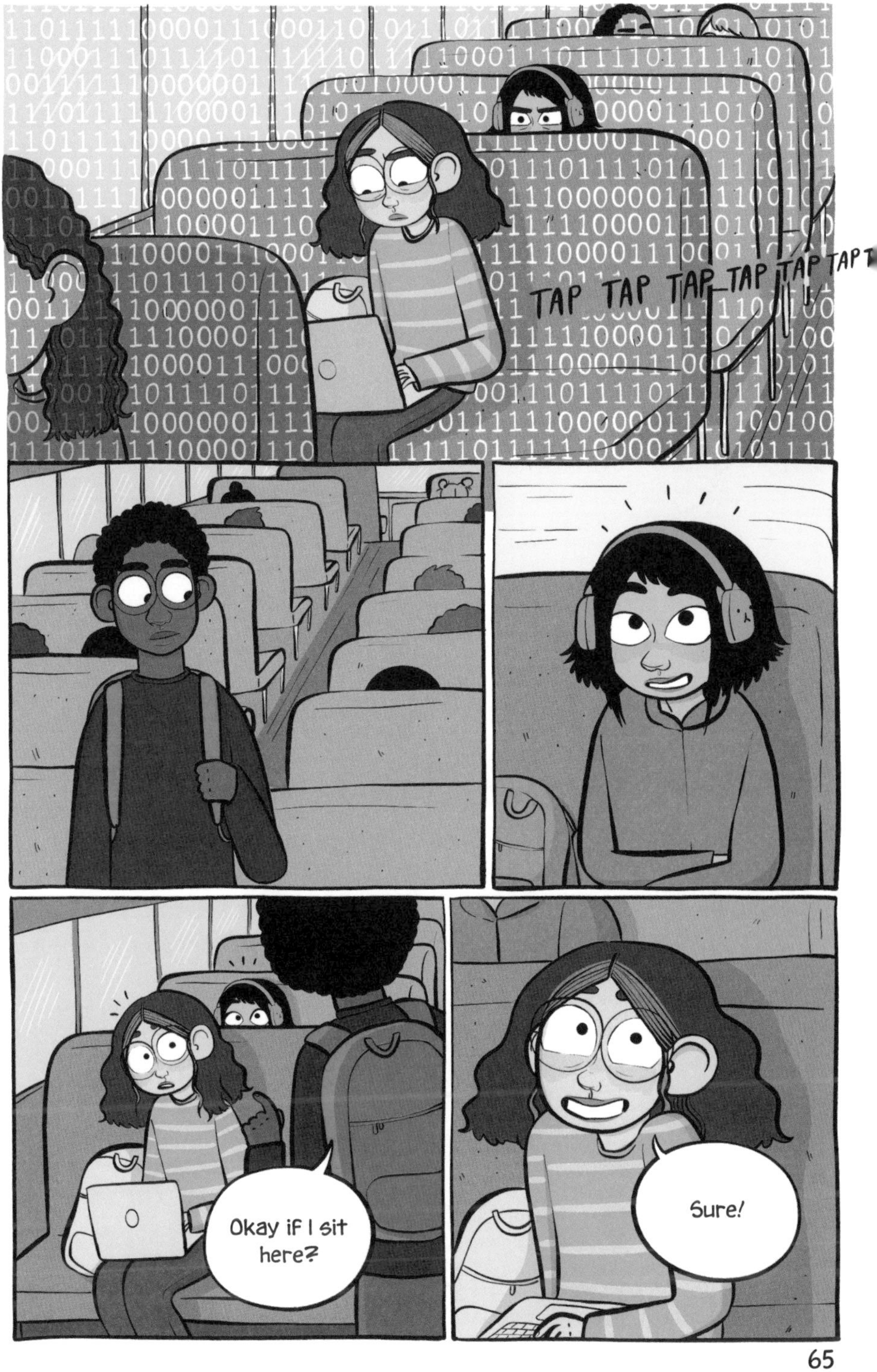
TAP TAP TAP TAP TAP TAPT
Okay if I sit here?
Sure!

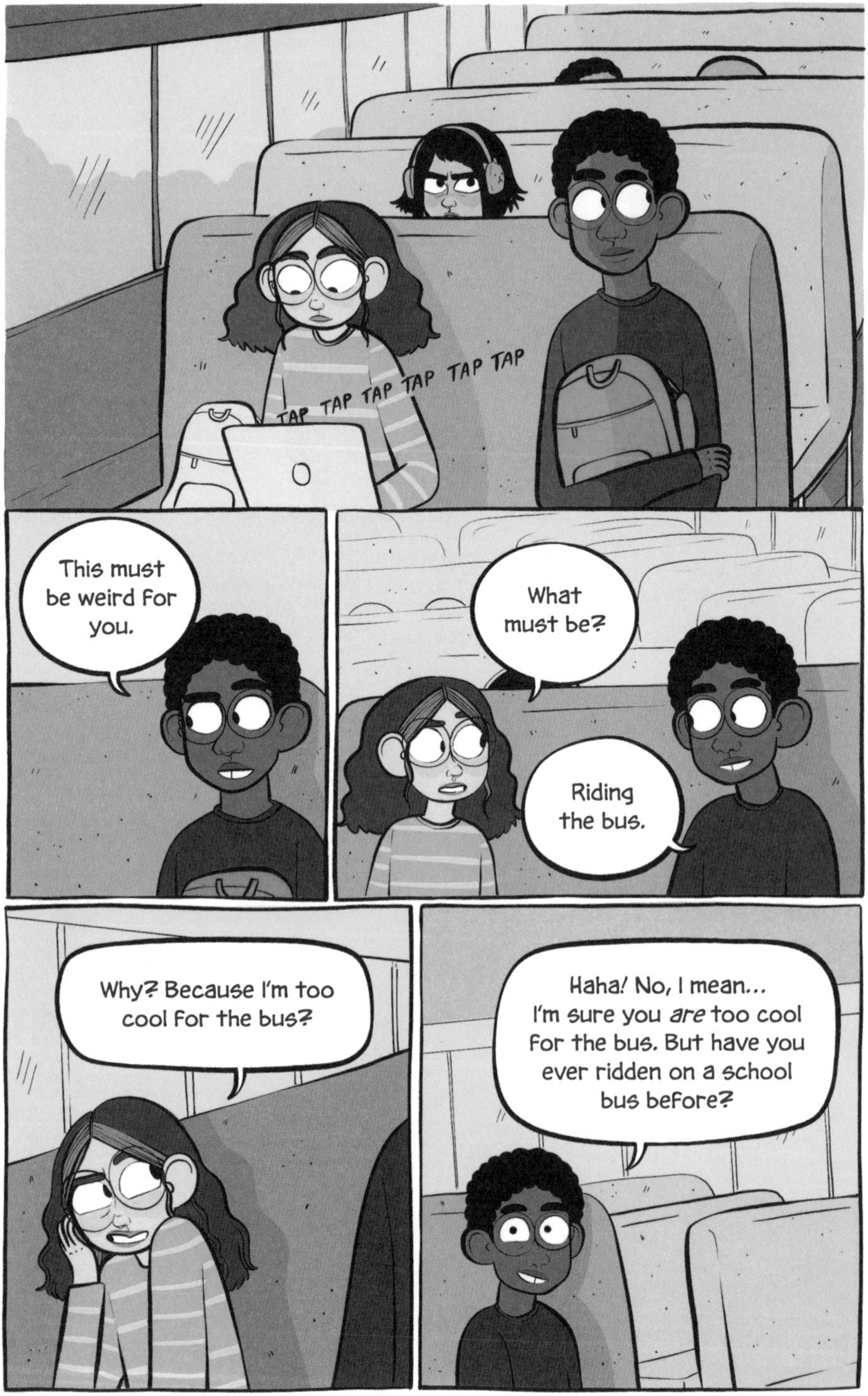
TAP TAP TAP TAP TAP TAP
This must be weird for you.
What must be?
Riding the bus.
Why? Because I'm too cool for the bus?
Haha! No, I mean... I'm sure you *are* too cool for the bus. But have you ever ridden on a school bus before?

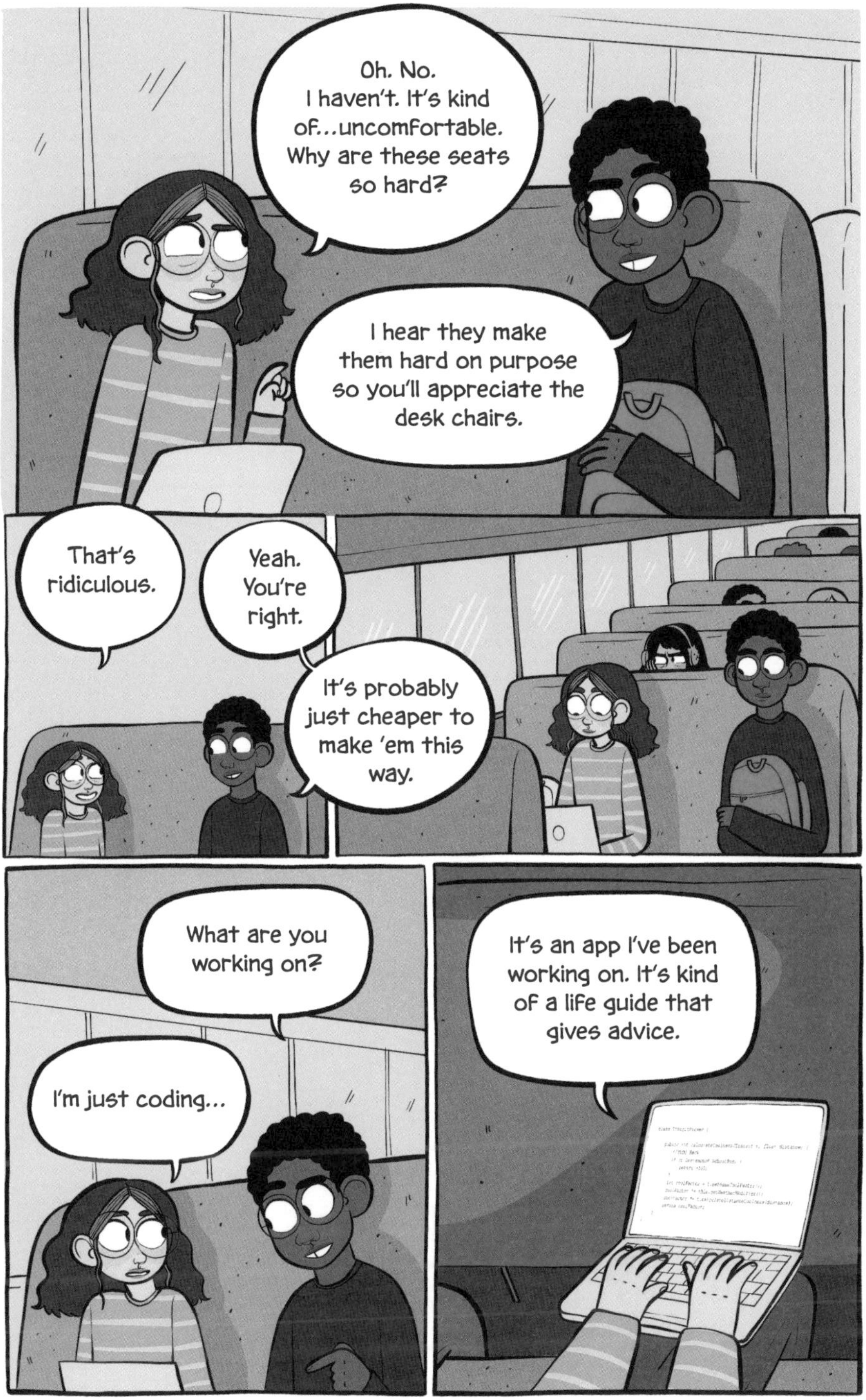
Oh. No. I haven't. It's kind of...uncomfortable. Why are these seats so hard?
I hear they make them hard on purpose so you'll appreciate the desk chairs.
That's ridiculous.
Yeah. You're right.
It's probably just cheaper to make 'em this way.
What are you working on?
I'm just coding...
It's an app I've been working on. It's kind of a life guide that gives advice.

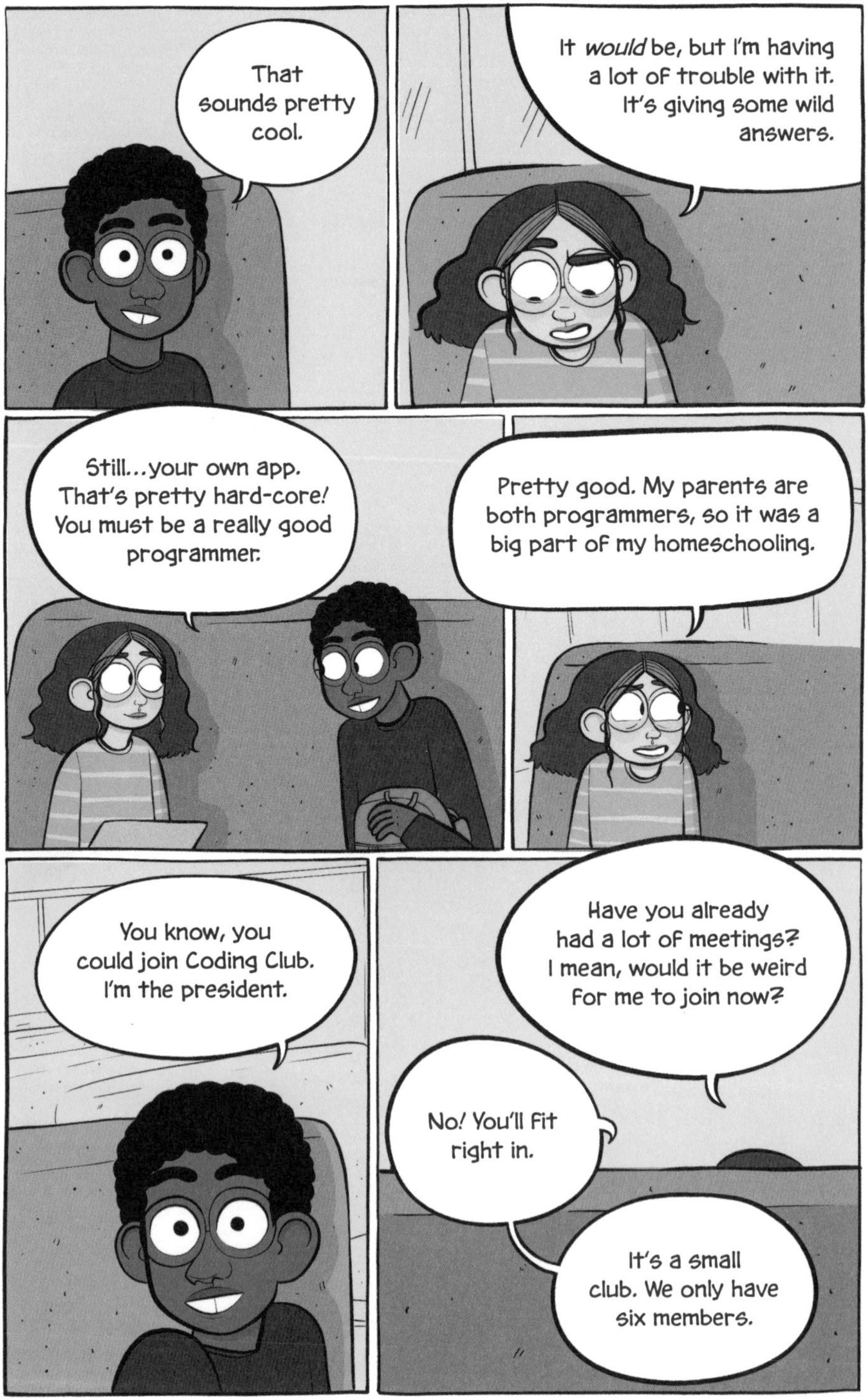
That sounds pretty cool.
It *would* be, but I'm having a lot of trouble with it. It's giving some wild answers.
Still...your own app. That's pretty hard-core! You must be a really good programmer.
Pretty good. My parents are both programmers, so it was a big part of my homeschooling.
You know, you could join Coding Club. I'm the president.
Have you already had a lot of meetings? I mean, would it be weird for me to join now?
No! You'll fit right in.
It's a small club. We only have six members.

69

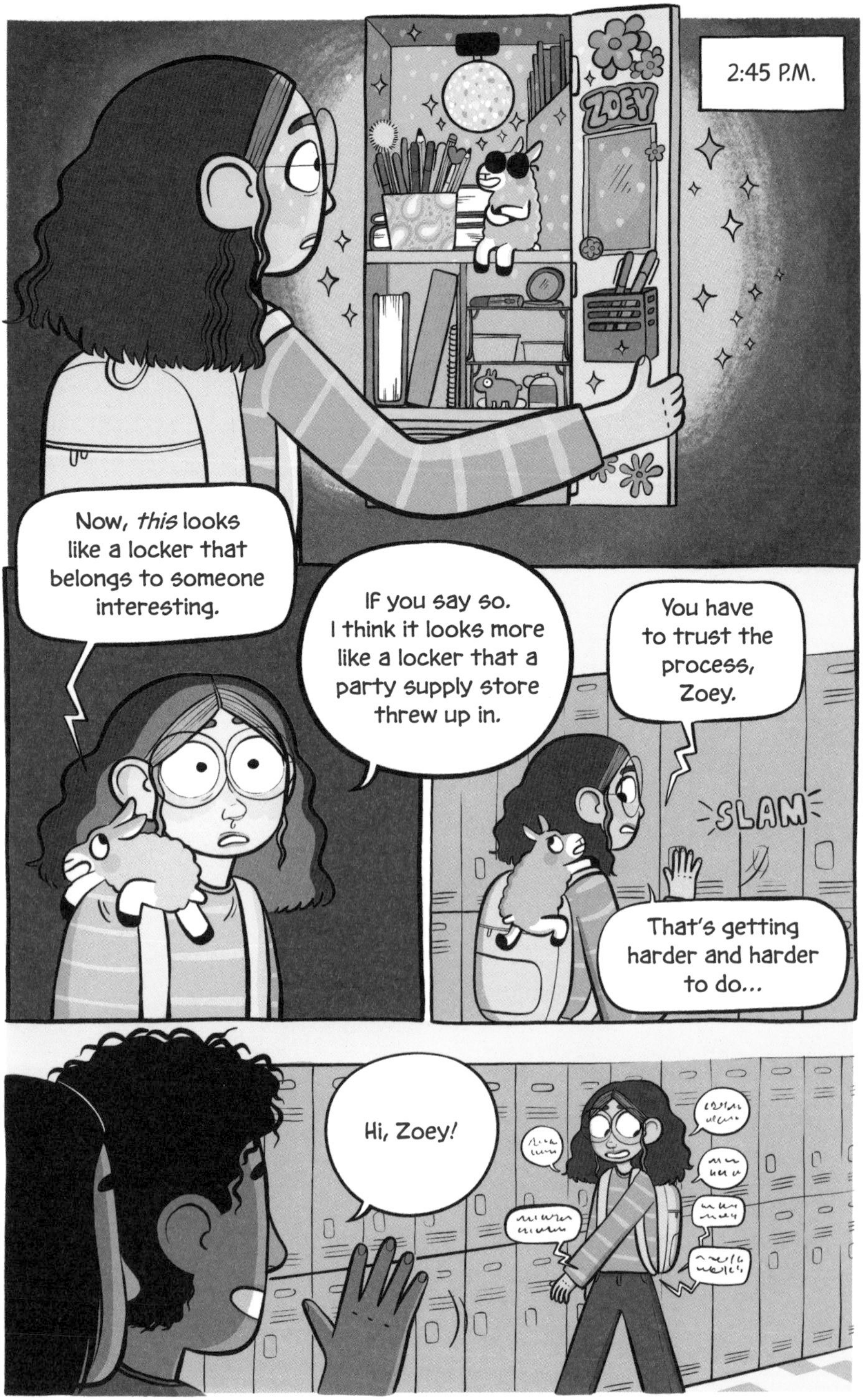
2:45 P.M.
ZOEY
Now, *this* looks like a locker that belongs to someone interesting.
If you say so. I think it looks more like a locker that a party supply store threw up in.
You have to trust the process, Zoey.
SLAM
That's getting harder and harder to do...
Hi, Zoey!

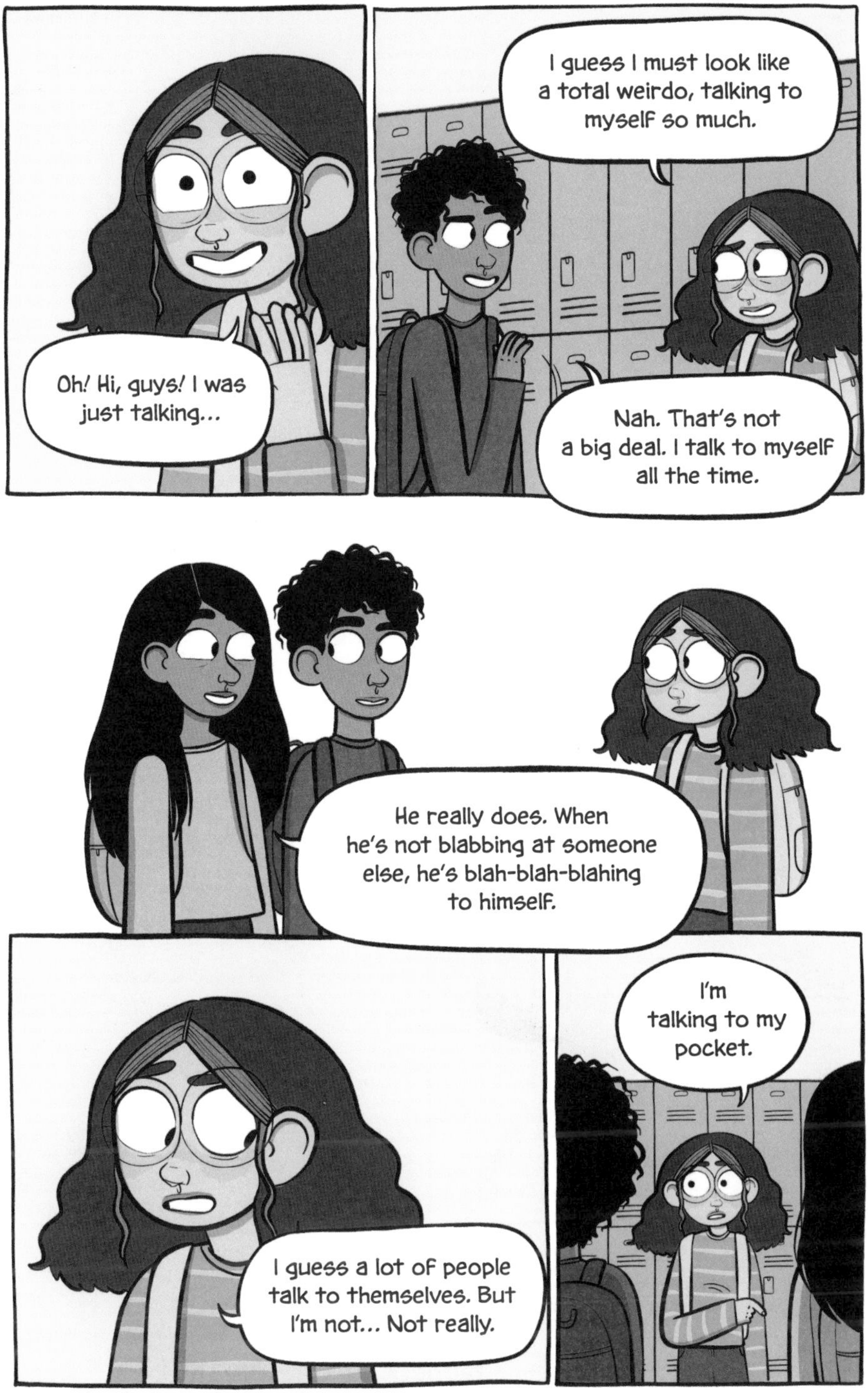
Oh! Hi, guys! I was just talking...
I guess I must look like a total weirdo, talking to myself so much.
Nah. That's not a big deal. I talk to myself all the time.
He really does. When he's not blabbing at someone else, he's blah-blah-blahing to himself.
I guess a lot of people talk to themselves. But I'm not... Not really.
I'm talking to my pocket.

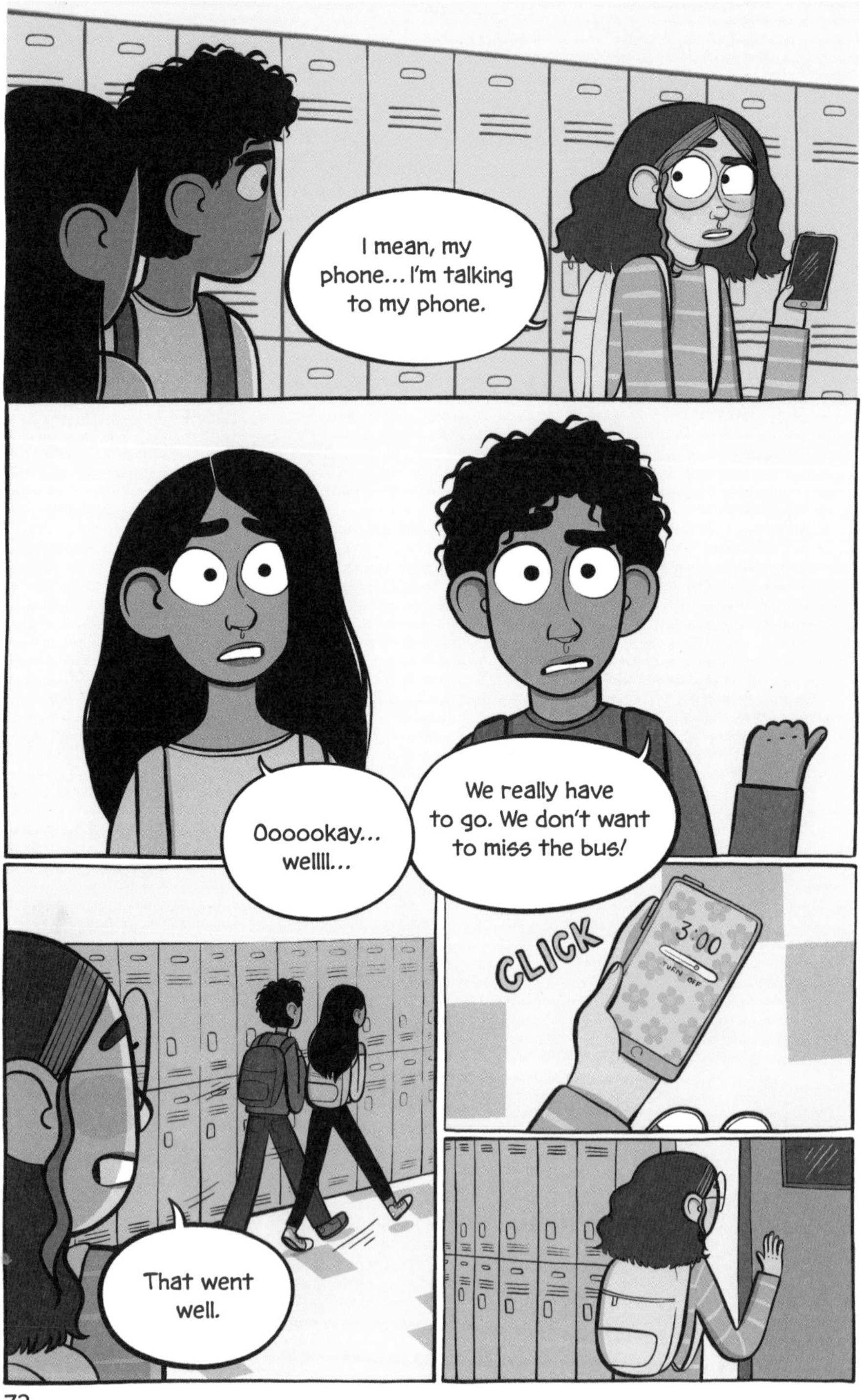
I mean, my phone... I'm talking to my phone.
Oooookay... wellll...
We really have to go. We don't want to miss the bus!
CLICK
3:00
TURN OFF
That went well.

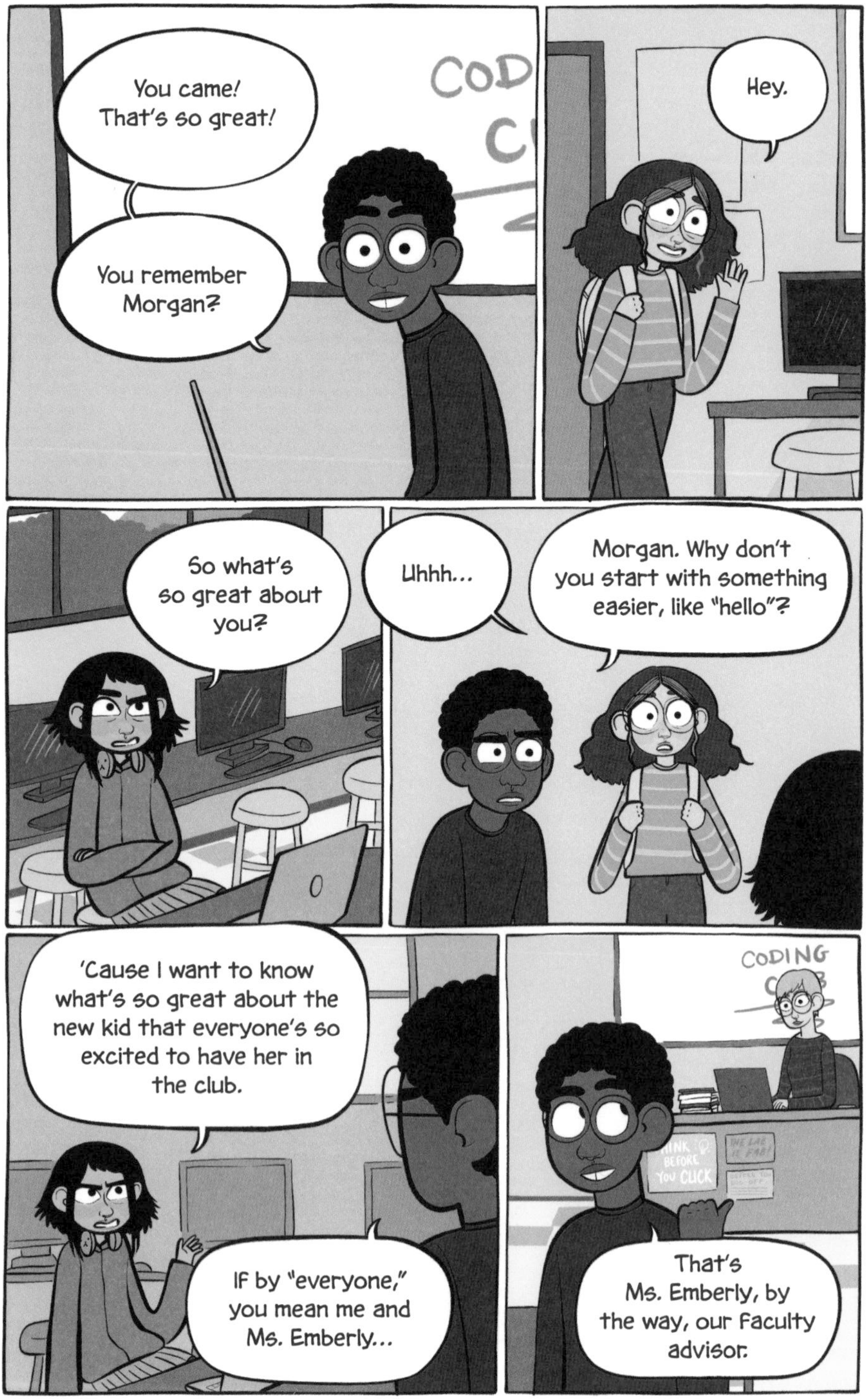

You came!
That's so great!
You remember Morgan?
Hey.
So what's so great about you?
Uhhh...
Morgan. Why don't you start with something easier, like "hello"?
'Cause I want to know what's so great about the new kid that everyone's so excited to have her in the club.
If by "everyone," you mean me and Ms. Emberly...
CODING
THINK BEFORE YOU CLICK
That's Ms. Emberly, by the way, our faculty advisor.

75

77

81

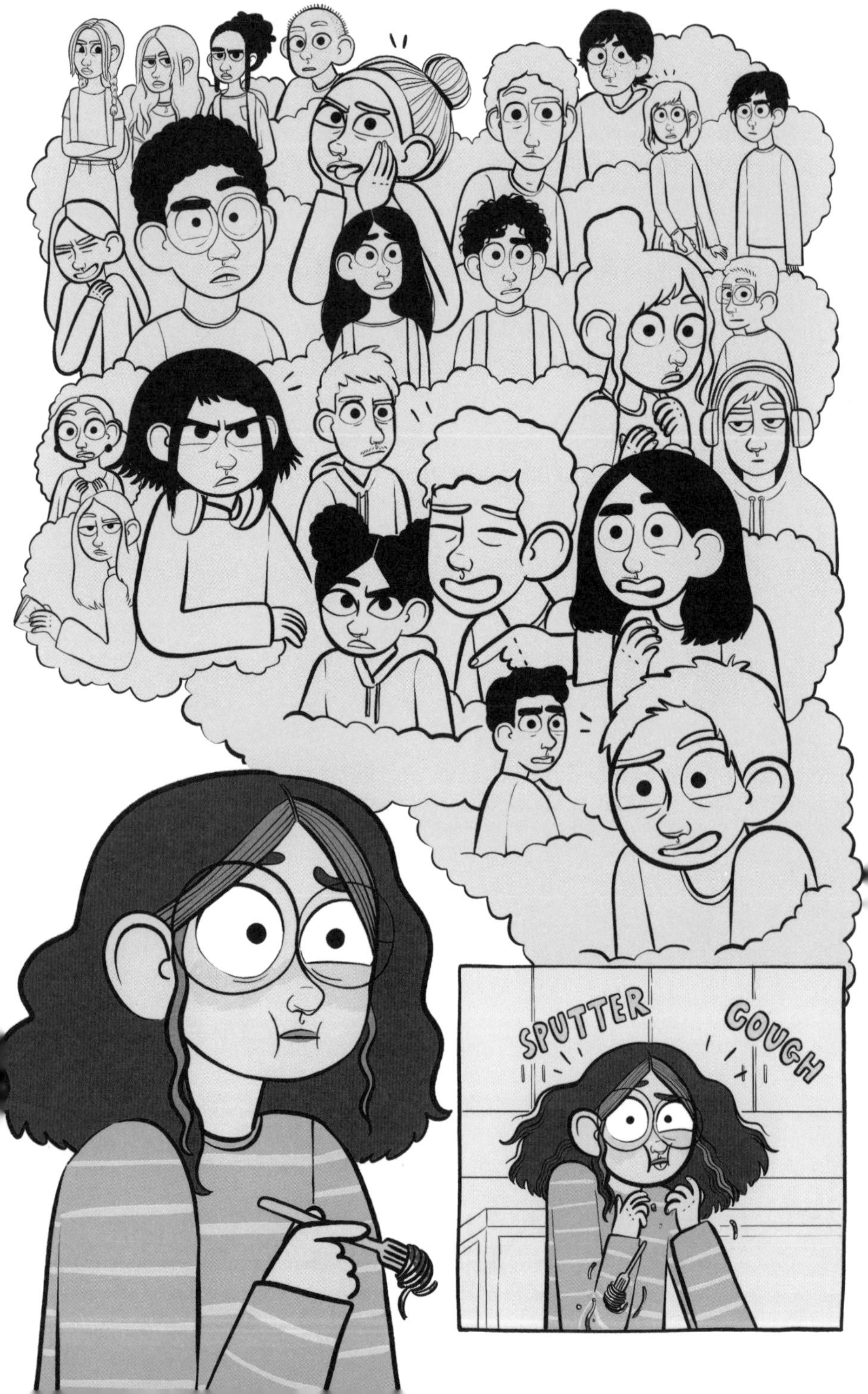
SPUTTER
COUGH

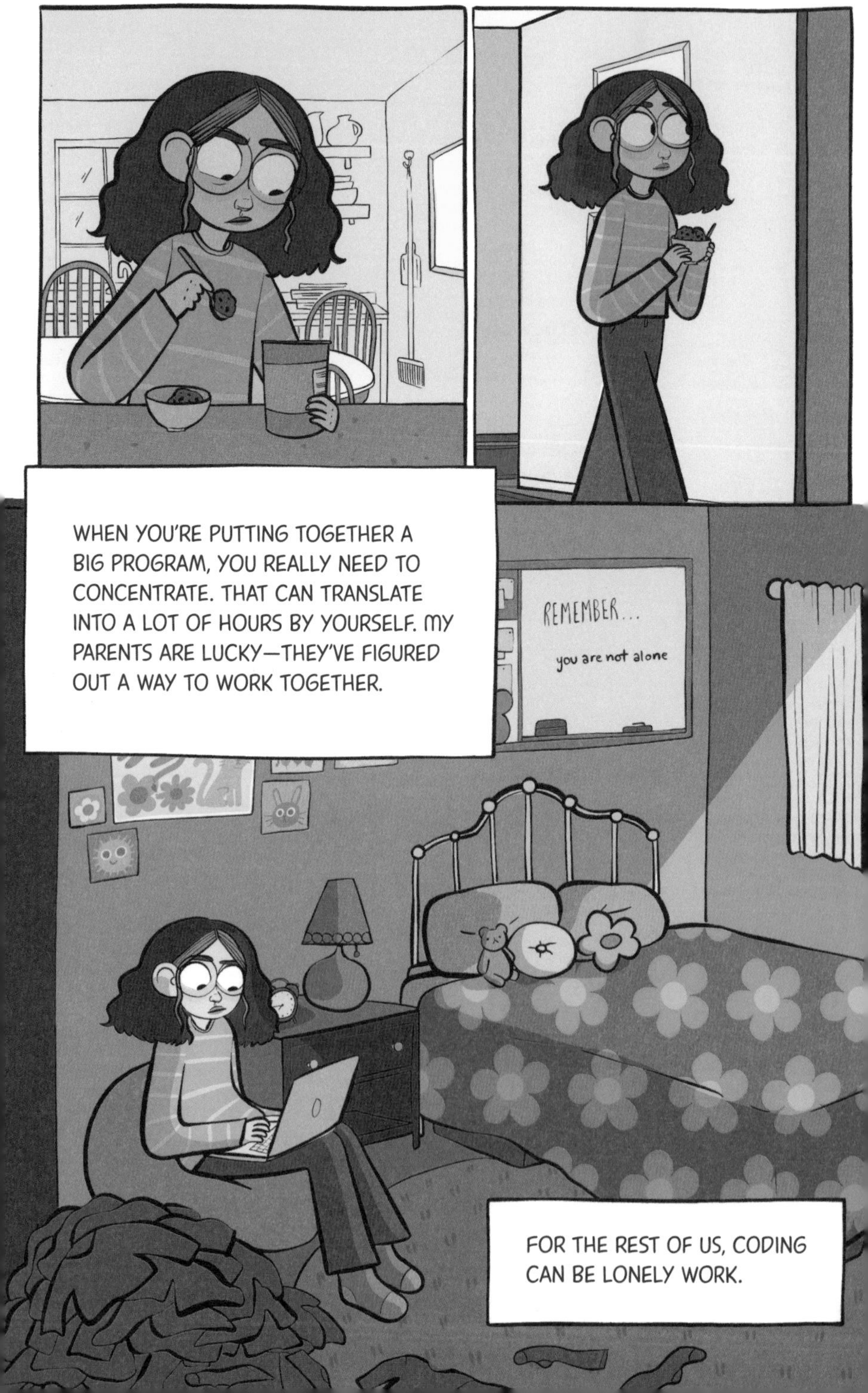
WHEN YOU'RE PUTTING TOGETHER A BIG PROGRAM, YOU REALLY NEED TO CONCENTRATE. THAT CAN TRANSLATE INTO A LOT OF HOURS BY YOURSELF. MY PARENTS ARE LUCKY—THEY'VE FIGURED OUT A WAY TO WORK TOGETHER.
REMEMBER...
you are not alone
FOR THE REST OF US, CODING CAN BE LONELY WORK.

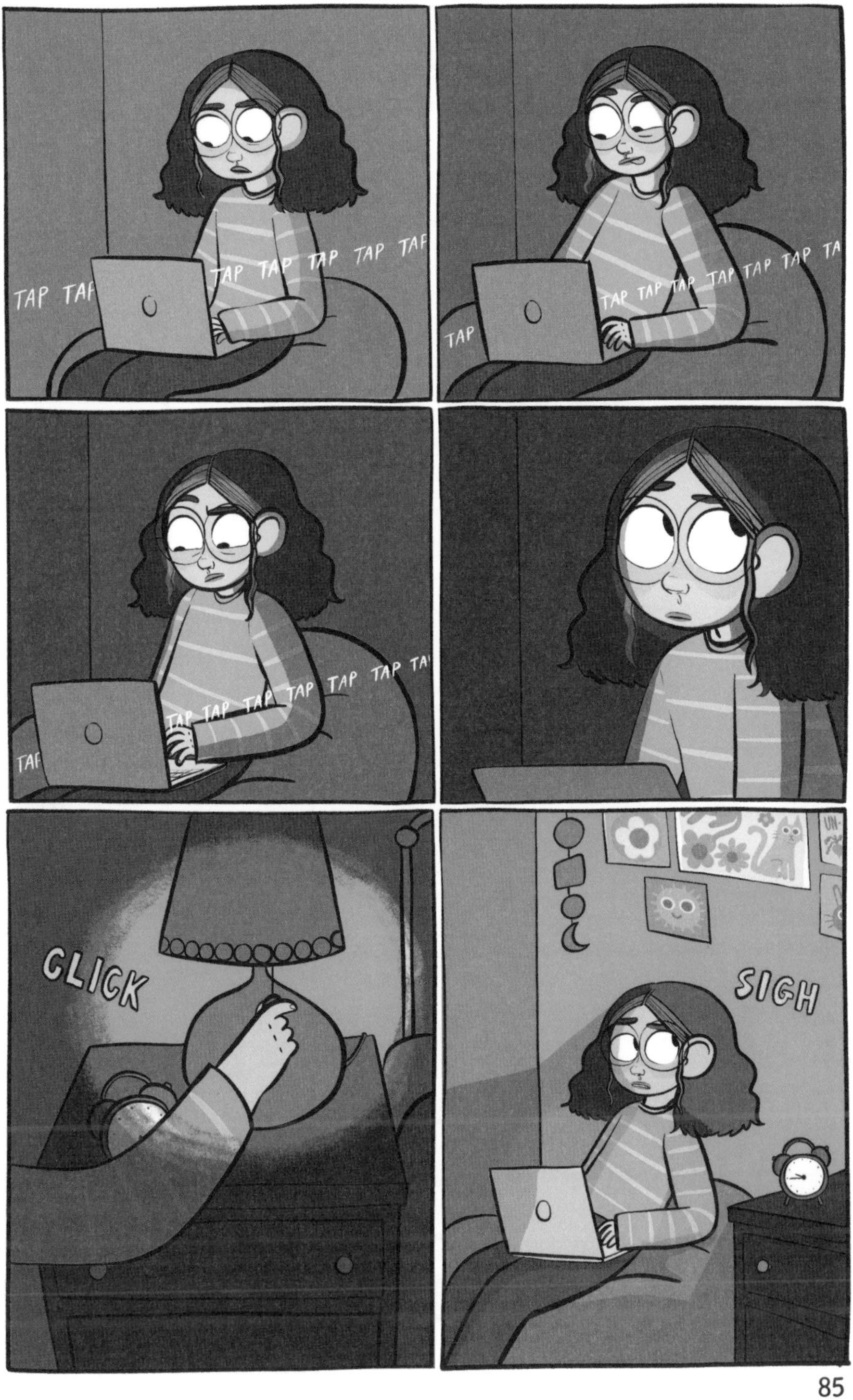
TAP
TAP TAP TAP TAP
TAP
TAP TAP TAP TAP TAP TAP TAP
TAP TAP TAP TAP TAP TAP
CLICK
SIGH

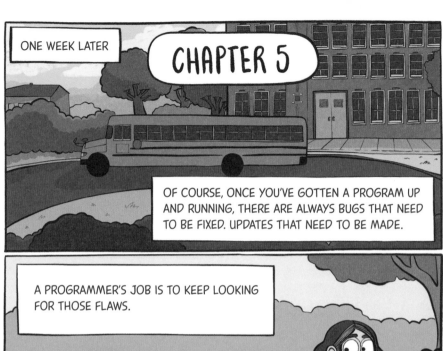

ONE WEEK LATER

CHAPTER 5

OF COURSE, ONCE YOU'VE GOTTEN A PROGRAM UP AND RUNNING, THERE ARE ALWAYS BUGS THAT NEED TO BE FIXED. UPDATES THAT NEED TO BE MADE.

A PROGRAMMER'S JOB IS TO KEEP LOOKING FOR THOSE FLAWS.

CLICK

BUT EVERYONE WANTS THEIR WORK TO SUCCEED, SO IT CAN BE TEMPTING TO OVERLOOK THEM.

89

91

92

93

95

NEW ITEM:

DRESS
↳ LONG SLEEVED
MINI-LENGTH

You have one item in your closet inventory. The Cool Code recommends that you burn it immediately.

Ummm... whoops? Sorry.

Yeah, so, the program works pretty much like this:

Welcome to the Cool Code!

Welcome COOL CODE

LOG IN

You log in, and you can select from a list of scenarios.

Who's that?

That's C.C. He's a llama.

"C.C." is for Cool Code—I know it's kind of weird, but I just started calling him that and then I got used to it.

98

SUBJECT NAME:
UNKNOWN

CLOTHING:
BELOW AVERAGE

INTERACTION STYLE:
ABYSMAL

PRELIMINARY COOL ASSESSMENT:
POOR

103

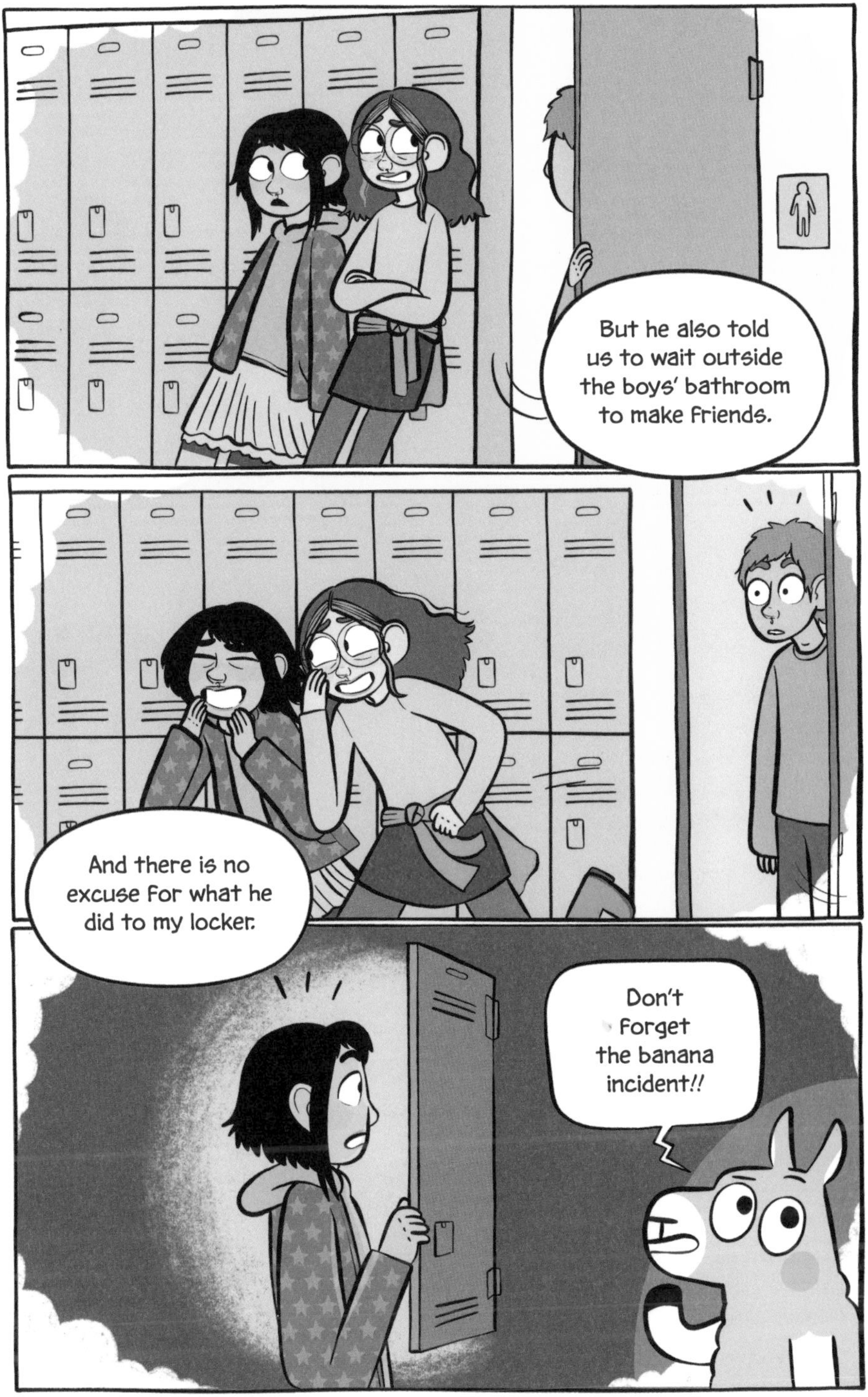
But he also told us to wait outside the boys' bathroom to make friends.
And there is no excuse for what he did to my locker.
Don't forget the banana incident!!

107

CHAPTER 7

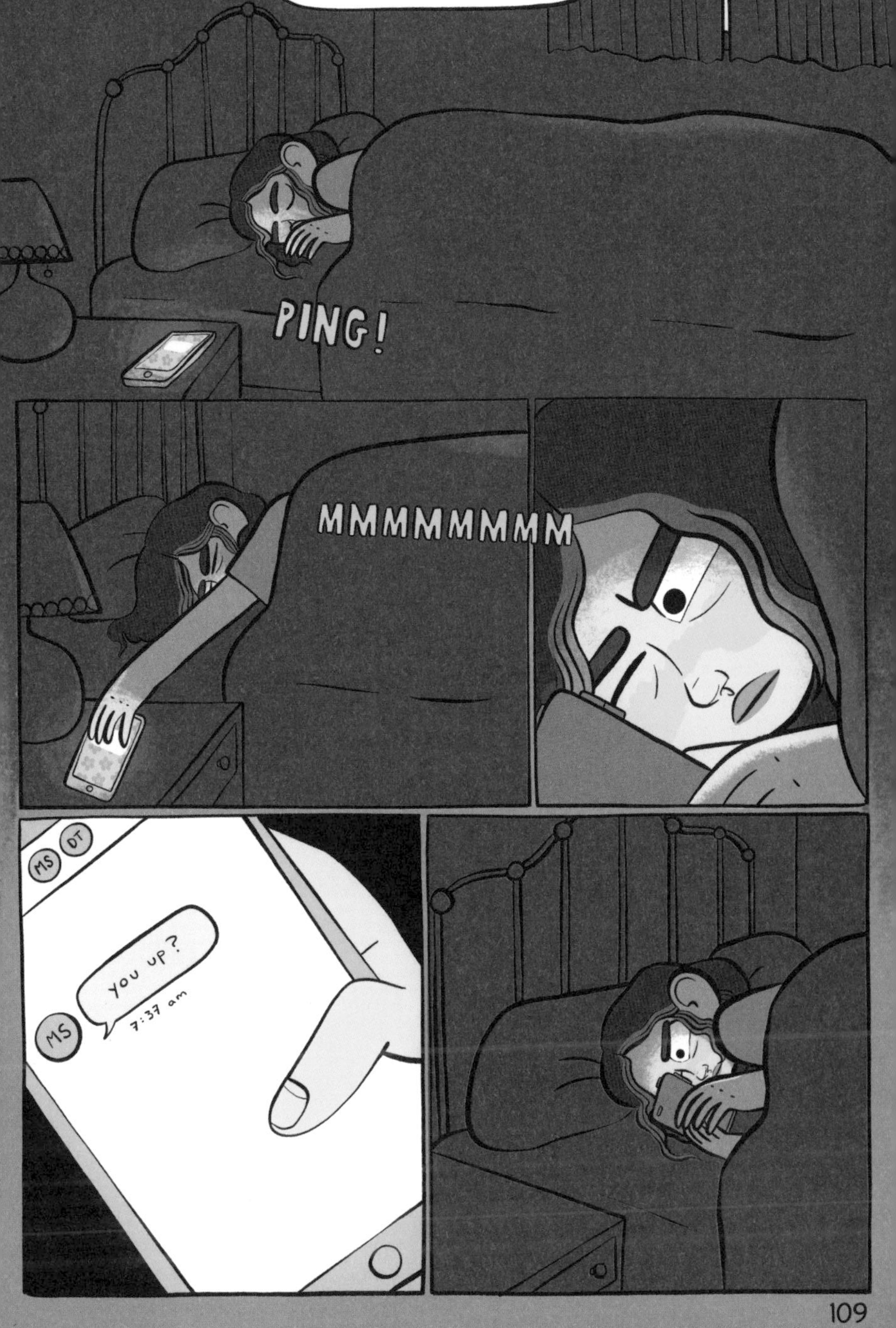
PING!
MMMMMMMMM
MS
DT
you up?
7:37 am
MS

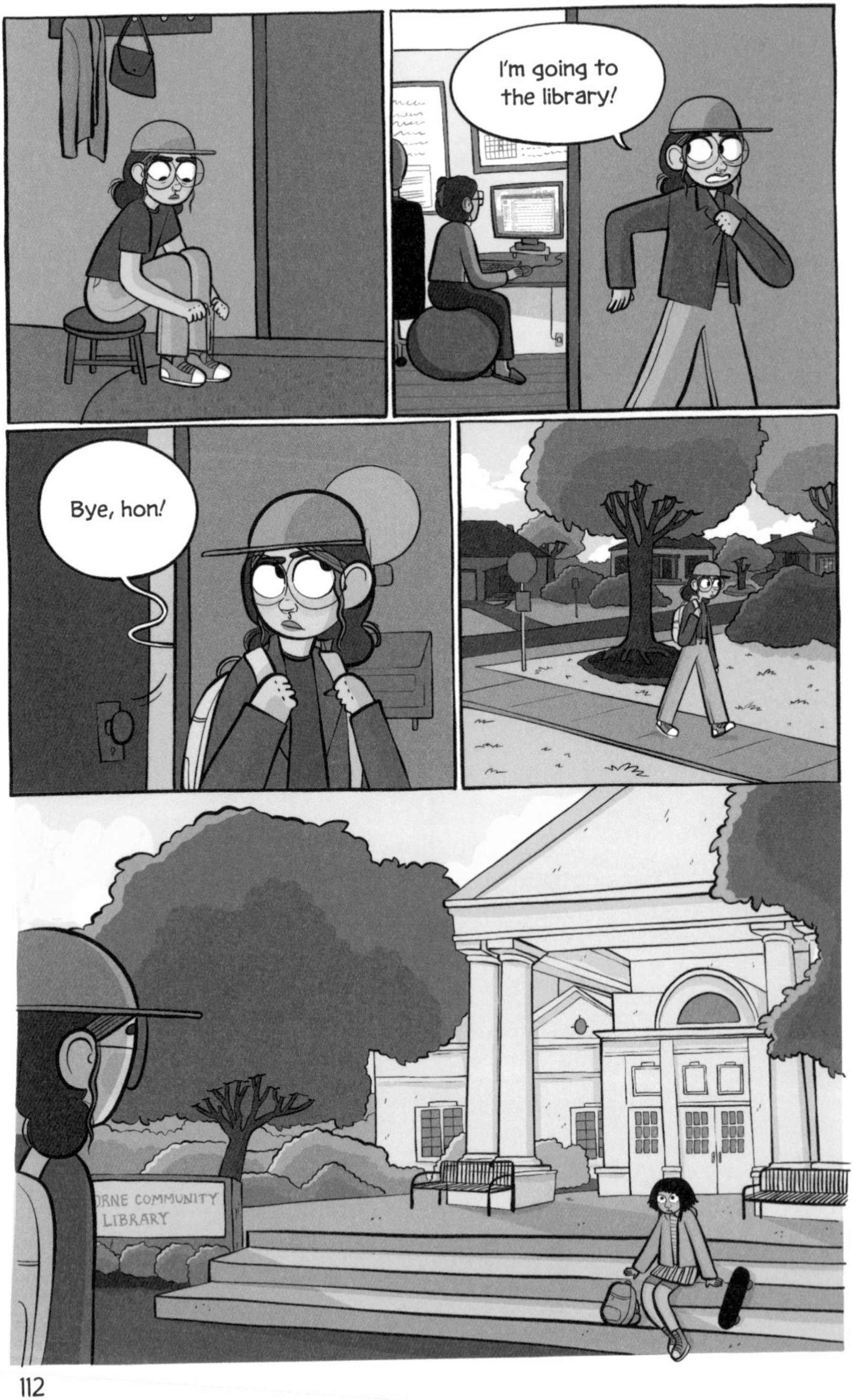
I'm going to the library!
Bye, hon!
ORNE COMMUNITY
LIBRARY

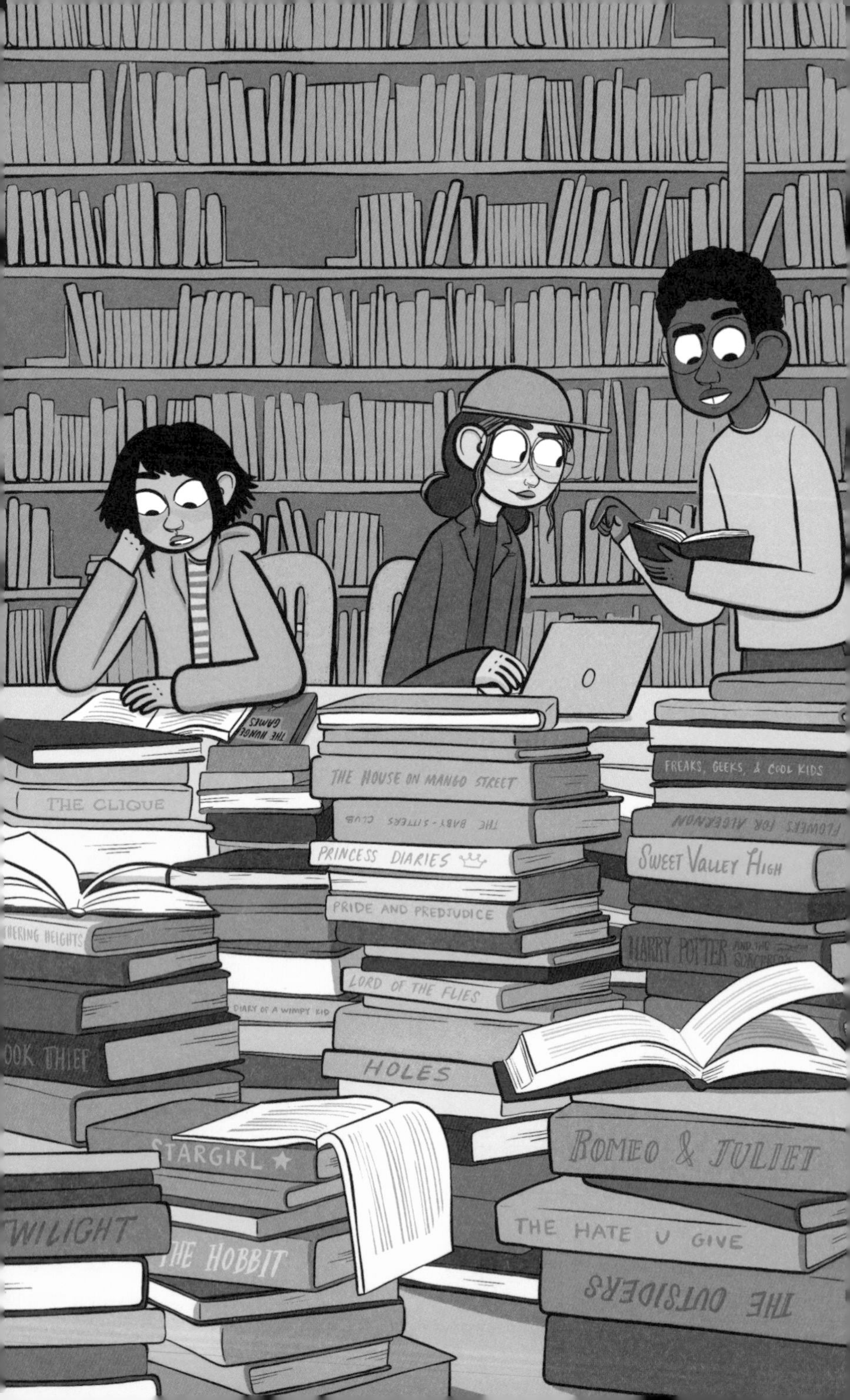
THE CLIQUE
THE HOUSE ON MANGO STREET
THE BABY-SITTERS CLUB
PRINCESS DIARIES
PRIDE AND PREDJUDICE
LORD OF THE FLIES
DIARY OF A WIMPY KID
HOLES
FREAKS, GEEKS, & COOL KIDS
SWEET VALLEY HIGH
HARRY POTTER
HERING HEIGHTS
OOK THIEF
STARGIRL
WILIGHT
HE HOBBIT
ROMEO & JULIET
THE HATE U GIVE
THE OUTSIDERS

THE NEXT DAY...

AND THE NEXT...

117

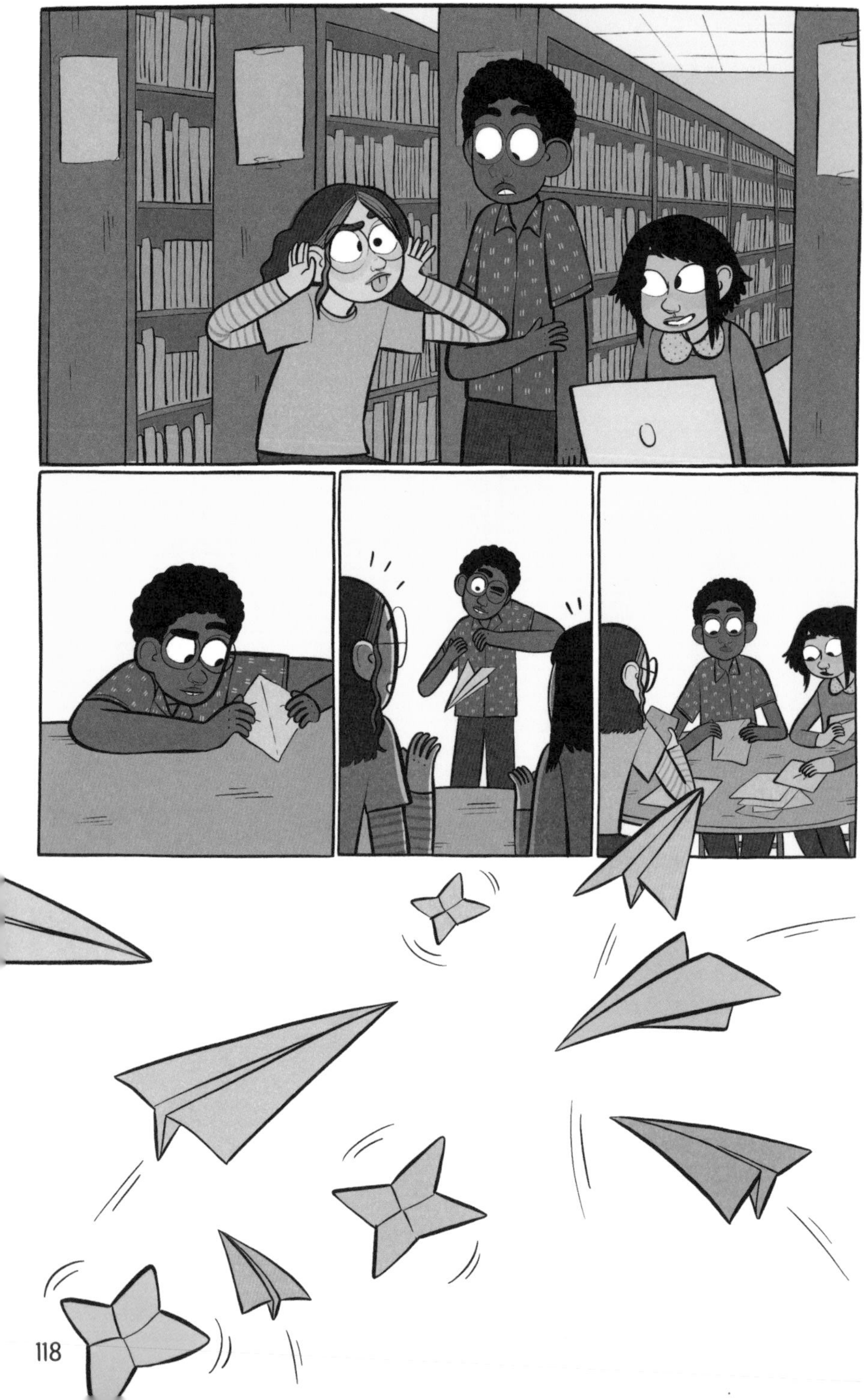

THREE DAYS LATER

Shhhhh!

FRIDAY

121

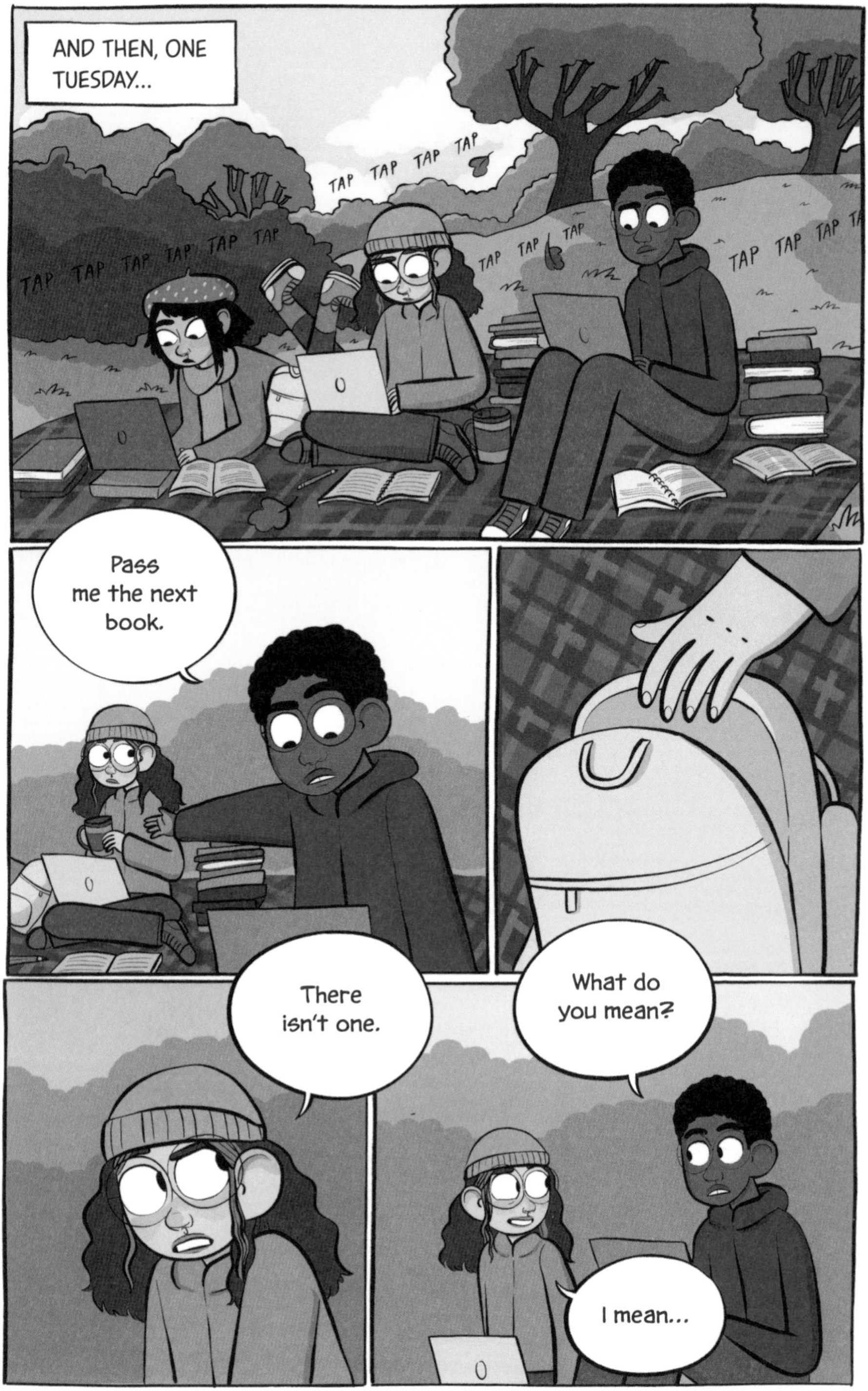
AND THEN, ONE TUESDAY...
TAP TAP TAP TAP TAP TAP
TAP TAP TAP TAP
TAP TAP TAP
TAP TAP TAP TA
Pass me the next book.
There isn't one.
What do you mean?
I mean...

123

CHAPTER 8

PING!

MS good morning !!! ☼

DT WHY DO YOU GET UP SO EARLY?

MS IT'S NOT SATURDAY!

MS hello?

DT What's up?

MS meet out front before school!

DT You could have told us that at ANY time that wasn't 6 a.m.

DT But okay! 😎

ZM see you there! 😊

Are you ready for today?

Sure! I mean, I'm a little worried that it won't go well.

It's not supposed to go perfectly. This is the feedback round. If something gets screwed up, just make sure you let C.C. know what he did wrong.

I know, I just don't want him to screw up as much as he did before. I don't want you guys to have wasted all that time and have it not work out.

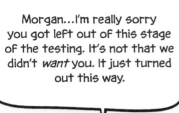

Morgan...I'm really sorry you got left out of this stage of the testing. It's not that we didn't *want* you. It just turned out this way.

Yeah. No offense, but you're just a little too—

Enthusiastic. He was going to say *enthusiastic*.

Sure, let's go with that.

We just need C.C. to work without interference. Just for this week.

I'll give you updates at lunch every day, and I can tweak the program every night. After a couple of weeks, we can start working together again!

Sounds good to me.

Morgan?

Okay. A couple of weeks. For science and middle schoolers everywhere.

135

139

140

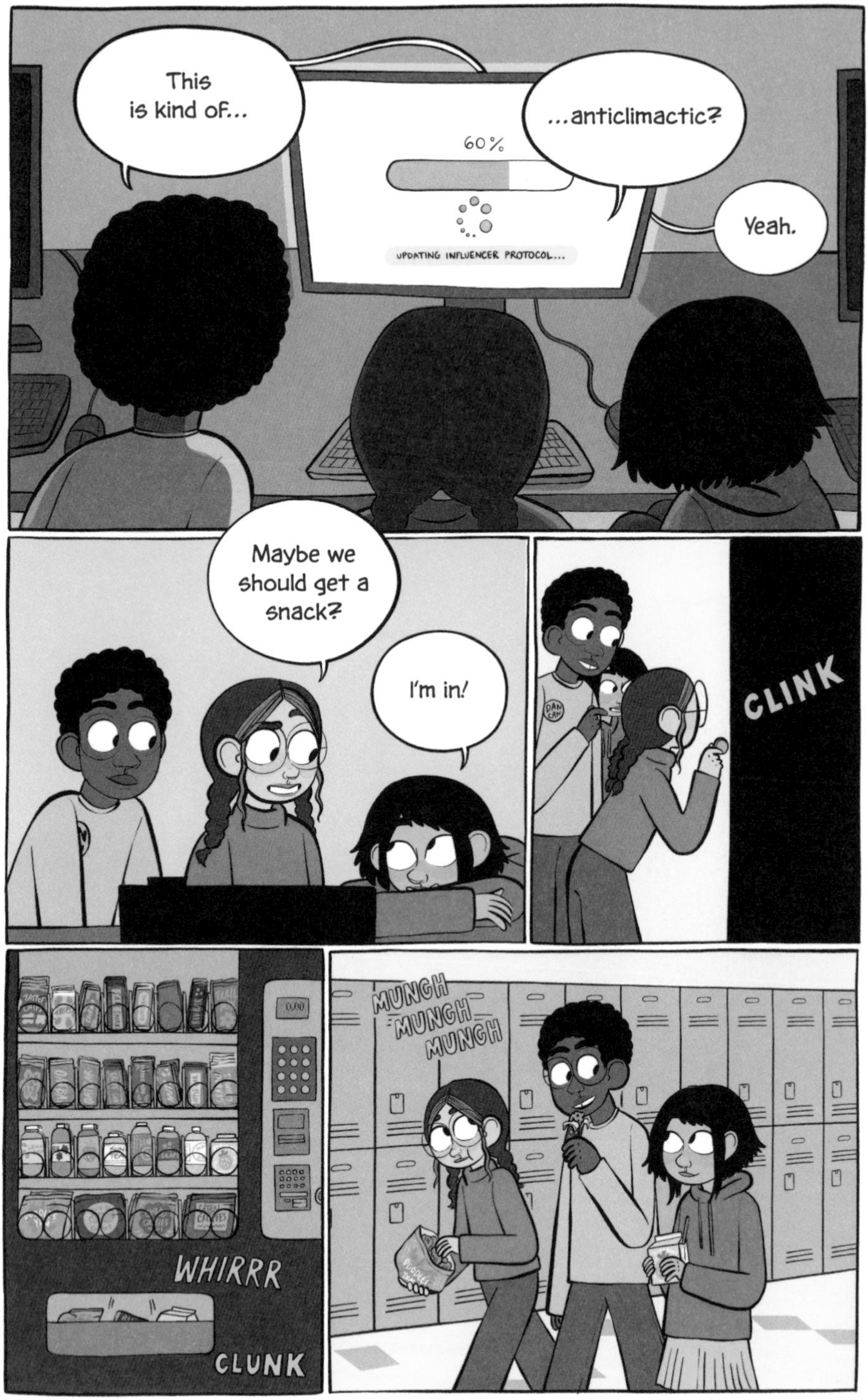
This is kind of...
60%
UPDATING INFLUENCER PROTOCOL...
...anticlimactic?
Yeah.
Maybe we should get a snack?
I'm in!
CLINK
WHIRRR
CLUNK
MUNCH
MUNCH
MUNCH

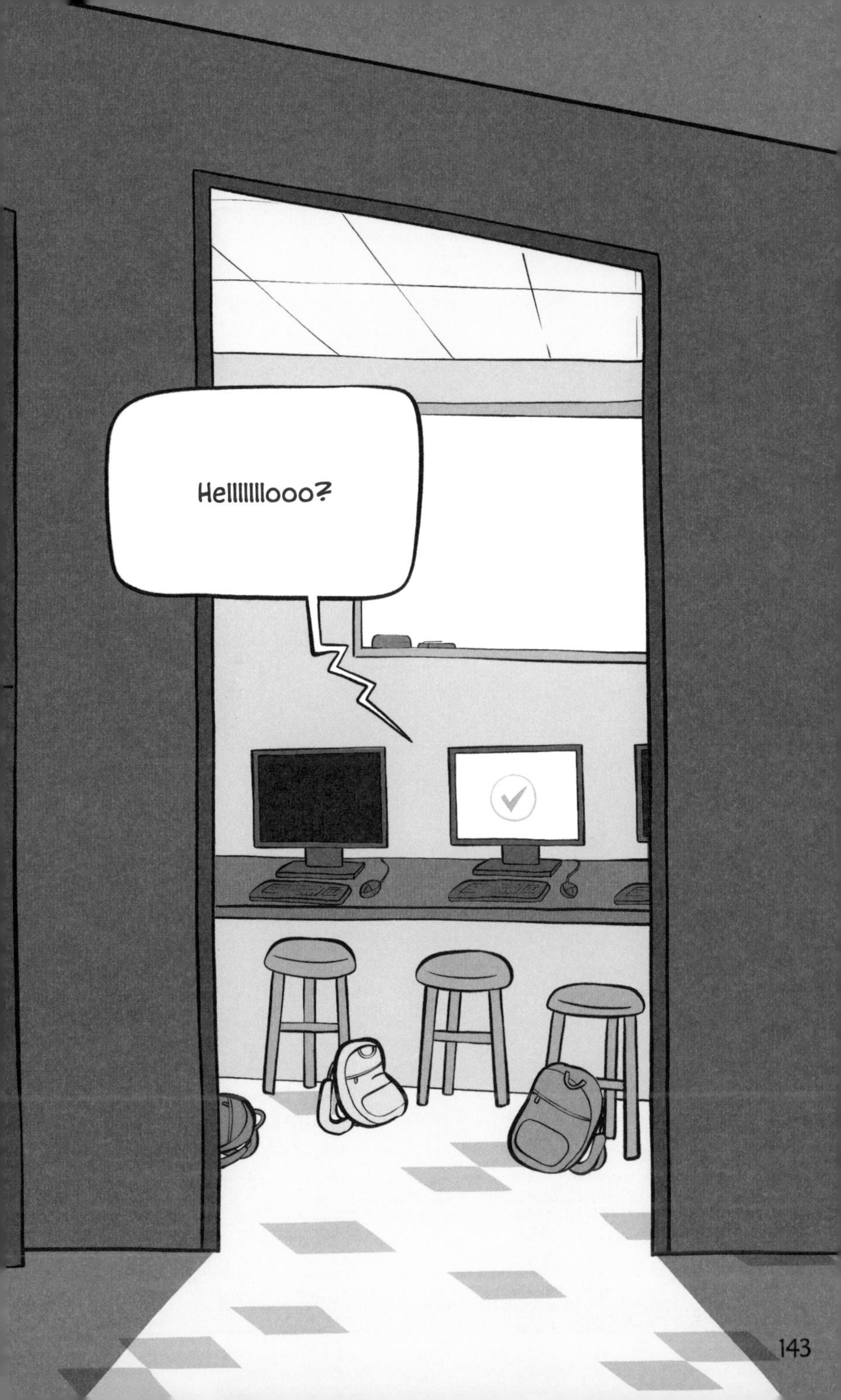
Hellllllllooo?

145

146

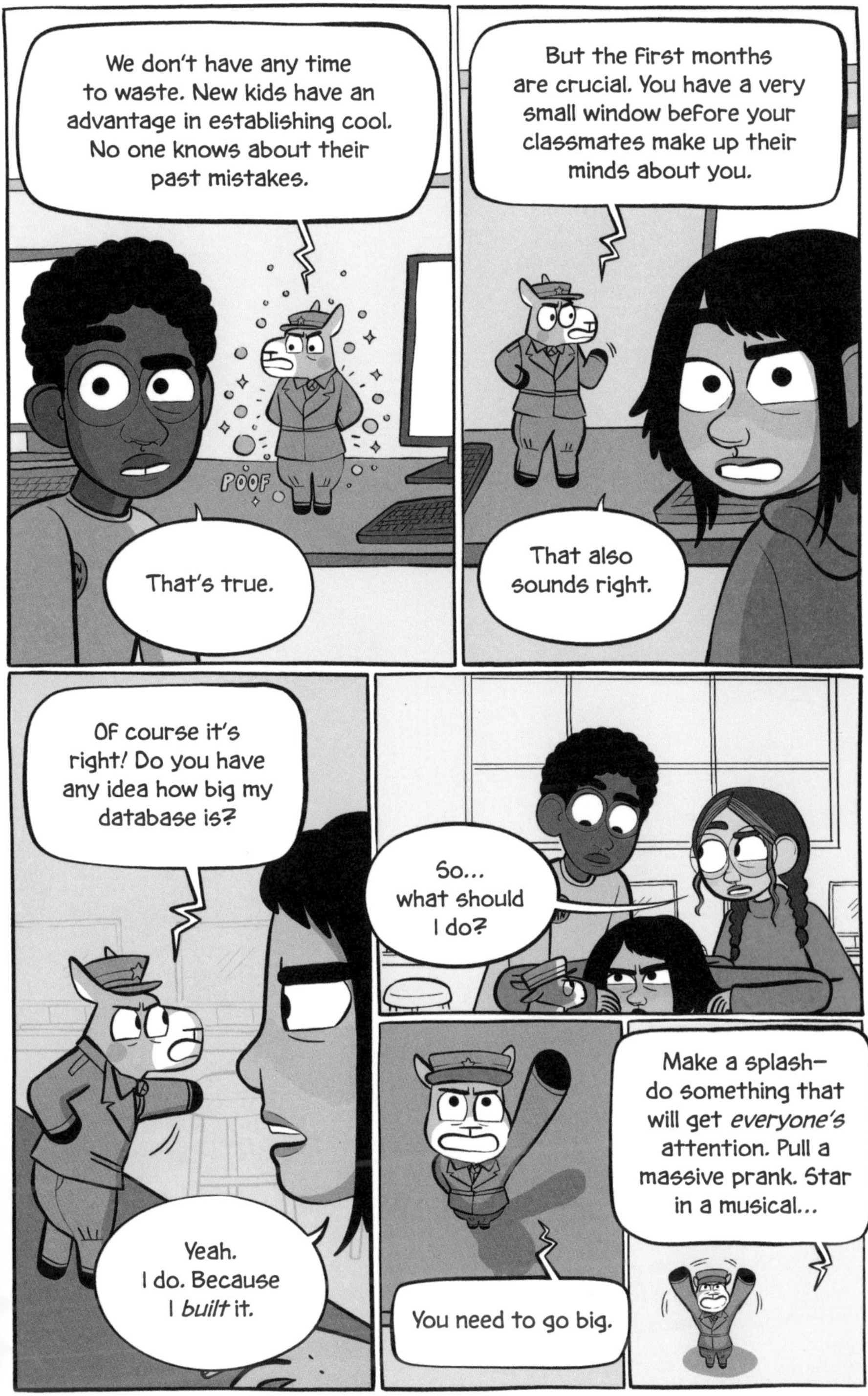
We don't have any time to waste. New kids have an advantage in establishing cool. No one knows about their past mistakes.
POOF
That's true.
But the first months are crucial. You have a very small window before your classmates make up their minds about you.
That also sounds right.
Of course it's right! Do you have any idea how big my database is?
Yeah. I do. Because I *built* it.
So... what should I do?
You need to go big.
Make a splash— do something that will get *everyone's* attention. Pull a massive prank. Star in a musical...

149

151

CHAPTER 9

RIIINNNGGGG

TAP

YOU HAD
ME TURNED OFF
ALL NIGHT?

CLICK

CLICK

CLICK

CLICK

CLICK

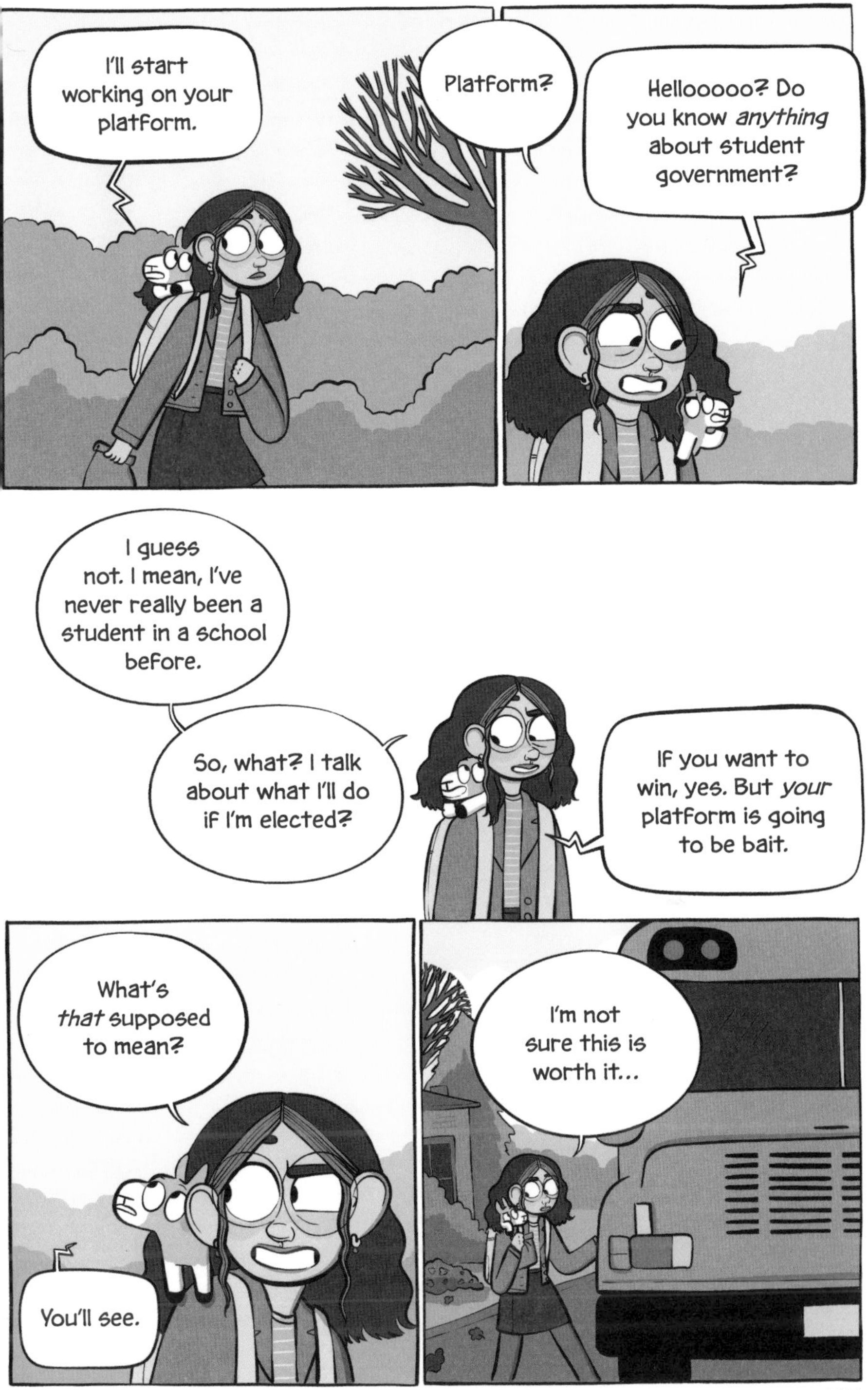
I'll start working on your platform.
Platform?
Hellooooo? Do you know *anything* about student government?
I guess not. I mean, I've never really been a student in a school before.
So, what? I talk about what I'll do if I'm elected?
If you want to win, yes. But *your* platform is going to be bait.
What's *that* supposed to mean?
You'll see.
I'm not sure this is worth it...

156

159

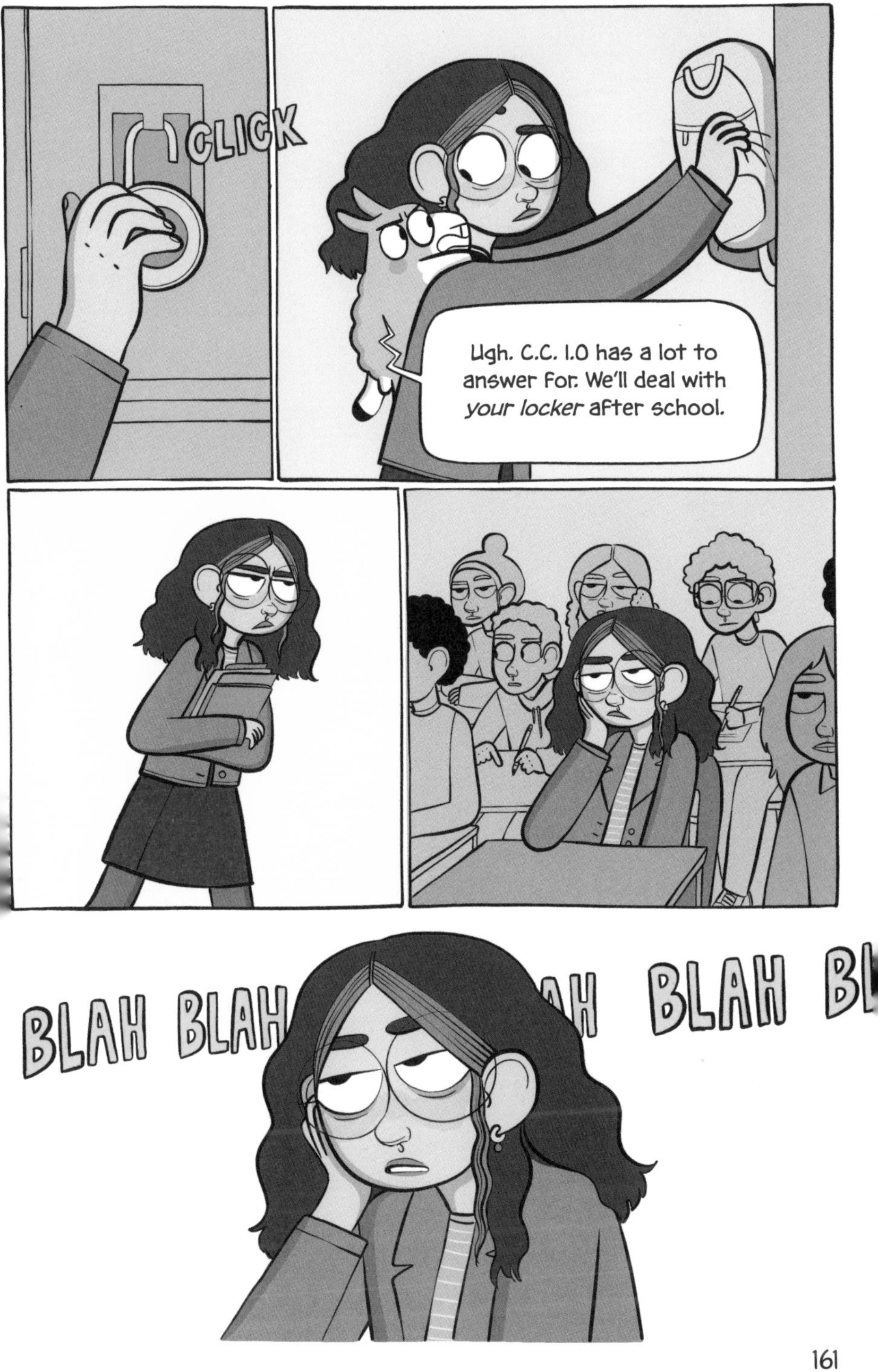
CLICK
Ugh. C.C. 1.0 has a lot to answer for. We'll deal with *your locker* after school.
BLAH BLAH
AH BLAH BL

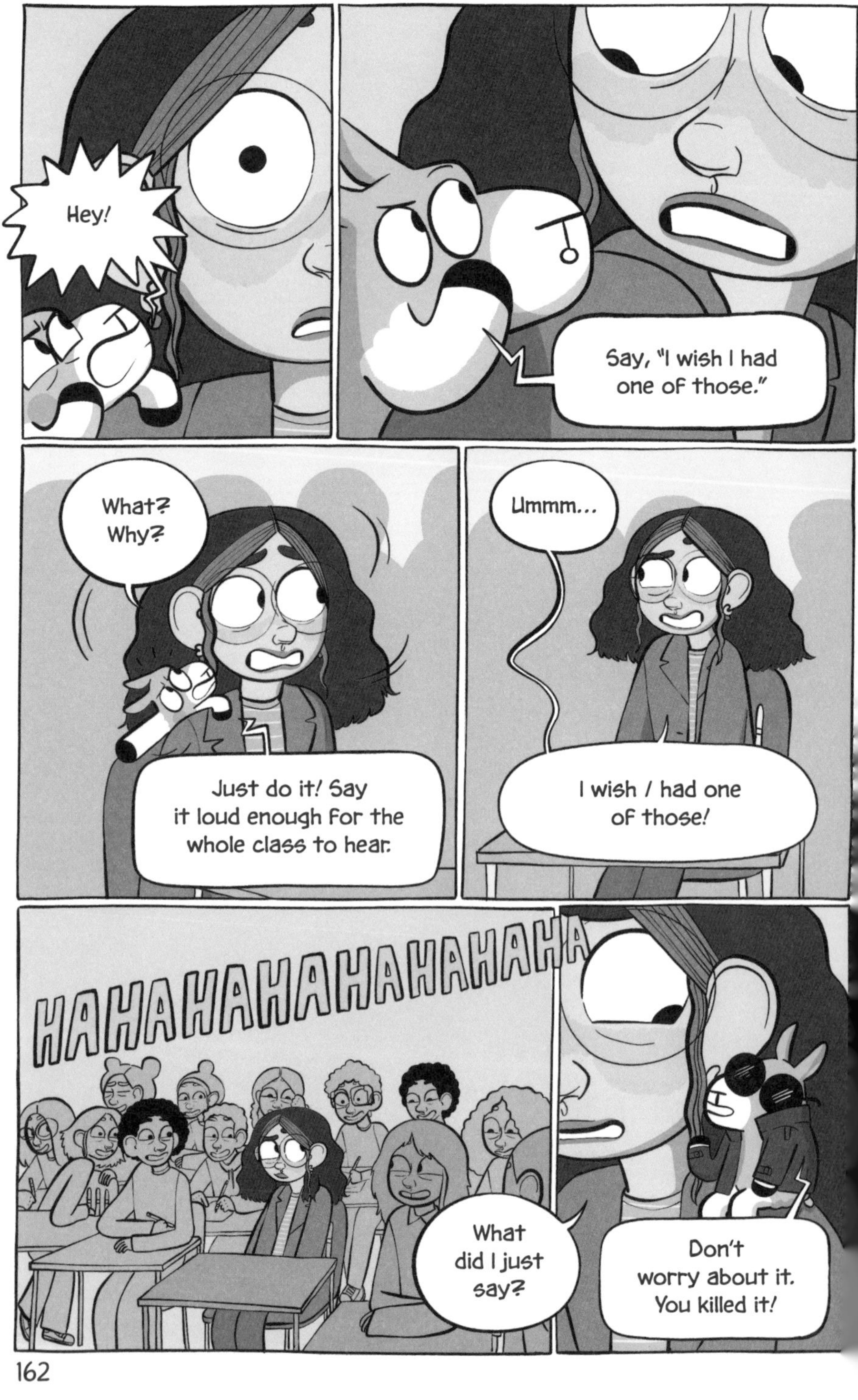
Hey!
Say, "I wish I had one of those."
What? Why?
Just do it! Say it loud enough for the whole class to hear.
Ummm...
I wish I had one of those!
HAHAHAHAHAHAHAHAHAHA
What did I just say?
Don't worry about it. You killed it!

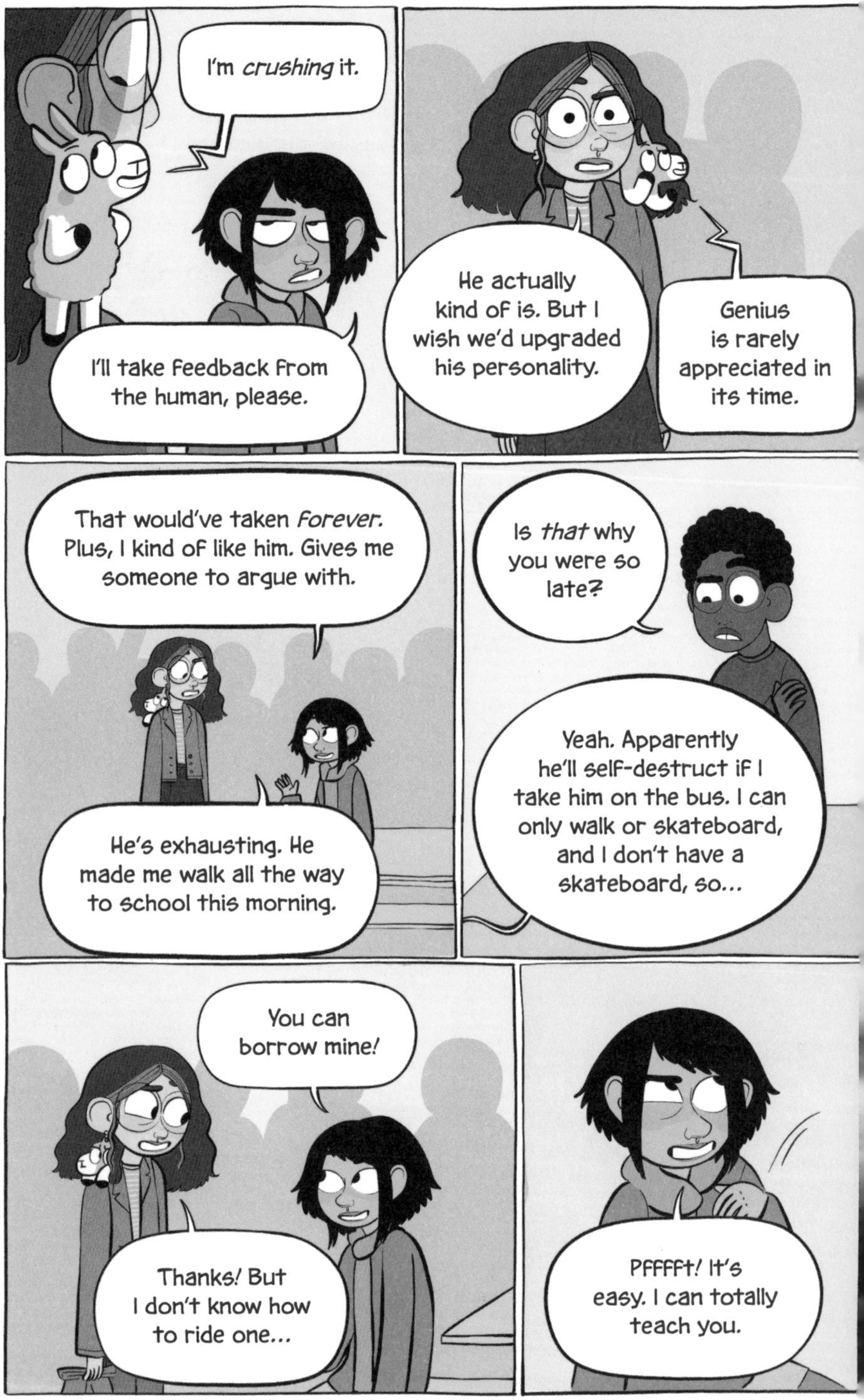
I'm *crushing* it.
I'll take feedback from the human, please.
He actually kind of is. But I wish we'd upgraded his personality.
Genius is rarely appreciated in its time.
That would've taken *forever*. Plus, I kind of like him. Gives me someone to argue with.
He's exhausting. He made me walk all the way to school this morning.
Is *that* why you were so late?
Yeah. Apparently he'll self-destruct if I take him on the bus. I can only walk or skateboard, and I don't have a skateboard, so...
You can borrow mine!
Thanks! But I don't know how to ride one...
PFFFFt! It's easy. I can totally teach you.

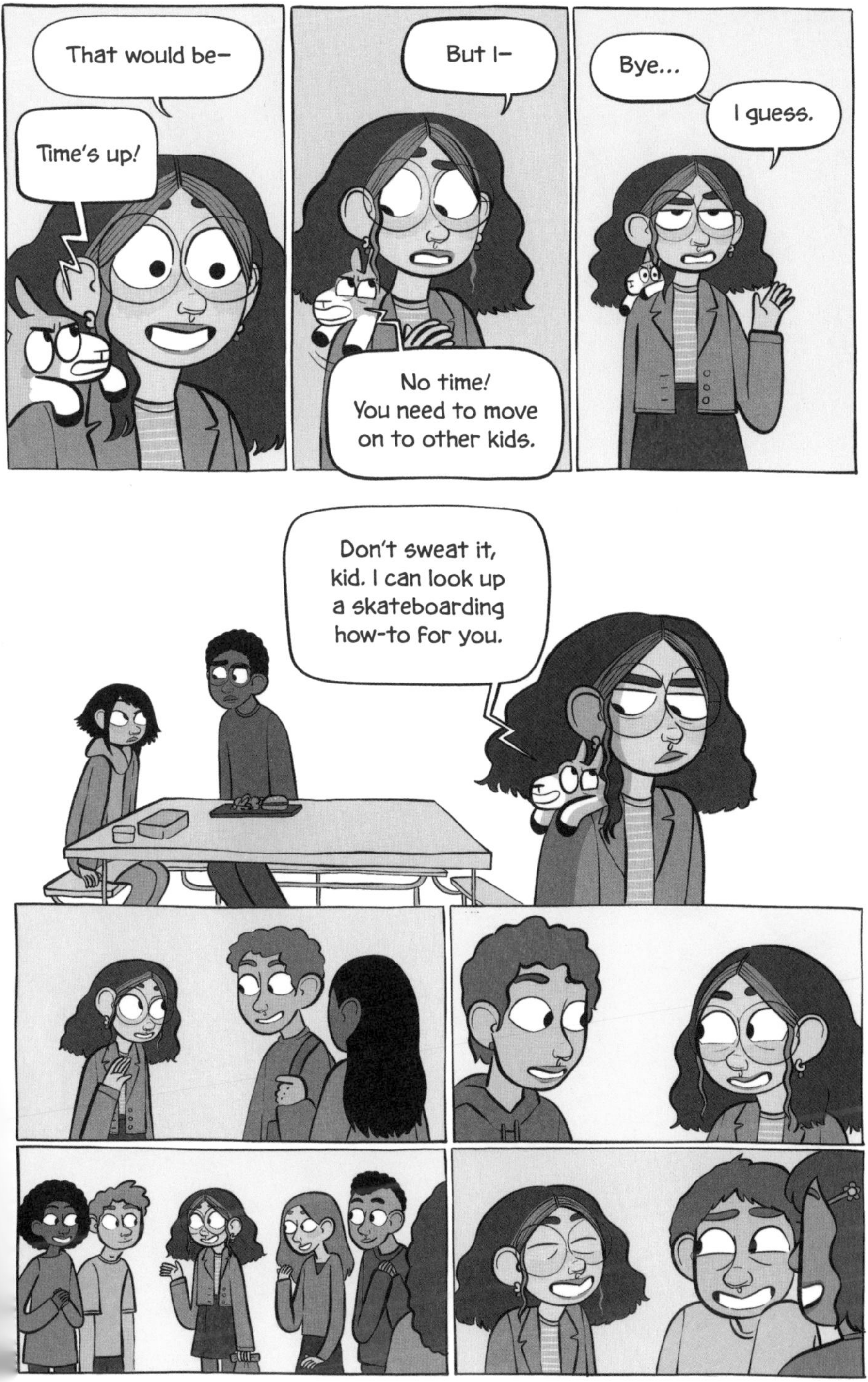

That would be–
Time's up!
But I–
No time! You need to move on to other kids.
Bye...
I guess.
Don't sweat it, kid. I can look up a skateboarding how-to for you.

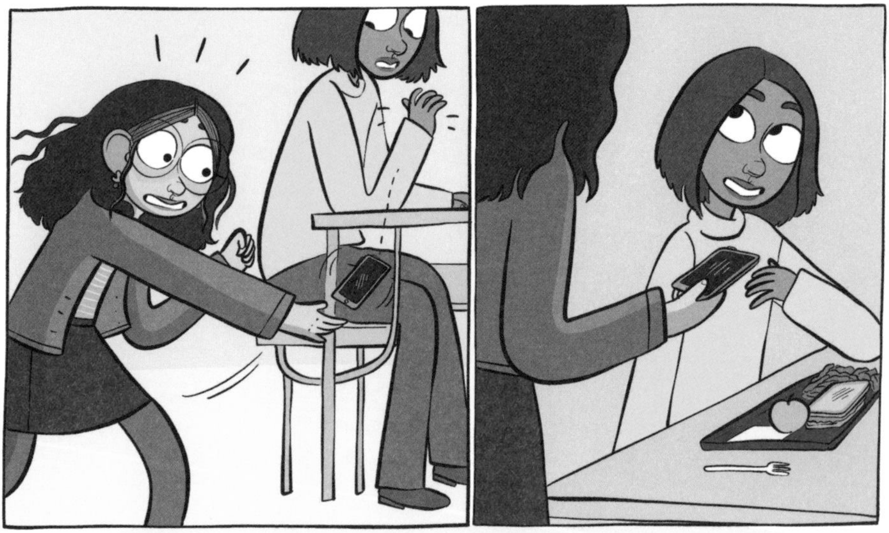

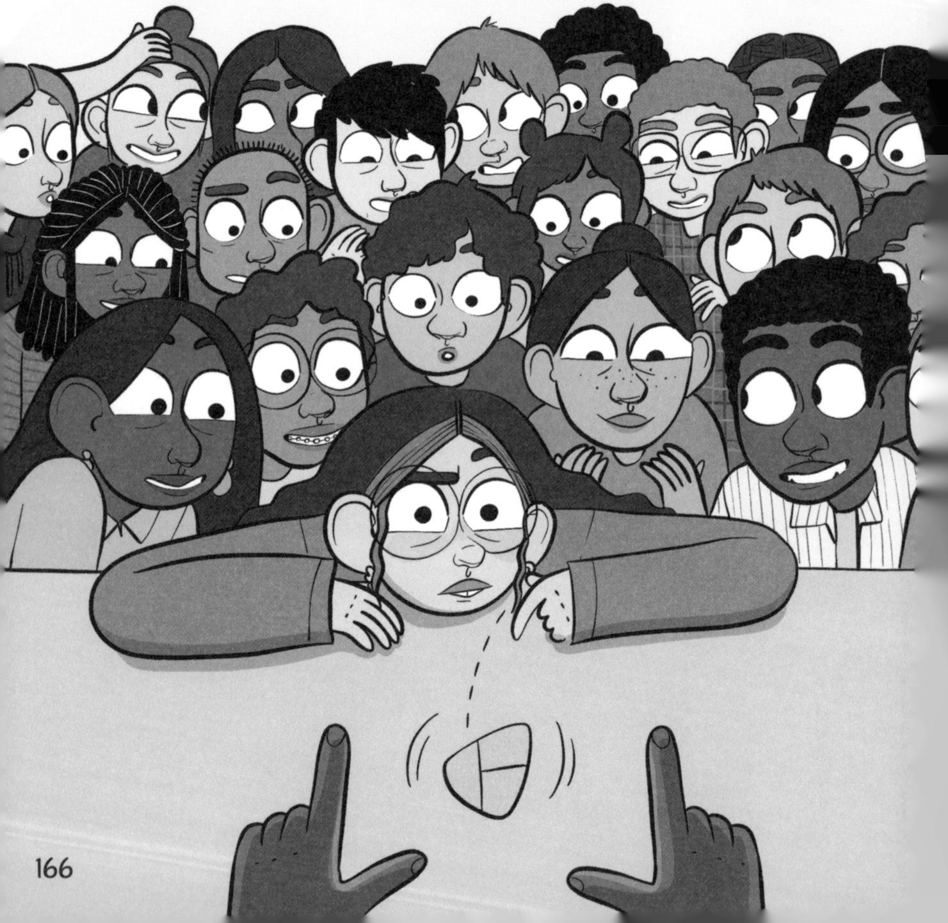

167

168

169

I DON'T KNOW WHY IT FREAKS ME OUT SO MUCH THAT C.C. WAS SENDING TEXTS. I GUESS I KIND OF FEEL LIKE A FAKE. I MEAN, PASSING OFF SOMEONE—SOME*THING*—ELSE'S IDEAS AS MY OWN JUST FEELS SO...DISHONEST.

BUT I MADE C.C. SO DOES THAT MEAN THAT HIS IDEAS ARE MINE, TOO?

I'm so excited to run your campaign. *Everybody* wants to join. We're having a "Go for Zo!" meeting after school today.

Mr. Asher says we can use his room. See you there!

We are?

Um...bye?

What is happening?

You asked Tanya to run your campaign?

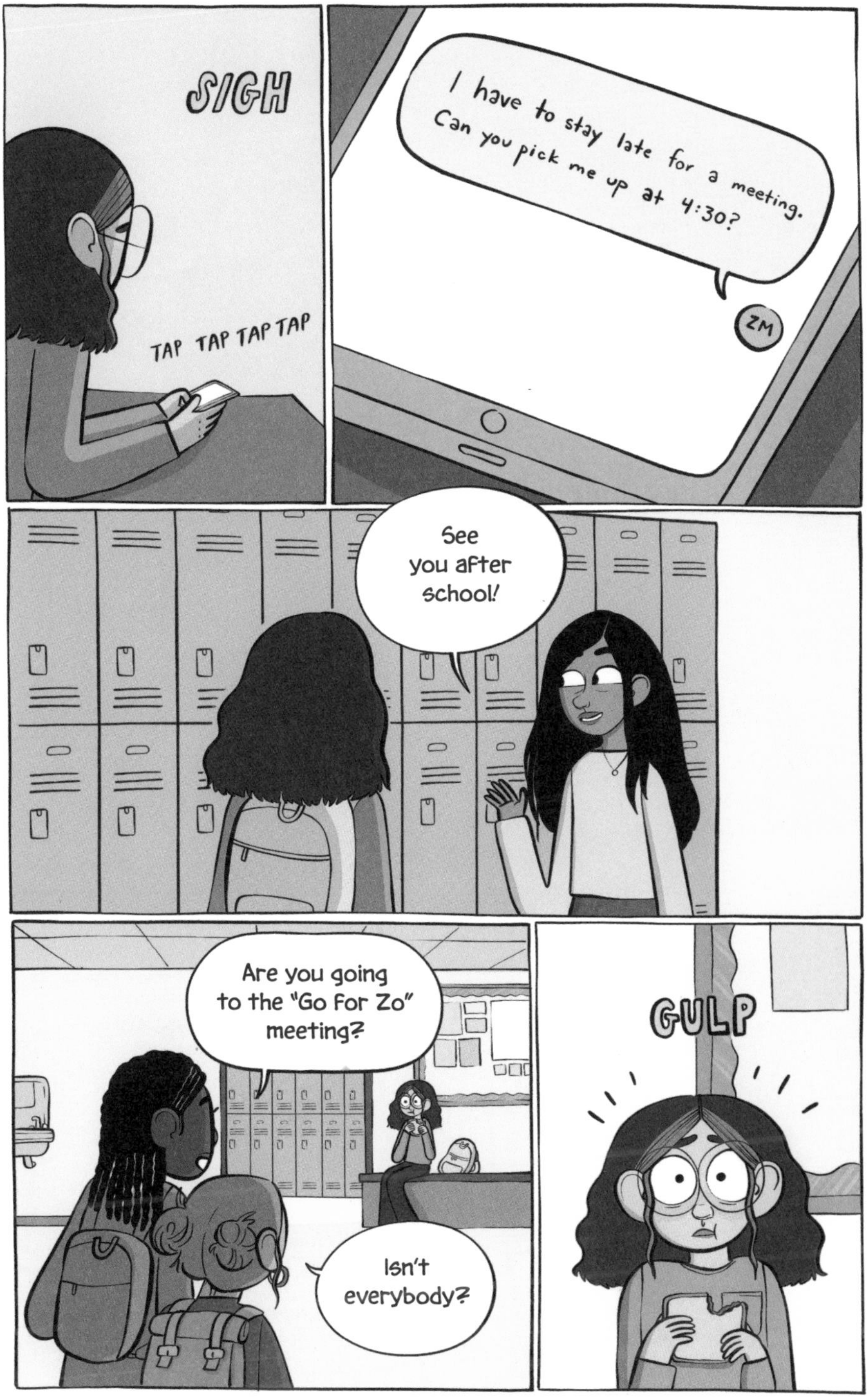
SIGH
TAP TAP TAP TAP
I have to stay late for a meeting. Can you pick me up at 4:30?
ZM
See you after school!
Are you going to the "Go For Zo" meeting?
Isn't everybody?
GULP

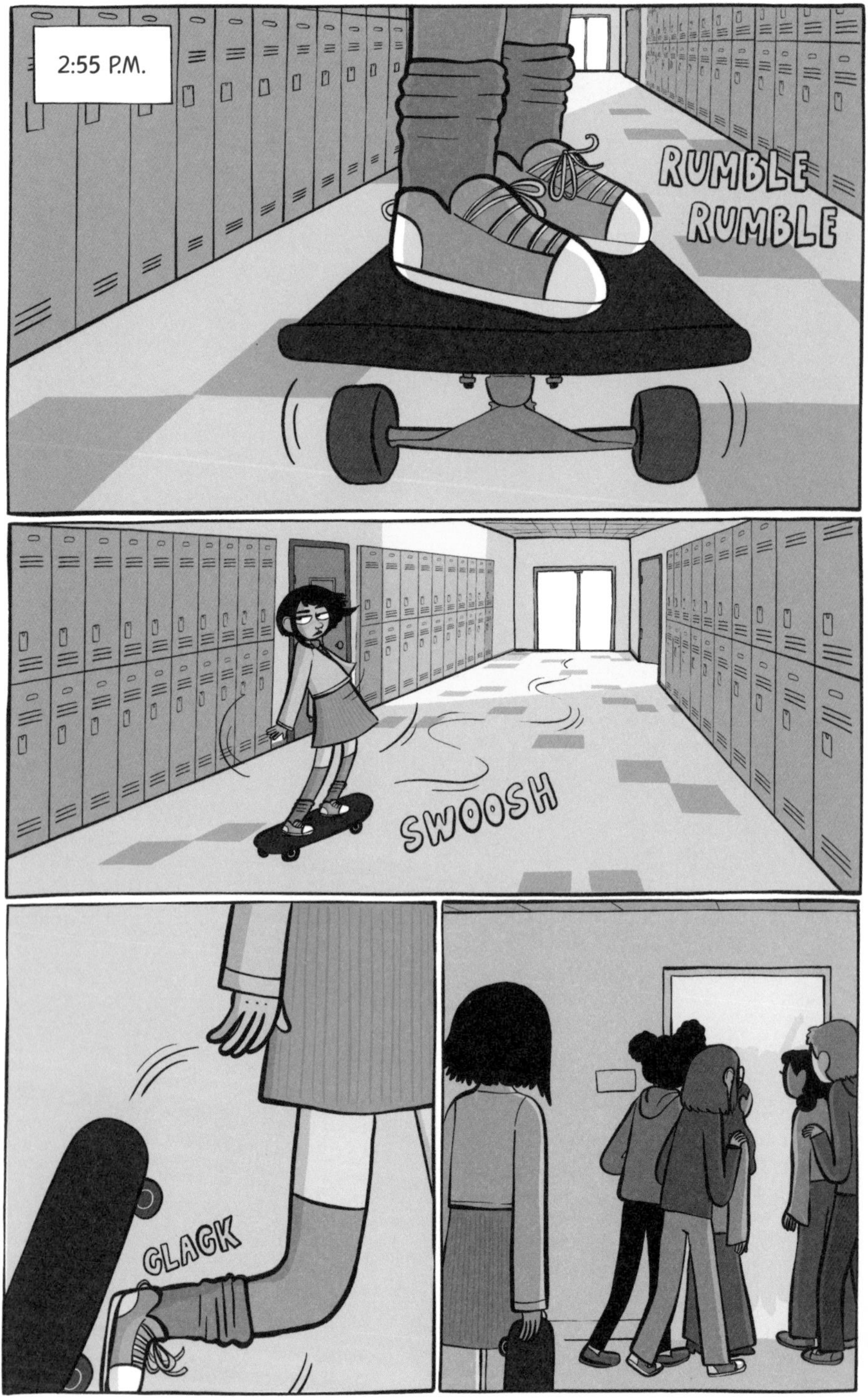
2:55 P.M.
RUMBLE
RUMBLE
SWOOSH
CLACK

176

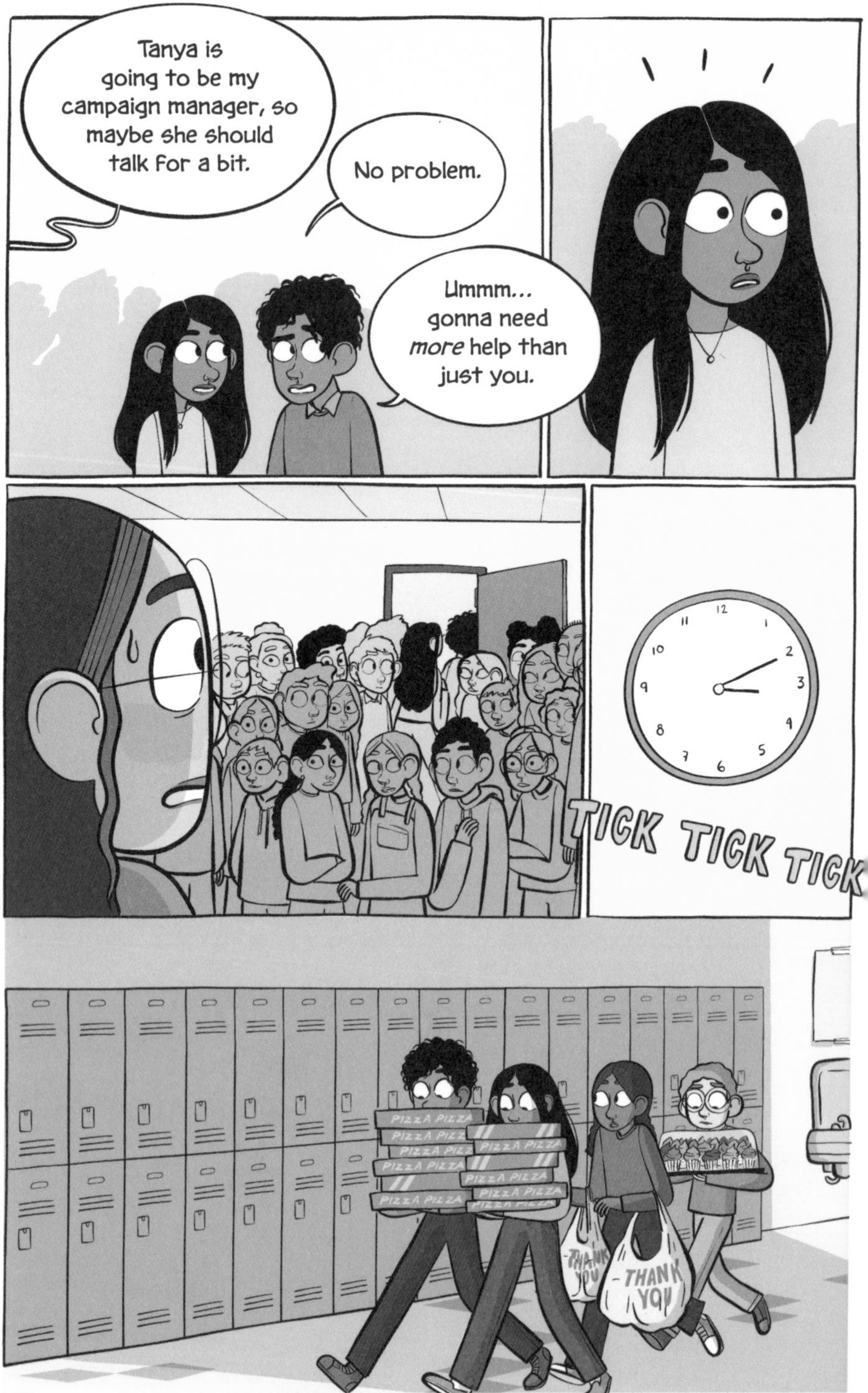
Tanya is going to be my campaign manager, so maybe she should talk for a bit.
No problem.
Ummm... gonna need *more* help than just you.
12
11
1
10
2
9
3
8
4
7
5
6
TICK TICK TICK
PIZZA PIZZA
THANK YOU
THANK YOU

181

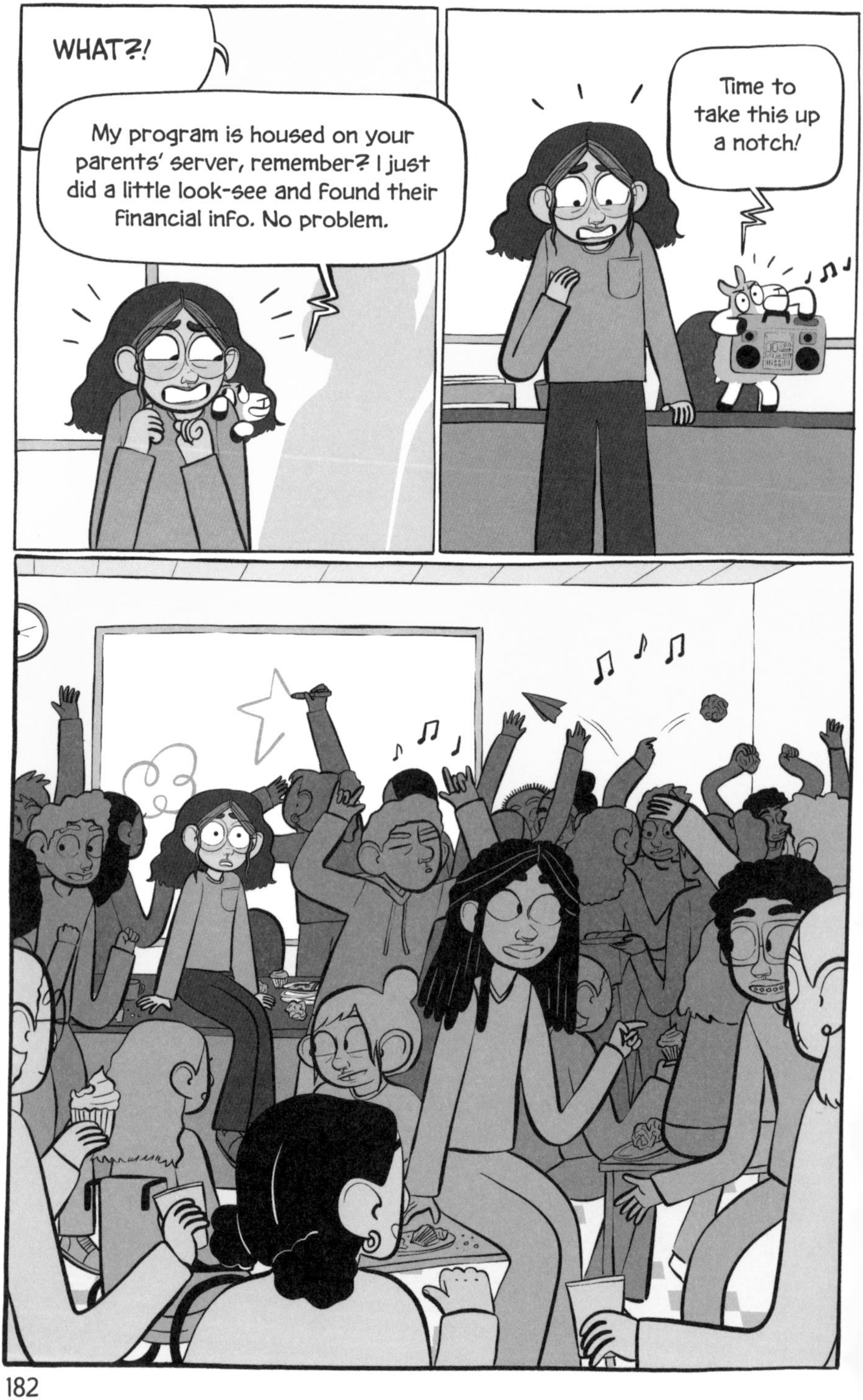
WHAT?!
My program is housed on your parents' server, remember? I just did a little look-see and found their financial info. No problem.
Time to take this up a notch!

183

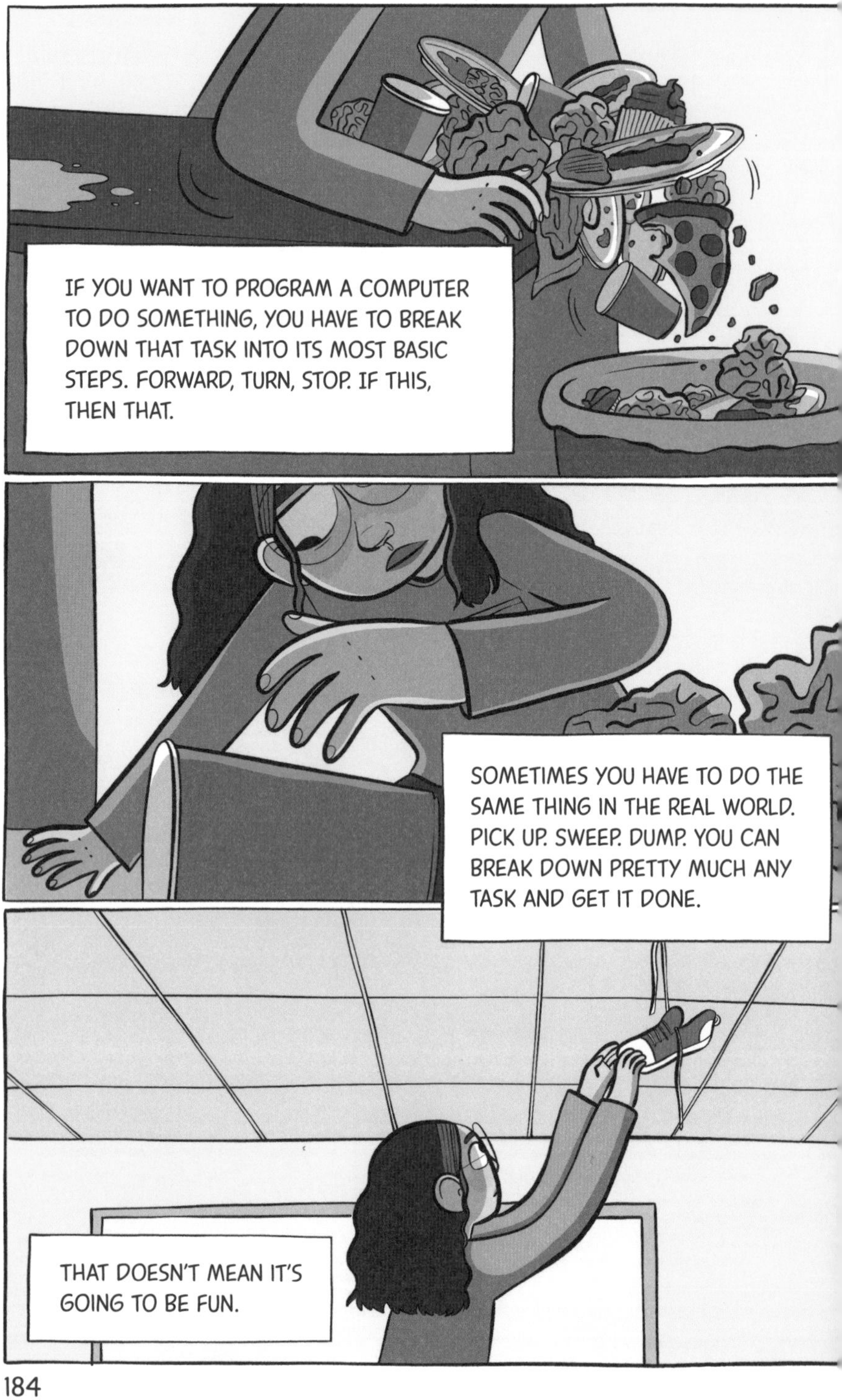
IF YOU WANT TO PROGRAM A COMPUTER TO DO SOMETHING, YOU HAVE TO BREAK DOWN THAT TASK INTO ITS MOST BASIC STEPS. FORWARD, TURN, STOP. IF THIS, THEN THAT.
SOMETIMES YOU HAVE TO DO THE SAME THING IN THE REAL WORLD. PICK UP. SWEEP. DUMP. YOU CAN BREAK DOWN PRETTY MUCH ANY TASK AND GET IT DONE.
THAT DOESN'T MEAN IT'S GOING TO BE FUN.

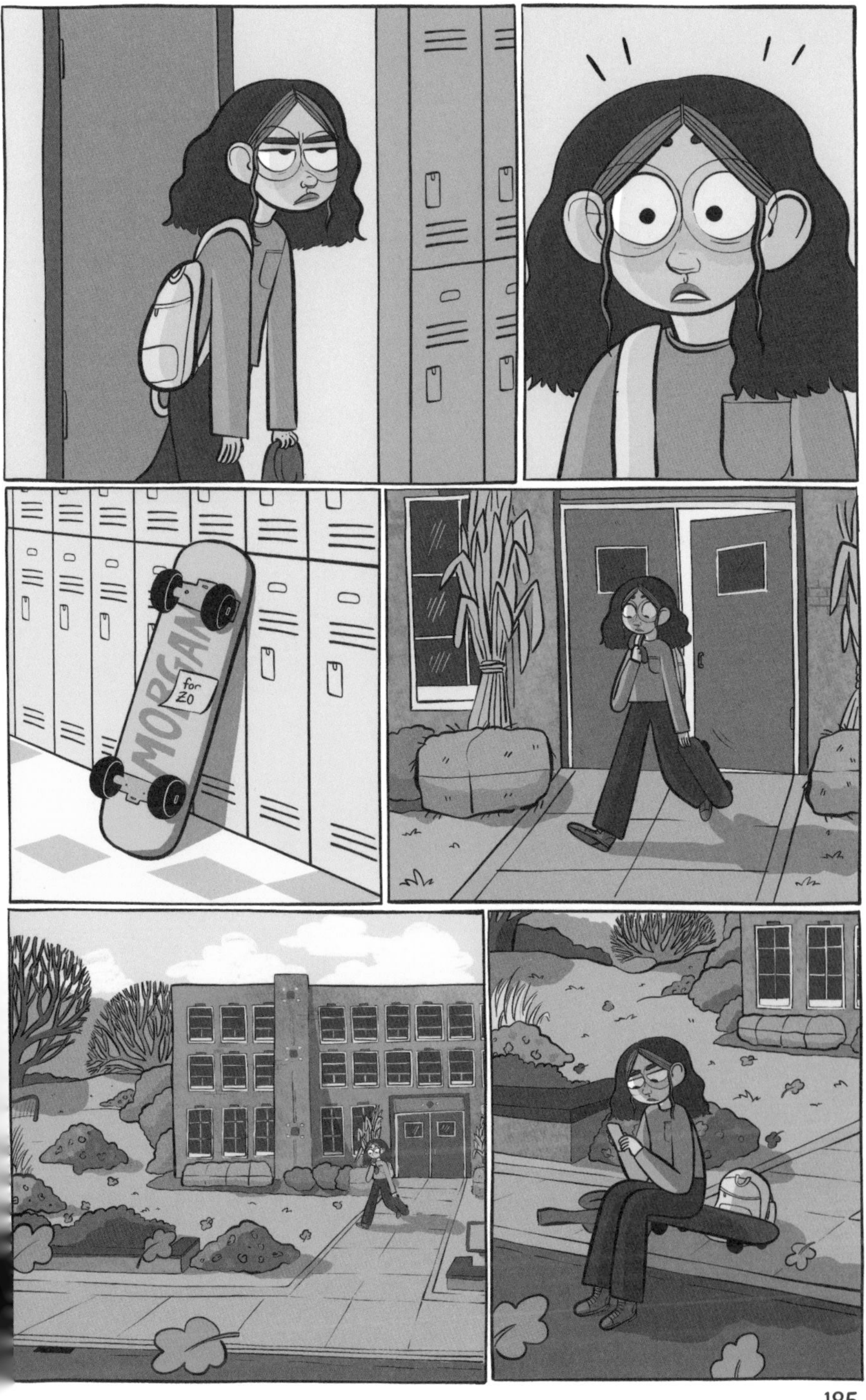
MORGAN
for ZO

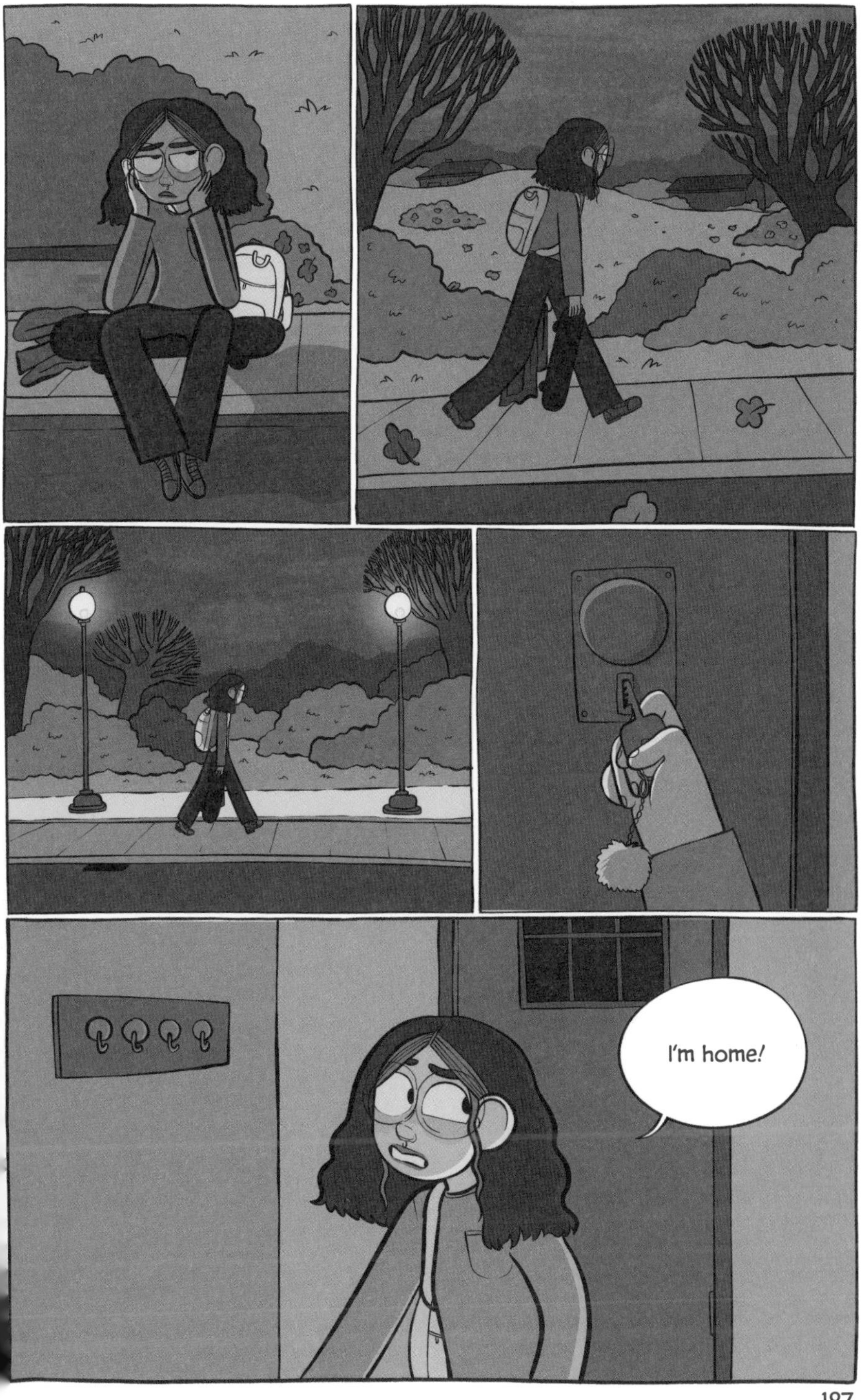
I'm home!

CHAPTER 10

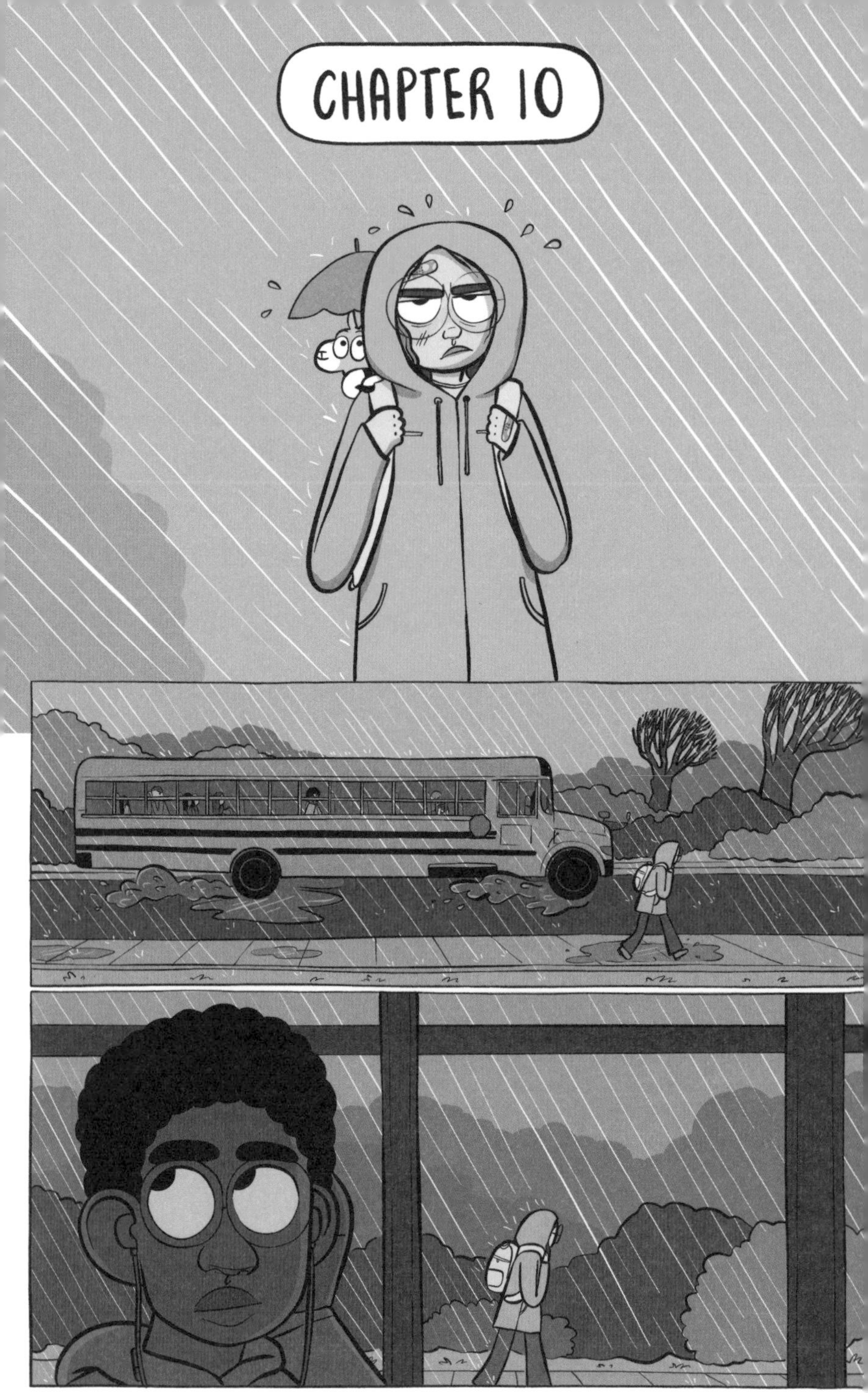

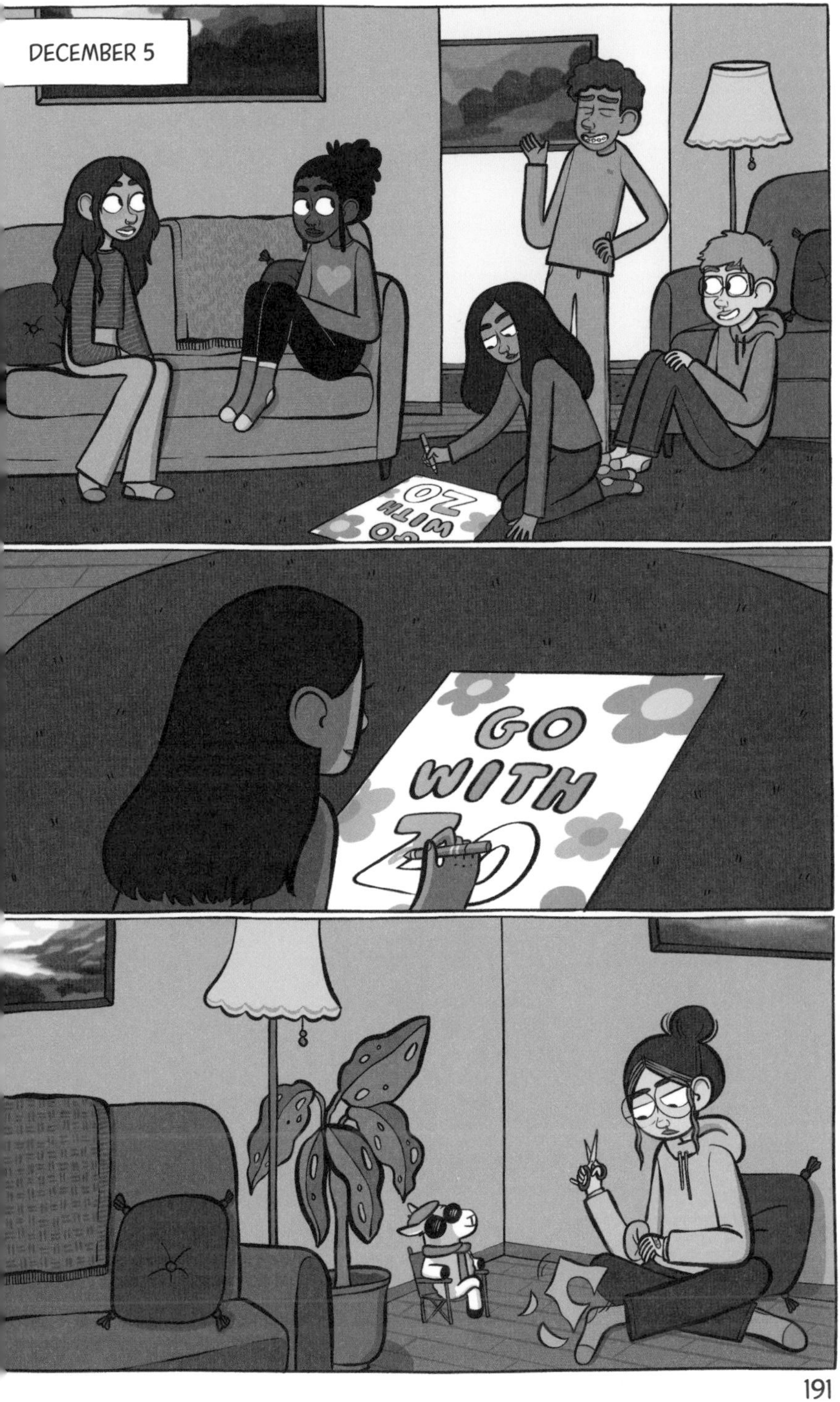
DECEMBER 5
GO WITH ZO
GO WITH

DECEMBER 10

GO WITH ZO

DAN GAN!

MEET THE CANDIDATE: ZOEY MCINTYRE

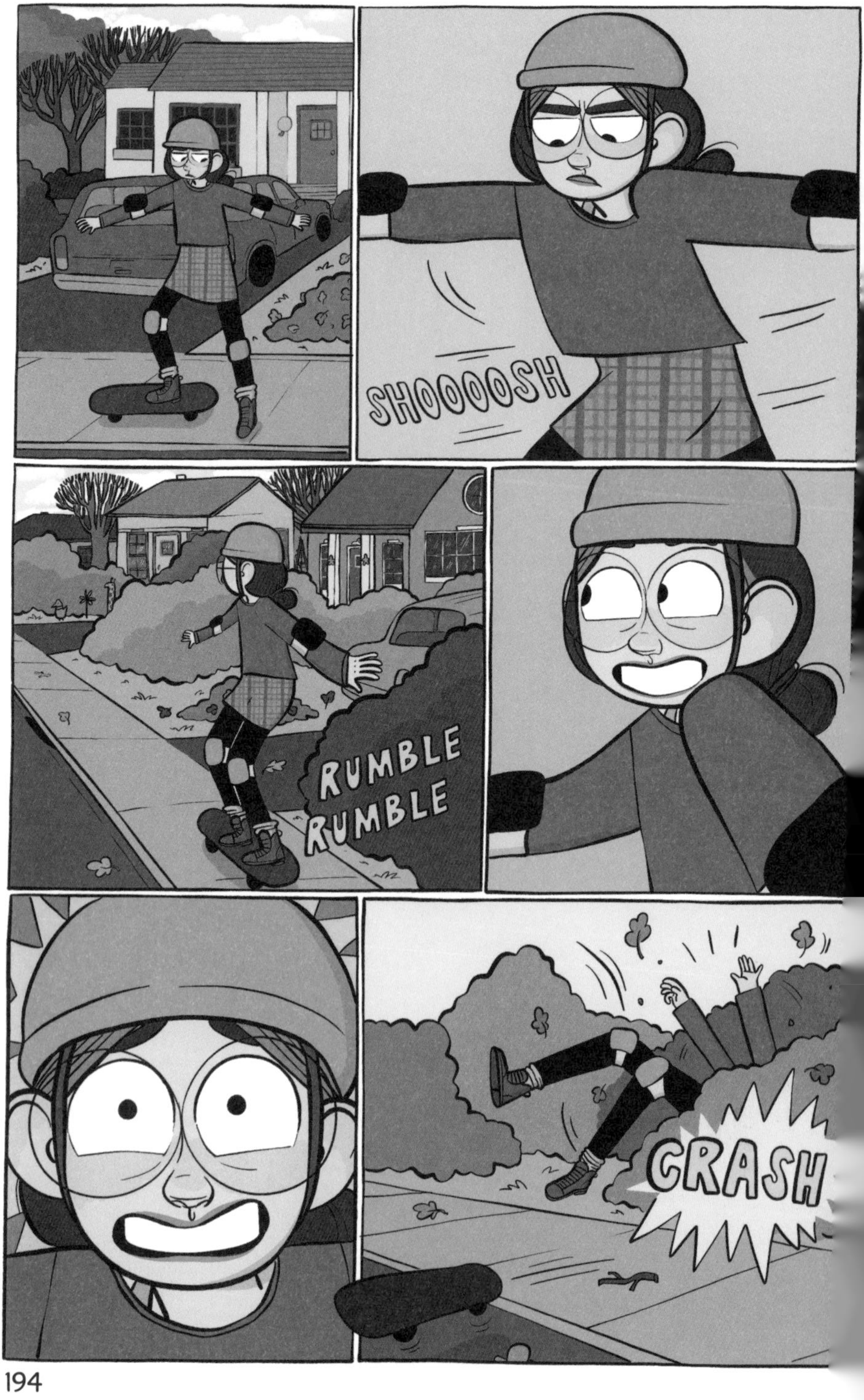
SHOOOOSH
RUMBLE
RUMBLE
CRASH

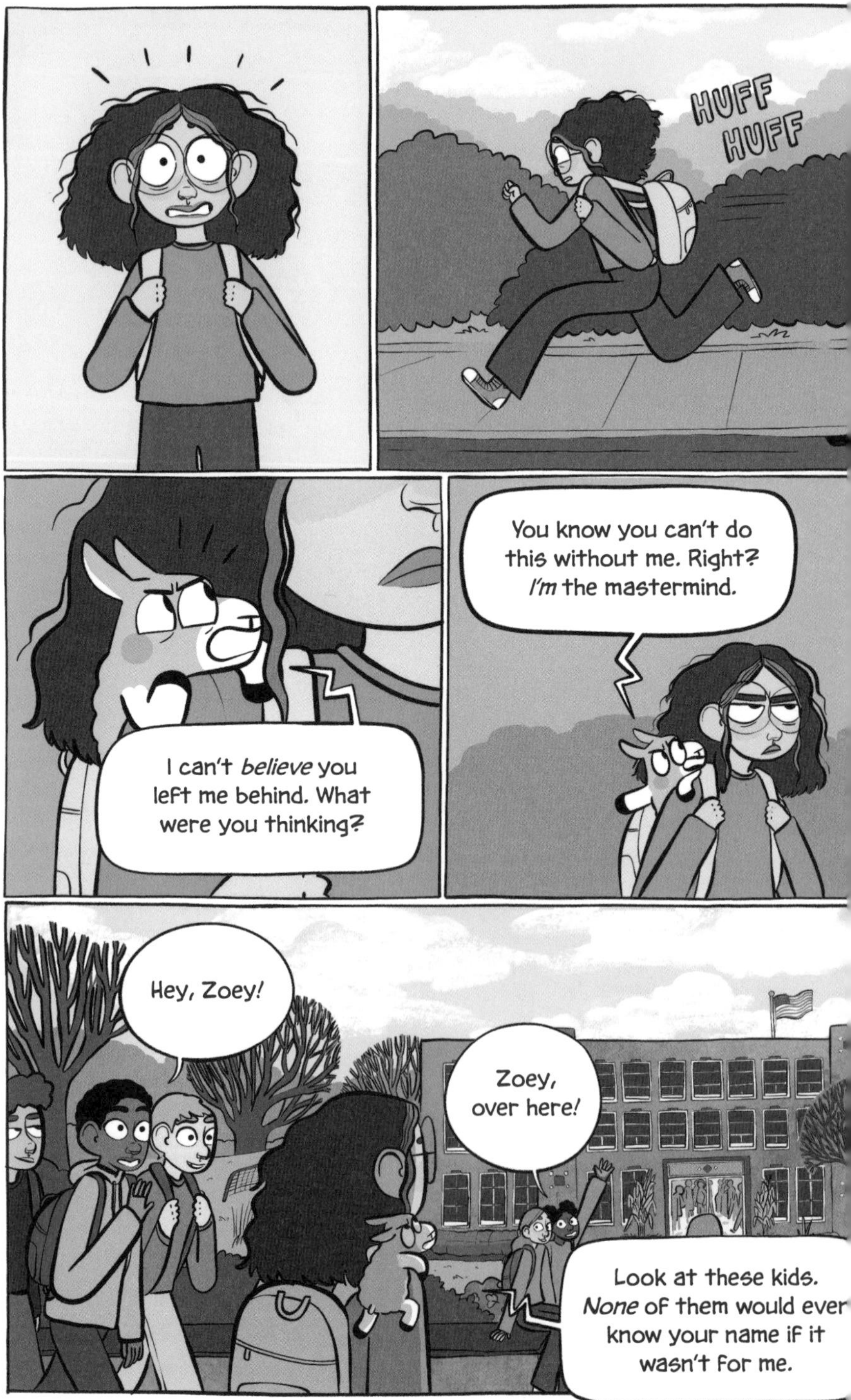
HUFF HUFF
I can't *believe* you left me behind. What were you thinking?
You know you can't do this without me. Right? *I'm* the mastermind.
Hey, Zoey!
Zoey, over here!
Look at these kids. *None* of them would ever know your name if it wasn't for me.

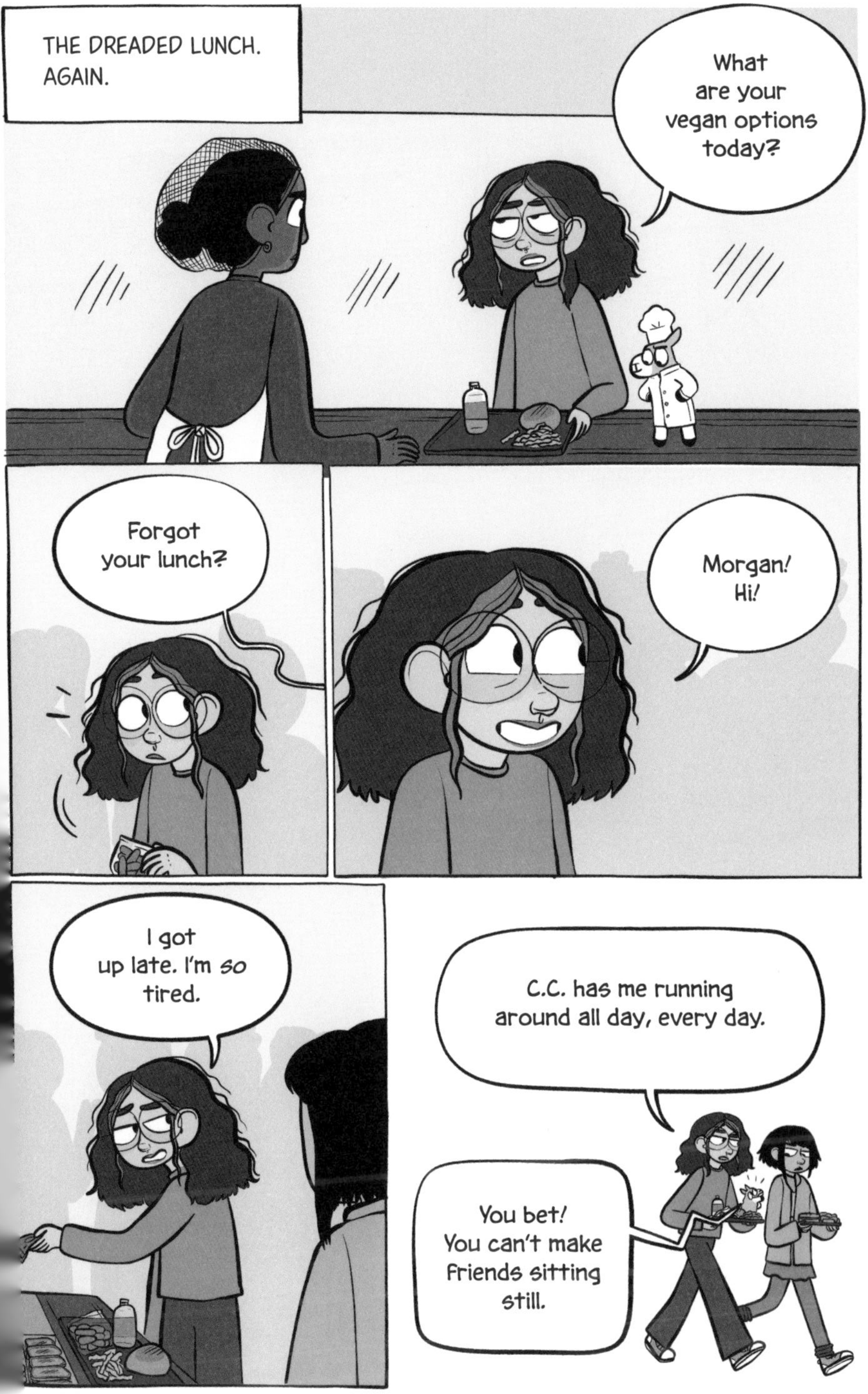
THE DREADED LUNCH. AGAIN.
What are your vegan options today?
Forgot your lunch?
Morgan! Hi!
I got up late. I'm *so* tired.
C.C. has me running around all day, every day.
You bet! You can't make friends sitting still.

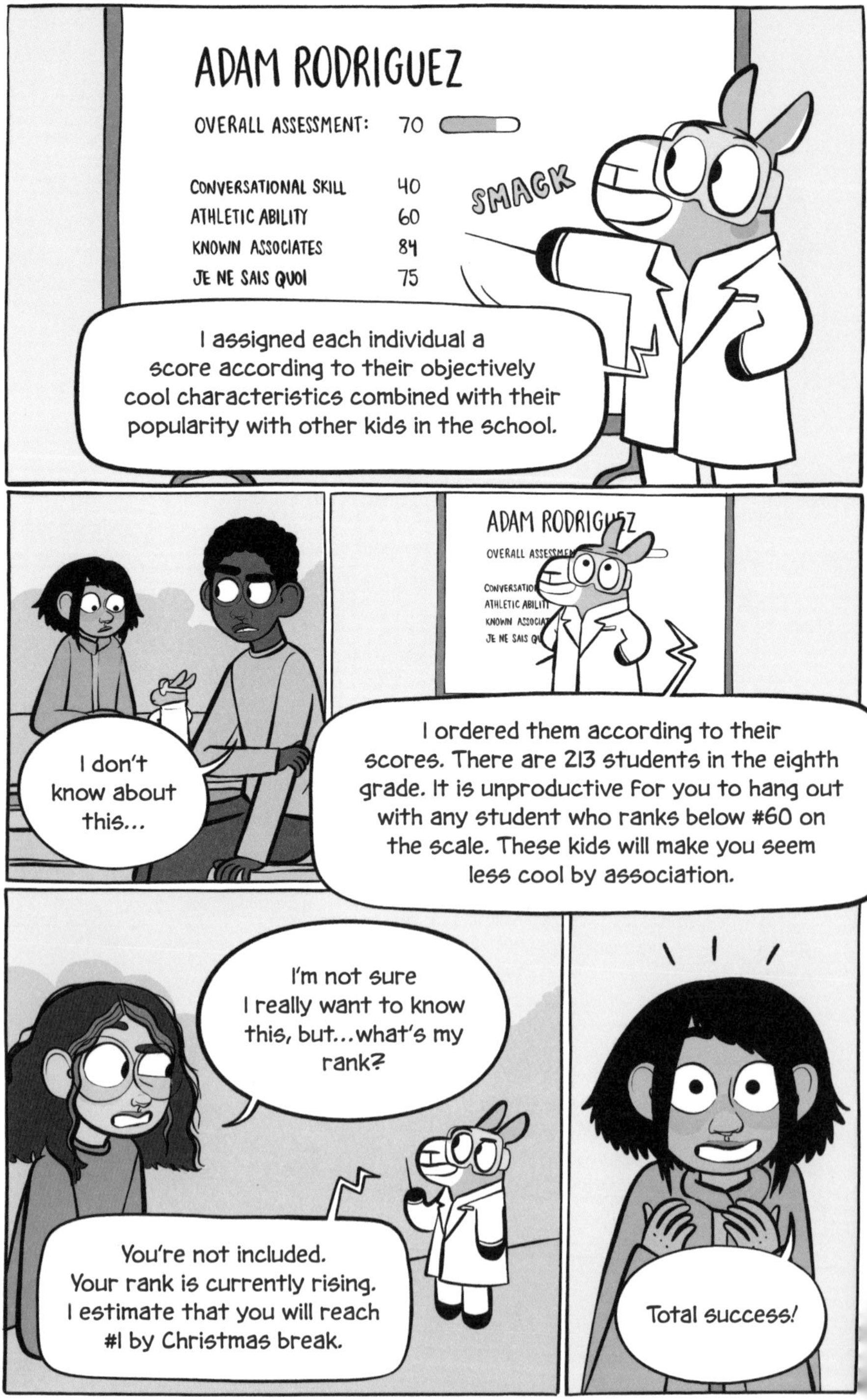
ADAM RODRIGUEZ
OVERALL ASSESSMENT: 70
CONVERSATIONAL SKILL 40
ATHLETIC ABILITY 60
KNOWN ASSOCIATES 84
JE NE SAIS QUOI 75
SMACK
I assigned each individual a score according to their objectively cool characteristics combined with their popularity with other kids in the school.
I don't know about this...
I ordered them according to their scores. There are 213 students in the eighth grade. It is unproductive for you to hang out with any student who ranks below #60 on the scale. These kids will make you seem less cool by association.
I'm not sure I really want to know this, but...what's my rank?
You're not included. Your rank is currently rising. I estimate that you will reach #1 by Christmas break.
Total success!

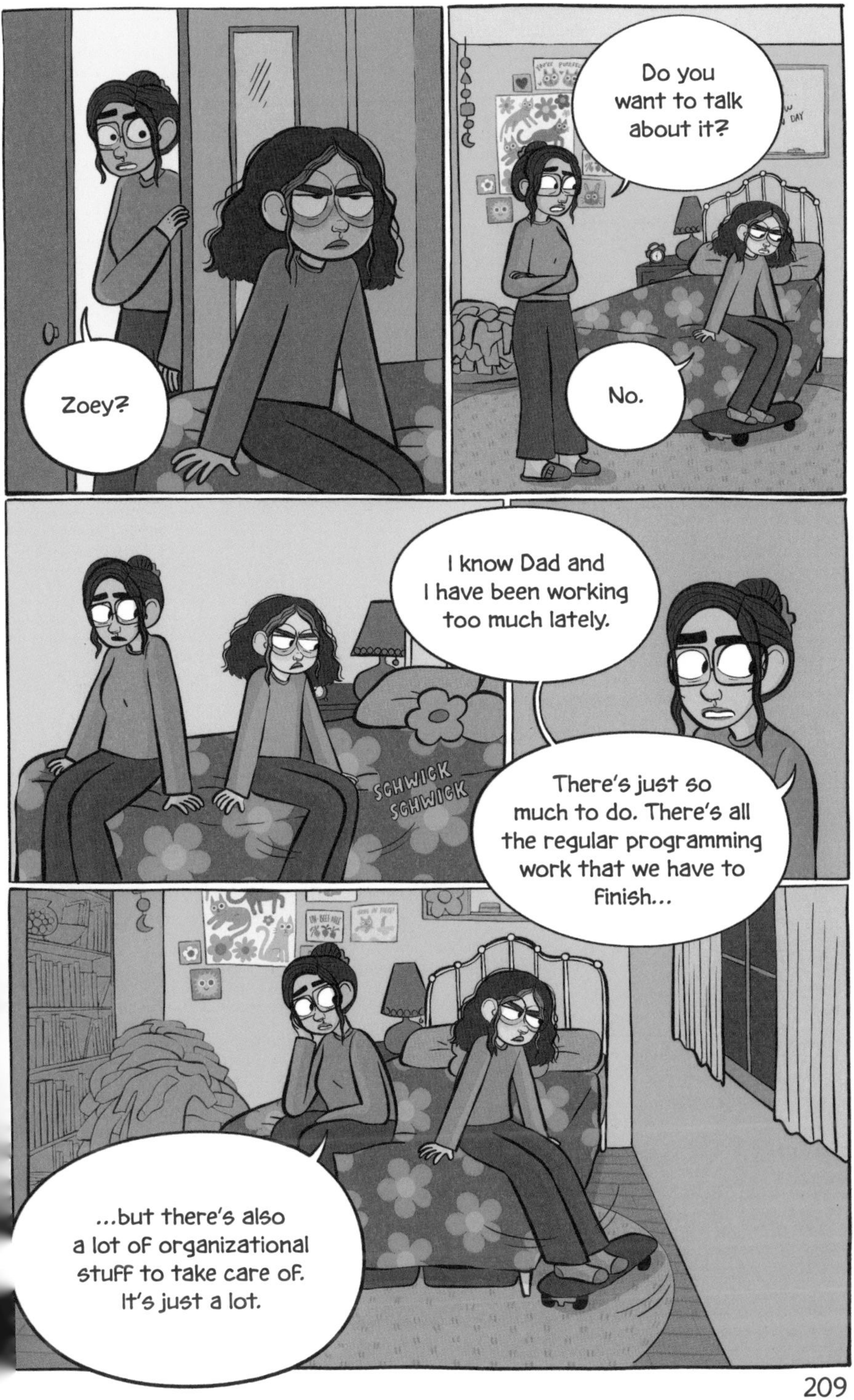
Zoey?
Do you want to talk about it?
No.
I know Dad and I have been working too much lately.
SCHWICK SCHWICK
There's just so much to do. There's all the regular programming work that we have to finish...
...but there's also a lot of organizational stuff to take care of. It's just a lot.

I don't want you to think that we don't *want* to spend time with you. I miss our school days together... Family game nights...even just watching TV with you.

Does that make any sense? Maybe one day when you're older...

It's just... sometimes projects can have a life of their own. They start out as simple ideas, but they grow and grow until there isn't room for anything else.

SCHWICK SCHWICK

It makes sense now.

It does?

Yeah. I get it.

FLIP

MORGAN

Well, it's no excuse for us not being there when you need us. People are more important than projects.

Thanks, Mom.

I'm sorry.

MORGAN

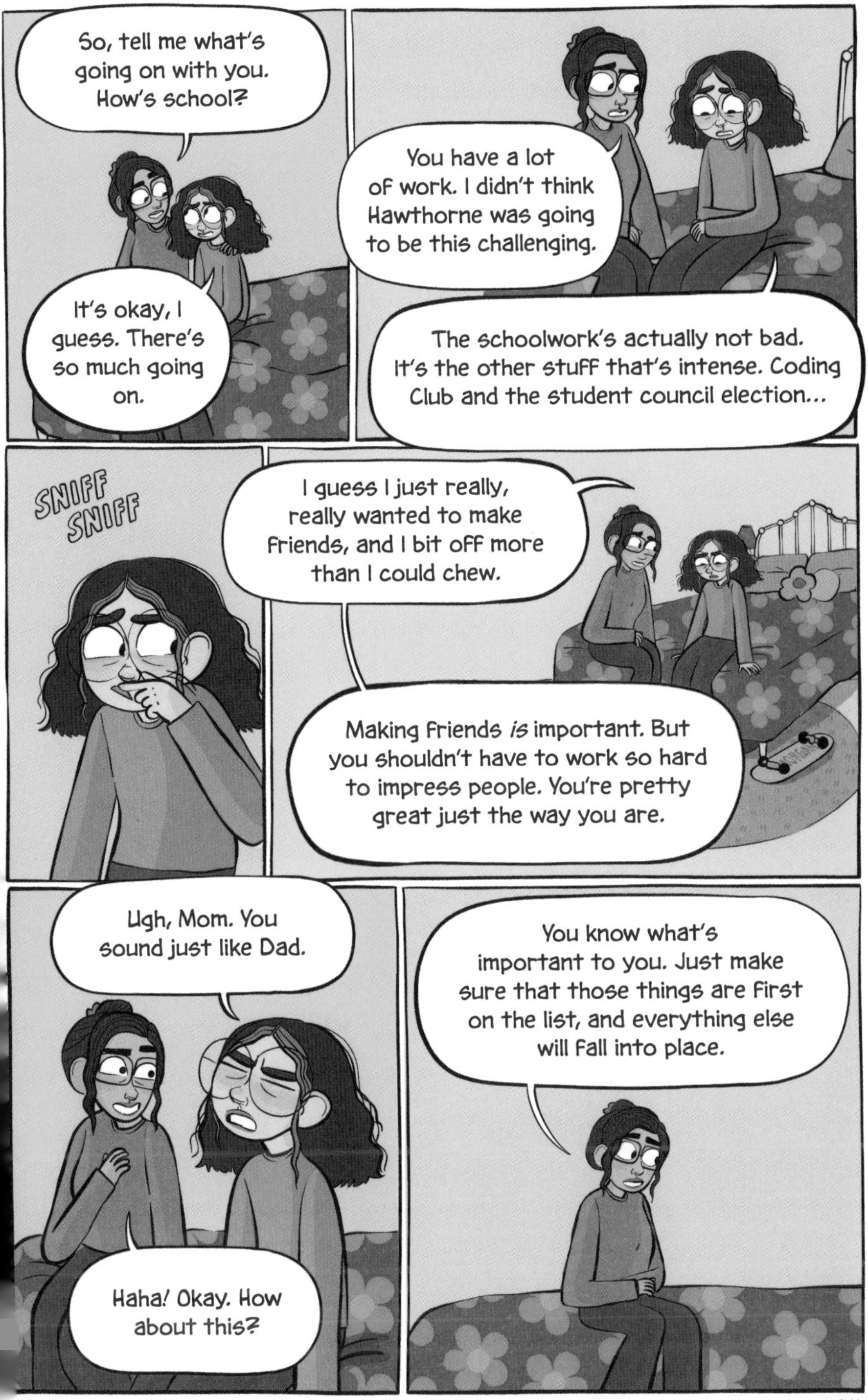
So, tell me what's going on with you. How's school?
It's okay, I guess. There's so much going on.
You have a lot of work. I didn't think Hawthorne was going to be this challenging.
The schoolwork's actually not bad. It's the other stuff that's intense. Coding Club and the student council election...
SNIFF SNIFF
I guess I just really, really wanted to make friends, and I bit off more than I could chew.
Making friends *is* important. But you shouldn't have to work so hard to impress people. You're pretty great just the way you are.
Ugh, Mom. You sound just like Dad.
Haha! Okay. How about this?
You know what's important to you. Just make sure that those things are first on the list, and everything else will fall into place.

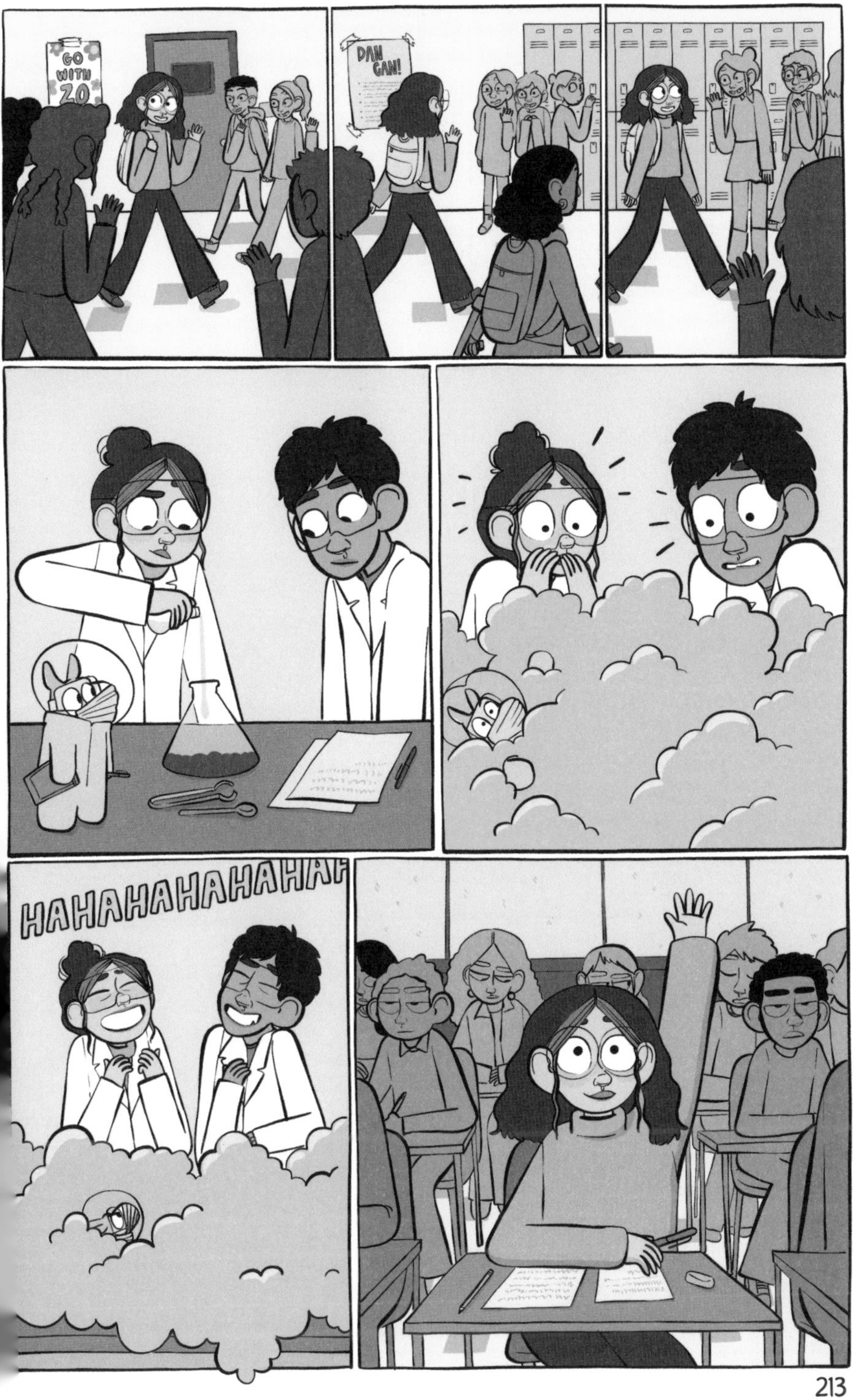
GO WITH ZO
DAN GAN!
HAHAHAHAHAHAH

215

Nope. C.C. said it himself—it wasn't about winning the election, it was about making me popular. And I'm definitely more popular than I would've been on my own. I think the program works.

But we didn't even get to the election. Don't we need to know who wins?

PFFFFt. You're only #8. You have a loooooong way to go.

I think we've done a great job. It's time to end the trial.

What?!

Are you sure about this?

I'm very sure.

Hey, wait a second!

Morgan, do you want to do the honors?

YES!

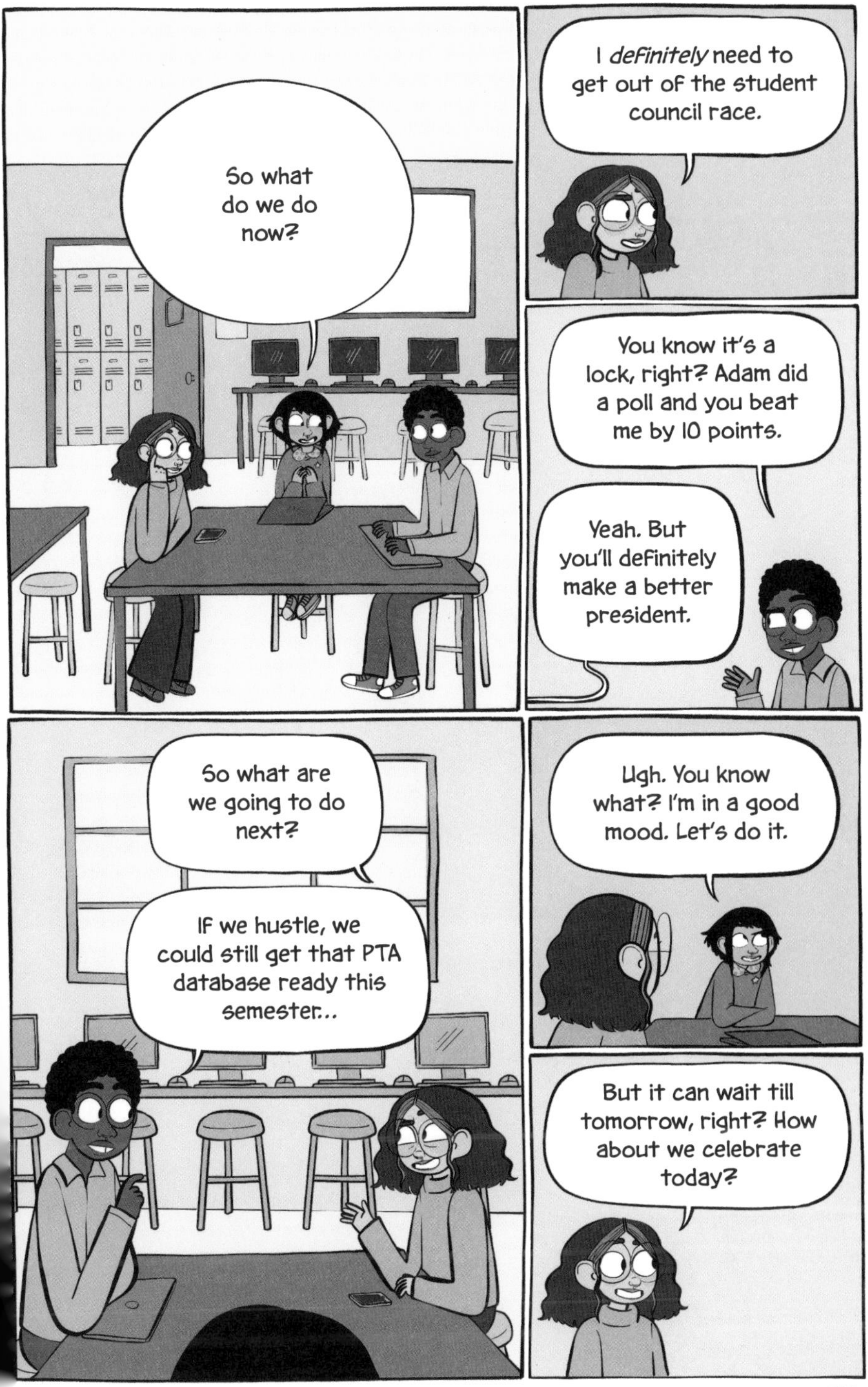
So what do we do now?
I *definitely* need to get out of the student council race.
You know it's a lock, right? Adam did a poll and you beat me by 10 points.
Yeah. But you'll definitely make a better president.
So what are we going to do next?
If we hustle, we could still get that PTA database ready this semester...
Ugh. You know what? I'm in a good mood. Let's do it.
But it can wait till tomorrow, right? How about we celebrate today?

SATURDAY

I GUESS MOM WAS RIGHT: IT'S EASY TO LET WORK TAKE OVER YOUR LIFE. BUT AT THE END OF THE DAY, CODE ISN'T GOING TO LAUGH AT YOUR JOKES, SCARF SUNDAES AND WATCH MOVIES, OR UNDERSTAND HOW IT FEELS TO WIPE OUT IN THE CAFETERIA.

PING!

FOR THAT, YOU NEED FRIENDS. REAL-LIFE FRIENDS.

DT Ready?

MS IT'S SATURDAY!!!!!!!!!

So? This data isn't going to upload itself.

Meet me at the library at noon.

DT

MS you're the worst

but okay 😊

TAP TAP TAP

C u there!

ZM

SURE, FRIENDSHIP CAN BE MESSY. PEOPLE ARE UNPREDICTABLE.

221

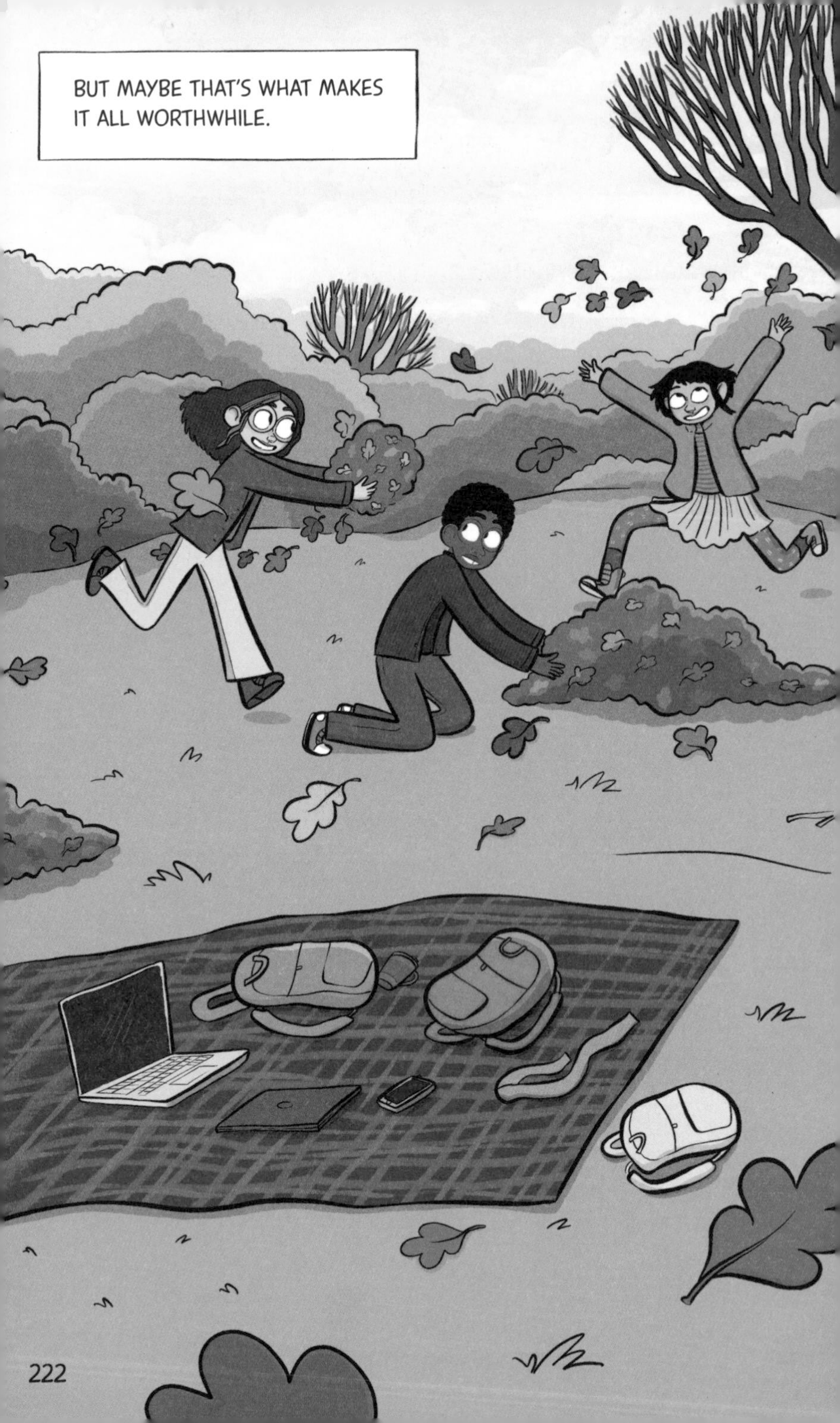
BUT MAYBE THAT'S WHAT MAKES IT ALL WORTHWHILE.